MISSION MULTIVERSE

MISSION MULTIVERSE

REBECCA CAPRARA

AMULET

AMULET BOOKS
NEW YORK

Cataloging-in-Publication Data has been applied for and may be obtained from the Library of Congress.

ISBN 978-1-4197-4823-3

Book design by Marcie J. Lawrence

Published in 2021 by Amulet Books, an imprint of ABRAMS. All rights reserved.

ABRAMS The Art of Books
195 Broadway, New York, NY 10007
abramsbooks.com

For AJ & FJ—
the most out-of-this-world kiddos

EARTH

DEV KHATRI'S RULES FOR SURVIVING MIDDLE SCHOOL WERE pretty simple: Don't speak up. Don't act out. Don't get your butt kicked.

During the last two months, he had learned these rules the hard way. Being the new kid was like wearing a flashing beacon on his head, alerting every bully to his presence. Except all Dev wanted to do was blend in, become invisible. That had been easy enough at his last school. But here in Conroy, Ohio, things were different.

It wasn't just school that was rough. Dev couldn't quite put his finger on it, but something about this town felt... off. Maybe it was the fact that Conroy lay along an active fault line and experienced frequent mini-quakes called *quivers*. Or maybe it was the intense and unpredictable weather patterns, dubbed *shivers*, with temperatures plummeting from balmy to subzero in a matter of hours.

Whatever it was, Dev believed his family had made a big

mistake leaving San Francisco. His parents, however, disagreed. Virtually all cities were coping with shifting weather patterns, and seismic activity was a natural and normal phenomenon, they said. Before the most recent tectonic realignment, San Francisco had experienced far worse quakes than Conroy, his mother pointed out.

More importantly, how could they pass up an opportunity to help advance scientific study in revolutionary and meaningful ways, especially at a time when Earth and its ten billion inhabitants were more vulnerable than ever? His parents, a physicist and a botanist, spoke of exploration, adaptation, and survival. Their visions for the future spanned timescales of light-years and expanded into universes—even multiverses—far away.

Dev appreciated the weight of these issues, but his concerns were a lot more . . . immediate. Like not getting his butt kicked by the lacrosse jocks, or heckled by the pop-collared prepsters, or lured into some argument about the ethical ramifications of interstellar colonization with the speech and debate kids. Like not making an utter fool of himself in front of Zoey Hawthorne-Scott.

He had met Zoey at marching band tryouts during his second week at Conroy Middle School. Typically paralyzed by stage fright, he'd been reluctant to join the group, but after the first practice he was hooked. It wasn't just that he got to spend time with Zoey; when he played the saxophone, he felt at home, despite the new city, new kids, new school. Plus, there was some unspoken nerd-to-nerd peace treaty that existed between the bandmates, which meant Dev could relax during practice without worrying some ninth grader was going to jump out from behind the tuba section and deliver an atom-splitting wedgie.

"Rise and shine! It's morning time!" His father knocked loudly on his bedroom door.

"Newton's first law: A body at rest wants to stay at rest," Dev grumbled sleepily.

"Good one!" his dad laughed. He paused for a minute, then began tapping out the words W-A-K-E U-P in Morse code with his knuckles.

"Message received. I'm awake," Dev called.

"Copy that! Breakfast will be ready in ten minutes. You need to fuel up for your field trip. I hear it's going to be *out of this world*! Pun intended. Get it?" He chuckled at his own dad joke.

Dev groaned and pulled a pillow over his head. It wasn't NASA that Dev had an issue with. NASA was cool. Out-of-this-world cool, to be precise. It was the fact that his father, Dr. Mohan Khatri, was the head interdimensional physicist at NASA's Gwen Research Center, the exact place Dev's class was headed later that day. And he knew that despite his father's good intentions, the statistical likelihood of him embarrassing Dev in some astronomically mortifying way was approximately 99.9 percent.

"Stupid field trip," he muttered to himself as he got dressed, wishing his wardrobe might reveal a portal to some alternate dimension where he could escape. Just for the day.

He opened his sock drawer and paused, staring at the neatly rolled rows of goofy socks. There were swirling galaxies stitched in shades of indigo and violet, metatron diagrams in fluorescent green and orange, even flying cheeseburgers orbiting cratered planets. Until recently, the socks had been something he and his father had shared. Okay, they didn't *share* them; that would've been gross. They each had their own identical sets. Before moving to Conroy, Dev and his dad would coordinate which pairs to wear each day of the week. A father-son bonding thing.

Dev looked down glumly at the open drawer. The socks fit, but Dev couldn't help but feel like he'd grown out of the tradition. He knew his dad would be wearing the classic rocket ship socks today, but Dev couldn't bring himself to wear his own set. Instead, he grabbed a boring, inconspicuous pair of black tube socks and slammed the drawer shut.

From the nursery across the hall, Dev's younger sister, Sejal, wailed, hitting an ear-splitting high note that could rival the school chorus's best soprano. He knew his mother was out in their backyard greenhouse taking morning assessments of her new cultivars, and his father was downstairs making breakfast and packing lunches, which meant diaper duty fell to Dev.

While he changed her, he hummed a jazzy version of "Twinkle, Twinkle Little Star." Sejal clapped enthusiastically. He wished all his performances could be met with such high praise. The marching band was preparing for regionals and would be up against some fierce competition.

"Excited for the big field trip today?" his dad asked as Dev carried Sejal into the kitchen and buckled her into her high chair.

"I am. But Dad, listen. Please don't do anything to embarrass me. Okay?"

His father looked shocked. "Who, me? How could I possibly do anything of the sort?"

"It's just that moving here has been tough. I'm finally starting to get in a groove and make some friends . . ."

"Yes!" His father thumped him on the back. "I'm really looking forward to meeting them today. I think your new friends will really get a *kick* out of these!" He hiked up the leg of his pleated chinos and stuck his foot out, wiggling his toes in a pair of socks with pi written out to the two-hundredth digit. "I know we discussed the rocket ships, but I thought these would make a stronger impression."

Dev blinked. "They definitely make an impression, that's for sure."

"Go change into yours, Dev-i-doodle!" his dad said brightly, using Dev's ridiculous childhood nickname. "So we can match!"

The probability of that happening was exactly 0.0 percent. "Oh, shoot! Mine are in the wash. Right, Mom?" Dev called out, knowing his mother was still in the greenhouse and nothing as trivial as laundry could distract her.

His dad shrugged. "Well, maybe next time. Need me to drive you to school today? The Tardis awaits." He couldn't resist a good *Doctor Who* joke.

Dev considered the offer. "Thanks, but I'll take the bus."

It would have been nice to get a ride to school, especially since Gage Rawley and the other bullies might be on board the bus. But the last time his dad had driven him to school, he'd insisted on walking Dev all the way inside, as though he were a helpless kindergartener. Then, his dad proceeded to introduce himself to Principal Brant, Janitor Howe, and even the electrician who was repairing some lights in the lobby. Worst of all, before he finally left, he hugged Dev in front of everyone, declaring loudly, "I love you to infinity, but not beyond, because infinity goes on forever-ever-ever-ever-ever-ever-ever-ever-ever..." Dev cringed at the memory and the teasing he had endured since.

"Good morning," his mother said, gliding into the room with a handful of fragrant herbs from the greenhouse.

Sejal squawked and launched a spoon into the air like a space missile. His father wiped splattered yogurt from his cheek, nudged his horn-rimmed glasses back up the bridge of his nose, and smiled warmly. "Pure entropy, as usual! Lack of order or predictability and gradual decline into complete disorder."

"I can see that," his mother said, completely unfazed. She turned to the blender on the counter and filled it with assorted ingredients, including the fresh herbs, then set the machine to pulse. A minute later, she handed Dev a thick, green smoothie in a tall glass.

He took a swig. He gagged. "Ack! What's in this? It's worse than yesterday's! Like lawnmower clippings mixed with ginger and toothpaste. And . . ." He wagged his tongue. "Chili powder? Ughhh!"

"Delicious, right?" his mother replied, polishing off a glass of her own. "Drink up, Dev."

"Not happening." Dev backed away from the kitchen island.

She reached her arms over her head, twisting from side to side, stretching her muscles. "The things that challenge us make us stronger," she said. "If you want to be a knight, you will need dragons to defeat."

"Maybe I don't want to be a knight. Besides, it's a smoothie. Not a dragon."

"It should be easy then, no? Defeat the smoothie, sweetie."

"Mom."

"What? You're not . . . scared, are you?" She stage-gasped, but her chestnut-brown eyes were playful.

"Of course not. It's just nasty, that's all."

"Ohh, so you *are* scared."

Was she calling him a coward? His pulse quickened. He locked eyes with his mother. She returned the stare, calm but forceful.

"You must learn to face your fears, Dev," she said. "It's the only way to grow."

He nudged his father, who had just finished cleaning up Sejal's latest breakfast propulsion experiment. "Dad, are you hearing this? Mom's turning a smoothie into a life lesson."

"Your mother is a font of infinite wisdom. You should listen to her." He gazed at his wife admiringly.

"Did *you* try this?" Dev asked his dad.

"Gosh, will you look at the time! I'm off to work! I hear we have a group of VIPs coming into the lab today." He winked at Dev, grabbed his car keys from the counter, then made a quick dash for the door, putting distance between himself and the universe's grossest smoothie.

Dev was about to follow when his mother stepped in front of him. "Not so fast."

"I've gotta go, Mom. Big day today. Can't be late."

She shook her head, her long black hair cascading from side to side. "Defeat. The. Smoothie."

"You are relentless." He grabbed the glass and chugged it down. As soon as he finished, he ran to the sink and washed away the awful taste with gulps of fresh water. Sejal cheered, tossing Oaty-Os like confetti. "Nice to know I have at least one fan," he said to his baby sister.

"You have more than that, sweetie," his mother said. She gave him a pat on the back and a kiss on the cheek.

"Ma! Really? You have got to stop doing that!"

"What?" She drew a hand across her chest.

"Calling me 'sweetie.' Kissing me. It's . . . it's . . . it has to stop. It's mortifying. You and Dad. Both of you need to just stop."

She exhaled. "Someday you'll learn that your family's love—and your father's unconventional sense of humor—are nothing to be embarrassed by."

Dev heard a hydraulic hiss and the squeak of wheels. Through the kitchen window, he watched as the electric school bus passed by. Above the red-leafed autumn trees, heavy gray clouds crowded the sky, hinting at rain.

Dev groaned. "Okay, okay. Love you too. But I need to go. Really. Especially now that I'll be walking to school." He gave his mother a quick hug, then blew a wet, sloppy raspberry on Sejal's cheek, which sent her into a fit of giggles.

"Have a good day!" his mother called. "May you defeat many dragons!"

"Sure, whatever!" he hollered back.

On his way out the door, he grabbed his saxophone from the bench in the hall. He wrapped a green poncho around the instrument case, as protection from the unpredictable Conroy weather, and stuffed a second poncho into his bag in case he needed one to wear. You could never be too prepared in this weird town.

He popped his earbuds in, tapped his music player, and let the sweet sounds of John Coltrane fill his head. If he hurried, he might be able to catch up with Lewis down the road.

Lewiston Wynner was not, as his name suggested, a winner. Sure, he had inherited the Wynner looks: sandy hair, olive skin, jade-green eyes. But to his father's great chagrin, he was not an elite athlete like the generations of Wynners who had reigned before. To his older brothers' endless amusement, he was actually fairly uncoordinated. Instead of playing lacrosse like them, Lewis ran track, half-heartedly at best, and only because sports were a family requirement.

Aside from frequently tripping over his own lanky legs and boat-sized feet, Lewis was best known for three things: playing drums, playing pranks, and having what had once been described as "devastatingly cute" dimples. His pranks often got him into trouble, and his dimples typically got him out of it. And his passion for percussion earned him a spot on the Conroy Middle School Marching Band, along with the not-so-coveted title of Band Geek. Never before had a Wynner been such a loser. At least according to his brothers, a fact that they reminded Lewis of daily, ever since he had opted for drumsticks over lacrosse sticks.

Speaking of his brothers, he could hear them lumbering down the hall.

"Sleeping beauty! Wakey-wakey!" Kingston called out. At seventeen, he was the oldest of the three Wynner boys and a total bruiser.

Instead of his usual dread, Lewis felt the giddy fizz of excitement. After a few failed attempts at basic retaliation pranks, he'd smartened up and recruited his new friend Dev to help design the ultimate Brute Brothers Takedown.

Lewis had met Dev on the first day of school when some lacrosse jocks pinned Dev to his locker, threatening some terrifying thing called a supersonic-atomic-bubonic-wedgie. Because his older brothers were captains of the varsity and junior varsity lacrosse teams, Lewis held some sway over the ninth-grade bullies. He told them to get lost or face the wrath of Kingston and Winston. Since then, he and Dev had formed a fast friendship built on a shared love of music, pranks, and sour gummies.

"Get up, band geek!" Winston, the middle brother, barked from down the hall.

Lewis hid, fully dressed, in a protective fort made of pillows and blankets. He peeked out, surveying the intricate contraption. He'd stayed up until two o'clock in the morning constructing each pulley and trigger, following the detailed diagrams Dev had sketched out after band practice.

Two beefy shadows approached. He could hear the *thwack, thwack* of their lacrosse sticks against their palms, ready to inflict their morning tortures.

"Moooooom!" Lewis hollered from beneath his fortress, playing the part. "Win and King are being goons again!"

He eyed the taut string across the floor, intended to trip Winston and send him face-first into a pie plate heaped with shaving cream. When Kingston followed a moment later, the overhead trigger would pull, setting off an elaborate chain reaction. He pictured the glorious scene in his mind: Foam darts raining down, a bucket of marbles spilling across the floor, a pail of maple syrup tipping onto their heads, the fan whirring, speakers blaring, a feather pillow tearing open, a glitter bomb exploding in a final crescendo. He held his phone steady, finger poised above the record button. The epic video would probably be viral by third period. His toes tingled with anticipation.

Kingston's voice drew nearer, snapping him out of his daydream. "You're gonna have to stand up for yourself someday. Why not get some practice?"

"I can stand up for myself just fine. And I stand up for my friends, too. Against *your* friends," Lewis replied, praying the prank would go off without a hitch.

"Can you bench-press two hundred pounds? Can you run the hundred-meter dash in fourteen seconds flat? Can you call yourself a state champ, an MVP, a true Wynner?"

Lewis frowned. "Those aren't the only measures of success."

"We have a legacy of greatness to uphold, baby bro," Kingston snickered. "You need to man up."

Lewis's stomach twisted. He hated when they talked like that. "It's possible to be a jock, not a jerk, you know."

"Sure, but what fun is that?" He could hear the slap of their high five. Then he spotted them, framed in the doorway. Kingston was about to tromp across the threshold when—

"Boys! Your seven-egg omelets are ready!" their mother called out.

Their ears pricked. "Protein!" they roared, and went racing down the polished oak staircase like a pack of slobbering hounds.

Lewis sat numbly in the center of his fort. His elaborate prank was untouched. There wasn't a speck of glitter, a single feather, or a sticky drip of maple syrup anywhere. His brothers were unscathed, stuffing their faces with fluffy omelets instead of writhing in the pain of total humiliation. What a letdown! Revenge would have to wait until tomorrow.

Disappointed, he stepped gingerly out of his fort and across the room, trying his hardest to place his clumsy feet as far away from the trip wires and glitter launchers as possible. It was never a good idea to leave a loaded prank unattended, but he didn't have the heart to dismantle the whole thing now.

By the time he made it downstairs, his brothers were shoveling the last bites of breakfast into their mouths. "Thanks for saving me some," he muttered, dodging their punches and grabbing a banana from the fruit bowl on the center island.

"Hello, Kingston," his mother said absentmindedly, scrolling through the neighborhood chat site, keeping up with whatever the Joneses were brag-posting about now.

"I'm Lewiston, Mom," he said, taking the farthest seat away from his brothers at the table.

"Yes, of course you are, dear." She never lifted her eyes from her phone.

Barrel-chested Victor Wynner strode into the room, dressed in a crisp navy-blue suit. All three boys sat up straighter. The ground shook with each of Victor's steps. Or was that another quiver? Lewis couldn't tell. Those little mini-quakes happened so frequently no one really paid much attention, except his friends Isaiah and Zoey.

"That looks good. Thank you, son." Victor lifted the banana straight out of Lewis's hand.

"Dad, hey, wait—"

"A busy man like me needs potassium. Big board meeting this morning, then hitting the links with the executive team." He crossed the room and began zippering his golf bag. The clubs shone.

"You'll be at our games tonight though, right?" Winston asked.

"Sorry, champ. Headed to Oarsville." Lewis watched as disappointment flashed across his brothers' brows. "I'm accepting an award for Top Sales Executive Management Strategic Consultant of the Year."

Lewis didn't have the slightest clue what that title meant, but his mother gushed, "Darling, that's remarkable. We are so proud! Boys, your father is *such* a winner." She snapped a photo of Victor with her phone, then immediately posted it online.

Lewis rolled his eyes.

His father smiled broadly, then gave Winston and Kingston thumps on the back. "You boys score a goal or two for me today, okay? Actually, make it a hat trick."

"You got it." Kingston flexed his muscles.

"And me?" Lewis asked hesitantly.

"You? Ahh...hmm." Victor scratched his head, like Lewis was a puzzle piece that didn't fit with the rest. "Do you have a track meet today?"

Lewis shrugged. "No, but I am going on a field trip."

"Right! Then I want you to win that field trip!"

"You can't win a field trip, Dad. It's not a competition," Lewis replied.

His father gave a toothy smile. "Everything is a competition. And don't forget: Wynners never lose!" That obnoxious family motto was actually embroidered onto pillows in the living room. Lewis despised it. What was so bad about losing, making mistakes, failing? Mrs. Minuzzi always said mistakes were part of learning. That made Lewis feel better, because he was really good at making them.

Without further ado, Victor Wynner gathered his briefcase and golf clubs, then marched out the door to load up his sleek, top-of-the-line sedan. Winston and Kingston followed.

"I'd better get going, too," his mother said breezily, putting her phone down long enough to sweep her blond hair into a ponytail. "Yoga class at nine. Pedicure at ten thirty. Charity lunch at noon. Laser facial at two . . ." It was hard work being the fittest, most fashionable housewife in Conroy.

"Did you pack me anything for lunch?" Lewis asked, grabbing a second banana. He scarfed it down before anyone could steal it away.

"I did. It's right here." She pointed, but the counter was empty. Just then, they heard the peal of gravel and the honk of Kingston's Jeep horn.

Great. He'd lost his lunch and his ride to school.

His mother flipped through her wallet. "Here. See if the

lunch lady can make change, okay?" She slid a hundred-dollar bill across the granite countertop. Lewis wasn't sure if there would be a food court or cafeteria at the Gwen Research Center, but he pocketed the bill quickly. A rumbling stomach would be a small price to pay, considering this outrageous lunch money could buy the latest Maxcroft game pack or a week's supply of candy for the entire marching band.

"I can drop you at school on my way to yoga," his mom said, mussing his shaggy locks. "Now, where are my keys?" She rummaged through her designer gym bag.

Out the window, Lewis caught a glimpse of a short kid with wavy brown hair swinging a bundled-up instrument case. He was wearing earbuds and sort of walk-dancing down the sidewalk. Dev wasn't anything like Lewis's brothers, and Lewis liked that. He was soft-spoken and a little shy, but he was funny and smart and a total wiz when it came to electronics. Just last week, he'd repaired Lewis's broken gaming console when his brothers accidentally crushed it while wrestling in the living room. Best of all, Dev didn't put Lewis on some dumb Wynner pedestal and compare him to the rest of his family.

"Thanks, but I'll walk. See ya!" He tossed his backpack over his shoulder, grabbed his drumsticks, and ran to catch up with Dev.

EARTH

"PLEASE TELL ME YOU ARE NOT WEARING THAT TODAY." TESSA
eyed her twin sister's clunky beige sneakers, tall white socks,
boring black leggings, and boxy T-shirt. "We may be identical, but clearly all the style genes went to me."

Like her sister, Zoey had warm brown skin and wore her
long hair in dozens of thin braids, but that's where the sim-
ilarities stopped. "What's so bad about this?" Zoey asked.
"It's functional. I can move in it. I can groove." She twirled
and busted some marching band dance moves.

Tessa crinkled her nose. "Let me explain in nerd terms
so you understand: In the theory of infinite universes,
somewhere I am a brain surgeon, somewhere Chihuahuas
are the dominant species, somewhere we were never born,
and maybe, possibly, somewhere those shoes are fashionable. But here on Earth, that ensemble is just not working."

Zoey blinked.

"If you wear that, I'll be unstylish by association," Tessa

said flatly. She turned to her reflection in the mirror and carefully blended a swipe of shimmery highlighter over her cheekbones.

"Aha. So this isn't about *me*, it's actually about *you*. Surprise, surprise. How could I forgot that planet Earth revolves around the one and only Tessa Hawthorne-Scott?"

Tessa dabbed her lips with gloss. "Don't hate me 'cause you ain't me."

"I have a field trip and marching band practice today. What's wrong with being comfortable? You want me to dress like I'm going to a pageant? How can you even walk in those things?" She pointed at her sister's feet.

"What? You mean my studded kitten heel booties? They're fabulous. A little pain is a small price to pay." She flashed a mega-watt smile, but there was an emptiness, a sadness behind it. "Plus, you never know when the press might snap a photo." Ever since their mother had been elected mayor of Conroy, the Hawthorne-Scott family had been under a microscope. The pressure was . . . a lot.

Tessa slipped a purple eChron smartwatch onto her right wrist. After the girls' phones had been hacked two months ago, their mother insisted they use these devices instead. From the outside, they looked like normal watches, except the eChrons were government-issued with encrypted data storage and special software that allowed the family to message each other over a secure network. Tessa and Zoey mostly used them to send each other snarky texts and goofy cat GIFs.

On her other wrist, Tessa clasped a wide, silver cuff bracelet to hide her scar. Beneath the puckered skin, a metal plate and pins held her damaged bones together, the result of an accident when she was seven.

"You don't have to wear that," Zoey said tenderly, pointing to the bracelet. All these years later, she still felt guilty. It had been *her* idea to play on the tractor at their grandmother's farm, back when Conroy was still known for its abundant corn and soybean crops.

"It's my signature accessory," Tessa sassed back. "Plus, I don't want my friends to think I'm a freak." She ran a finger glumly over the bracelet.

"Real friends wouldn't think that."

"Yeah? What would you know about *real* friends? Please tell me you don't mean your band buddies, like that conspiracy-theory weirdo, Isaiah? And what's the redhead's name? Mallory? Maxine?"

The sympathy Zoey felt for her sister a moment earlier dissolved. "Her name is Maeve. You are rude. And she is not my buddy." Zoey bit her lip. "Not anymore at least." She didn't want to talk about Maeve. Ever since the incident at the pharmacy, things had been complicated. And when Maeve went out for drum major—and got it!—their friendship became more strained than ever.

"Ohh, so she's, like, your arch nemesis now?" Tessa prodded, sniffing for gossip.

Zoey frowned. "Not exactly."

"Frenemy?"

"Drop it, okay? You don't know anything about her."

"I know she's the most obnoxious girl in seventh grade. Maybe in the whole school. Plus, Hailey heard from Blake that—"

"Enough, Tess!"

"I'm just looking out for your reputation," Tessa said.

"I can handle myself just fine, thanks," Zoey shot back, her skin tingling with anger. "And speaking of reputation, what would happen to *yours* if everyone found out where you got those earrings? Or that lip gloss?"

Tessa gaped, shocked by the sudden turn in conversation. "You wouldn't."

"Do you really want to find out?" Zoey planted her hands on her hips.

"You're the worst!"

"At least I'm not a kleptomaniac. Imagine if the press got wind of *that*? Mom would literally disown you."

Tessa glared, her hazel eyes narrowing to furious slits. Her twin sister did the same.

"It was a dare. It was one time."

Zoey tilted her head, unconvinced. She knew her sister could never resist a dare.

"Fine. Maybe twice," Tessa said. "But it was harmless. Okay? And you swore—*you promised*—you wouldn't say anything."

"My silence was contingent upon your benevolence."

"Ugh." Tessa rolled her eyes. "Just because you're in

honors English and I'm not doesn't mean you have to be so, so . . ." She struggled to find the word.

"Condescending?" Zoey said in a know-it-all voice.

"Some days I can't even believe we're related," Tessa snapped.

"Same, sis. Same."

There was a crack of thunder outside. Both girls jumped. Rain sluiced down their bedroom windows in heavy sheets. It had been sunny half an hour ago, but the weather in Conroy was seriously moody.

Tessa stood and straightened her cropped denim jacket as though it were a suit of armor. "I think you're jealous that I'm more popular than you."

Zoey scoffed. "You couldn't pay me to hang out with Gage and Blake. Maybe *you're* jealous that I have better grades. I'm the one with *real potential*, remember?" she blurted, repeating a line from an interview her mother had given the media during her last campaign.

Tessa froze, her perfectly made-up face drooping into a frown. "That quote was taken out of context, and you know it. Now you're just being mean."

Thunder boomed outside. The lights dimmed, then brightened.

Zoey's voice rose louder. "You pretend to be soooo cool, but really, you're desperate for everyone else's approval. And you think you can get it by wearing fancy labels, or putting down the people who actually care about you." She shook her head, dark braids whipping her flushed cheeks. "Good luck, Tess. See how far that gets you!"

"Girls! Volume, please." Their father appeared in the doorway, his shirt streaked with colorful paint from his latest mural. His expression was unusually stern. He held a finger to his lips. "Your mother is on an important call down the hall. The local news station is asking for an official statement about the rolling blackouts."

"You mean the flickers?" Zoey glanced at the light fixture overhead. "They're nothing. They last a few seconds, minutes at most, and then the power gets restored." Her friend Isaiah had been tracking them in his Journal of Strange Occurrences, but so far, he hadn't detected any discernable patterns.

"Even so, they're happening more frequently. It's starting to affect small business owners, especially those without solar generators."

"Why is that Mom's problem?" Tessa asked.

"If it concerns the city of Conroy, it concerns your mother. Which means it also concerns us." He looked at both girls kindly. "You know I don't mind you speaking your minds or exercising your vocal cords, but when Mom is working, you two need to take it down a notch."

"Mom is always working," Tessa said under her breath.

He nodded. "Yes, your mother works hard. For our family. For the people of our city. Let's be supportive. Okay?"

"By supportive, you mean quiet," Tessa replied sullenly.

"At this particular moment, yes." He studied her face.

"Is there something bigger going on here that I should know about?"

Just then, Valerie Hawthorne stepped into the room. At five feet ten inches tall, she cut a striking figure, feminine and strong, in a crimson pantsuit with a silk scarf draped smartly around her neck. She focused inquisitive eyes on her dueling daughters.

Tessa gulped.

"Everything copacetic?" she asked, which was more of a command than a question. As mayor of Conroy, their mother had a high-powered job, and she had equally high expectations of her daughters.

Zoey stepped forward, playing the part of the good-mannered, responsible kid. "Yes, of course. Sorry about the noise, Mom. *Someone* was trying to give unsolicited fashion advice, which sort of . . . spiraled. It won't happen again. We promise."

Tessa nodded in agreement.

"Good." Before their mother could say more, the phone rang. She left to answer it, with their father following behind.

When they were alone again, Zoey turned to Tessa. She felt bad; her outburst had cut too deep. She loved her sister, but she didn't always understand her. And no one could push her buttons the way Tessa did. She was about to apologize when Tessa narrowed her kohl-lined eyes.

"You think you know me so well?" Tessa hissed, simmering. "You couldn't last one day in my shoes." She stamped a kitten-heeled foot.

A new expression fell over Zoey's face. It was the same look their mother had leveled at Hank Clementi the day he told her on live television that the city of Conroy would never elect a Black woman as mayor. It was a look that was always followed by action.

"I couldn't last a day in your shoes, huh? Is that...a dare?" Zoey countered.

Just then, the ground beneath them shook.

"Did you feel that? We're doomed!" Isaiah Yoon declared, clutching his backpack to his chest as his mother pulled their electric station wagon up to a crumbling, desolate wasteland. He rubbed his eyes. No, wait. That was just the Conroy Middle School parking lot.

"It's only a field trip. Not the end of the world, Isaiah." Sylvie Yoon said, trying to be patient with her son. The windshield wipers banged back and forth, pushing the deluge of rain away. She reached into the backseat of the car, which was stocked with boots, snow shovels, flashlights, hats, gloves, bug spray, sunscreen, and more. The weather changed so dramatically in Conroy that it never hurt to be prepared.

"Here. Take this." She handed him an umbrella.

"Thanks, but I'm not worried about the rain, Mom."

"Try this then." She passed him a honey granola bar from the stash in her purse.

"I'm not hungry either. I'm worried that the ground could literally crack open and swallow us whole at any moment!" He pulled his journal out, jotting notes on an elaborate table he and Zoey had drawn.

"Oh, Isaiah." His mother's voice was gentle. "The quivers are minor seismic adjustments. Mostly harmless. Any geologist will attest to this."

It was true, but the quivers still unnerved him. When they struck, the earth trembled. Vases shook on shelves. Swimming pools sloshed. A car alarm might sound. That part was fine. But in recent months, the quivers had started sending vibrations through the air, too. Trees, buildings, even *people* seemed to warp and bend and shimmer before returning to normal.

The first time it happened, Isaiah had freaked out. But no one else thought anything was awry. No one else seemed to *see* what he saw. Kids at school called him crazy; he didn't like that. So he kept the visions to himself, confiding only in Zoey.

Mere moments ago, it had happened again. The ground lurched and the parking lot blurred, transforming for a split second into a completely different landscape—parched, barren, apocalyptic. His mother was seated beside him and yet she barely blinked.

"Are we going to talk about what's really going on?" she asked.

Wait, *had* she noticed the parking lot weirdness? Isaiah

paused, trying to read her expression. He opted for a diversion. "If this is about my math grade, I already asked Ms. Breese about the extra credit assignment."

"Isaiah." She looked at him in that no-nonsense way of hers. "You had a dream again last night, didn't you?"

"Mom, typical humans dream approximately seven times a night. But we only remember a fraction of them." He zipped up his black sweatshirt and pulled the hood over his head.

"You know what I mean. You're always so skittish and edgy after those nightmares."

"I am not skittish or edgy."

"You have used the word *doom* approximately ten times this morning and it's barely eight o'clock."

"Okay, fine. Guilty as charged!" He held up his hands. "Last night I had an anxiety dream, Mom. We have regional championships coming up for marching band. I have so much music to learn. Plus, midterms are looming, and Mr. Kimpton assigned a ten-page history paper. It's just a lot to deal with, you know?"

She pursed her lips. "I understand. Except last night, you were talking in your sleep. And you were thrashing. I tried to comfort you, but you were in such a deep sleep. It was like you were somewhere else entirely."

He stared at her, his gray eyes wide. "What did I say?"

She looked down at her hands, folded in her lap. Her cuticles were chewed raw. It had been a rough year for both of them. "You kept calling out for your uncle."

His stomach dropped. Isaiah's dad had passed away when Isaiah was just a baby, so Uncle Ming was the closest thing to a father Isaiah had ever known. The loss of his uncle last year affected him deeply. The therapists and counselors all said time would help heal Isaiah's wounds, but the dreams his mother mentioned had been getting worse, the memories morphing, shifting into darker, stranger realities. Instead of the past, they seemed to be taking place in the future. In a world where his beloved uncle wasn't really gone . . . yet still slipping away. Just beyond his reach. Isaiah felt cold, his skin prickling at the thought.

"Some days I think Uncle Ming was trying to tell us something. Something important."

"Of course he was," his mother said softly. "He was a photojournalist. His goal was to communicate and connect. To bear witness, to tell stories through images. To help build empathy and awareness."

"What about the letters?" In the months leading up to his uncle's disappearance, his emails to Isaiah had become vague and disjointed, with cryptic riddles and half-finished phrases. Postcards arrived from far-flung locales, written in hasty script, smudged with metallic pigments and strings of random numbers. Others bore drawings of a bizarre thirteen-sided symbol. Nothing made sense. When Isaiah showed them to his mother, she brushed them off, but her face had creased with worry.

"We've talked about that, honey," she said, her voice heavy, exhausted. "Documenting wars, extinctions, famine, and natural disasters takes a toll, even on the most seasoned journalists. It's tremendously challenging to work in that field so long, witnessing hardship and suffering. It affected my brother—your uncle—physically and mentally."

According to authorities, last September, Ming Yoon boarded a waverider during a typhoon in the Philippines and never returned. Investigators posited that he had suffered a breakdown. The correspondence with his nephew didn't contain encoded clues; there was no great conspiracy to expose. The strange letters were merely the result of a deteriorating mind and spirit.

Isaiah didn't buy it. His uncle had always been brave, bold, daring, but he'd never known him to be reckless. If his uncle got into that waverider in those conditions, there was a reason. *There's always more to the story*, his uncle used to say about his photographs.

"I know it's hard, honey. There are days when I feel lost, too. Days when I don't want to believe he's gone. But he is." His mother clasped a hand over his own. "We had a funeral. We said our goodbyes. It's time to move on with our lives. It's what your uncle would have wanted."

Isaiah nodded. But the dreams, the letters, the way light buckled and bent before his eyes during a quiver, it all hinted at something bigger. Something frightening. He couldn't help but believe there was a connection.

His mother gave his hand a squeeze. "You know what? I'm going to call Dr. Frayley. Set up an appointment. How's next Wednesday?"

"Mom. I don't need to see the grief counselor."

"Mourning is an ongoing process, sweetheart. It's perfectly normal to need help along the way."

The truth was, Isaiah wasn't in mourning. Not exactly. Because his uncle wasn't dead.

He was still out there, somewhere. Isaiah knew it. He just needed to figure out where *there* was.

Not again.

Maeve Greene's locker was the victim of a "spack-attack" for the third time in two weeks. The metal door was scrawled with cruel words and spackled with a sticky mixture of purple slime, toilet paper, putty, and something offensively odoriferous that vaguely resembled week-old tuna salad.

Maeve's face flushed, her eyes pricked. The hallway fell silent as the other kids watched, waiting for a reaction. In contrast to what was happening at home, a vandalized locker was the least of her concerns. *Chin up, buttercup. Show them weakness and they'll feed off it*, Gramps always said. Maeve blinked. She rearranged her face and tucked her shoulder-length red hair behind her ears. She straightened her shoulders.

"You know, I'm flattered that someone took time out of their busy schedule to make this . . . this . . . masterpiece for me. How thoughtful!" She made her voice extra loud and chipper, to hide the hurt. "Though what a shame they don't know how to spell."

She pulled a marker from her backpack. With a few lines, she turned the work *FREAK* into *BREAK* and added the word *DANCER* below. A true performer never missed an opportunity to shine. Then, to the shock and confusion of the kids in the hall, she dropped onto her back and spun around the linoleum floor like an electrocuted turtle. She popped up onto her shoulder, kicked her feet, then nailed a perfect headstand. Dumbstruck students stared in silence.

Instead of applause, someone muttered, "Just when I thought she couldn't get any weirder..."

Maeve stood up. She dusted herself off and rubbed her sore arm, watching forlornly as the hallway cleared out. "They wouldn't know entertainment if it punched them in the nose," she mumbled to herself. As she turned, she spotted Lewiston Wynner rounding the corner, with that new kid Dev at his side. They were looking down at Lewis's phone and laughing.

She stepped in front of them. "You!" Lewis skidded to a stop, nearly crashing into Dev. She jabbed a finger at Lewis's chest, then pointed to her locker. "Explain. Now."

"Huh?"

Maeve crossed her arms over her chest. "Do I have you to thank for this, Wynner?"

Lewis regained his balance and looked at the locker. He shook his head. "No way, Mae. I might be a prankster, but I am not a vandal."

"Is that so?" She studied his face.

He shrugged and slipped the phone into his back pocket. "Look, prankery is an art form. Much like the music we play in marching band, a quality prank needs to be carefully choreographed and rehearsed." He gestured at the disgusting locker door. "That is just a hot mess."

"A hot, smelly mess," Dev added, pinching his nose. "It's worse than my baby sister's diapers."

Lewis nodded, taking a whiff. "I'm actually insulted by your accusation, Maeve. My work is far superior."

She made a face, scrunching the constellation of freckles scattered across her cheeks. "How do I know you're not lying?"

"You could just...trust me." Lewis flashed his signature Wynner smile. His dimples usually came in handy during moments like this. A cluster of seventh-grade girls giggled nearby.

Maeve shot the girls a look. She tugged nervously on the sleeves of her plum-colored tunic, making sure the fabric covered the bruises running up her right forearm. Breakdancing probably hadn't been the best idea, especially with an injured arm. She grimaced, recalling last night's fight. The pills turned her mom into someone else, someone mad and mean and unpredictable. If Maeve couldn't trust her own mother to keep her safe, how was she supposed to trust some dimple-wielding trickster?

She shook her head. "Your Prince Charming act is not going to work on me."

Lewis huffed impatiently. "I swear. It wasn't me, okay? Maybe if you weren't such an in-your-face know-it-all, people wouldn't want to blast your locker."

At this, Zoey looked up from a locker nearby. She stole a glance at Maeve, whose face was flushing a deep shade of red. In the past, Zoey would have jumped in to defend her friend, but things had gotten so complicated between them. Plus she was dressed in her sister's ridiculous designer clothes, pretending to *be* Tessa as part of their stupid dare. Tessa wouldn't speak up for Maeve in a million years, and in order to win the bet, Zoey had to stay in character as her sister, undetected, until band practice this afternoon.

Meanwhile, Maeve was still arguing with Lewis. "I'm sure Principal Brant will be disappointed when I inform her of your role in the defacement of school property."

Lewis groaned. "I just walked into school with Dev like three minutes ago. We sprinted the last five blocks so we wouldn't get soaked by the rain. Then I nearly twisted my ankle when the sidewalk shifted. For the last time: I didn't touch your locker. Okay?"

"I can confirm. This is accurate information," Dev replied.

Maeve squinted at Dev. He was nice and he seemed sincere. Why he hung around with Lewis was a mystery. "Fine. But I've got my eye on you, Wynner. Don't think you're going to get away with this kind of monkey business during band practice. As the newly elected drum major, I'll be running a tight ship. Got it?"

"Loud and clear, Captain!" Lewis gave a goofy salute.

Dev nodded politely and shuffled toward his own locker. As the newest member of the band, he did not want to get on Maeve Greene's bad side.

"If the janitor sees that mess, you're doomed," a voice said behind her.

Maeve wheeled around. "Ah, yes. Isaiah Yoon. I should have known you would be the gloomy voice of pessimism on this already crummy morning."

"Realism, Greene. Not pessimism," Isaiah replied. Then, from behind his back, he produced a roll of paper towels and a spray bottle of some lemony cleaning solution. "Here. I nabbed these from the boys' bathroom. Thought you might need some help cleaning up."

"Oh." She blinked. Some days Isaiah seemed lost in the clouds, other days he was hyper tuned in, noting little things other people missed. Maeve gave a confused but grateful smile. She wasn't used to being on the receiving end of random acts of kindness. "Thanks."

"No problem. Hey, have you seen Zoey anywhere?"

Maeve looked up, trying to keep her expression neutral. "No. Why?"

Isaiah bit his lip. "No reason. Umm, did you notice anything weird this morning?"

She shrugged. "I heard on the news that another cow went missing from Miss Mary's Dairy Farm."

Isaiah had already noted this in his Journal of Strange Occurrences. It was the sixth missing cow in just as many weeks. Peculiar indeed, but not his primary concern, especially since he was lactose intolerant. "Anything else?" he probed.

"Other than this putrid tuna-salad-and-slime spack-attack?" she said, wiping down her locker.

"No, more doomy than that." He spritzed some lemon cleaner onto the sticky surface.

"*Doomy* is not a real word."

"It's the word of the day, actually."

She surprised herself by laughing.

In contrast, his face was serious. "Can't you feel it?"

"Feel what?" Maeve asked.

"Something's not right."

"It's called middle school, Isaiah. Awkwardness is just part of the experience. It'll be over soon enough."

Isaiah gasped, his eyes widening. "I knew it!"

She threw a wad of paper towels into the garbage. "I didn't mean 'it'll be over' in an end-of-the-world sort of way. I just meant we'll be in high school soon, then hopefully college, and eventually out in the wide world . . . adulting."

"Adulting? Ugh. That sounds extra doomy. I hope the world ends before I have to start adulting."

Maeve disagreed. She was counting the days until she could escape from Conroy. She didn't expect to run away from all her problems, but she desperately wanted to start fresh somewhere new.

"Did you feel the quiver this morning?" Isaiah pressed. "How about the flickers?"

She paused, another gloppy paper towel dripping in her

hand. Had there been a quiver this morning? Between the shouting, the dishes smashing, and the doors slamming, she hadn't noticed. All she could recall was the crazed look in her mother's eyes and her grandfather's threats to call the cops. Again. The words *rehab* and *probation* and other things she couldn't bear to think about. "It was a . . . busy morning." She made her face smooth and unreadable, cool as stone. Inside, her emotions were messier than her locker.

Before Isaiah could reply, the bell rang.

"Good morning, Conroy Cadets!" the intercom boomed. Since the city of Conroy was home to a large NASA field station, the school had adopted the Space Cadet—a cartoon astronaut—as their official mascot.

"Seventh-grade students in homeroom classes A through D will be attending today's field trip to the Gwen Research Center. Homeroom classes E through H will be visiting the center on Monday. All field trippers in today's group: Please check in with your first-period teachers, turn in any homework assignments, collect your weekend work packets, then proceed immediately to the rear exit. Buses bound for NASA will depart promptly in thirty minutes."

Zoey gathered a stack of textbooks and set off to class, teetering in her sister's uncomfortable shoes. She tried her best to strut down the corridor as though it were a runway, the way Tessa did so effortlessly. Unfortunately, she was pretty sure she looked more like a tipsy sailor stumbling down a pier. She caught Maeve's eye as she passed and gave her a small smile. Maeve stared back, bewildered by the gesture. Tessa Hawthorne-Scott had never given her the time of day . . .

"In addition," the loudspeaker blared, "Coach Diaz requests that all members of the marching band bring their instruments with them, as buses will drop musicians off for mandatory practice at Baxter Field directly following the field trip."

"That means you, band geeks!" Gage Rawley sneered at Maeve and Isaiah as he passed.

"Bring our instruments? Really?" Dev groaned. He did not want to lug his saxophone to NASA and risk his father requesting some impromptu solo in front of his classmates.

Lewis nudged Dev. "Quick, let's go. I don't want to get stuck sitting next to her." He tilted his head in Maeve's direction.

The bell rang a final warning.

"Again, the buses will depart in thirty minutes! Any students not on board will join Principal Brant for the day in a quiet and excruciatingly boring extended study period," the intercom announced.

Isaiah helped Maeve wipe the last of the purple slime from her locker. "If we don't hurry, we're doomed."

"Yeah. You go. I'll meet you there," Maeve said.

Once she was alone, she closed her eyes. For a brief moment, she let herself drift away, imagining a world where her life was different. Where she wouldn't need to put on a mask and pretend everything was perfect when it was far from it. Where no one vandalized her locker or called her names. Where her mother wasn't so explosive. Where her father acknowledged her existence. Where Gramps could retire and relax, like he deserved. Where her half sister, Bethany, wasn't such a pain in the butt. She knew it was a tall order, but sometimes it felt good to imagine a parallel version of her life.

"Thirty minutes, people!" the intercom boomed, breaking up her daydream. "Consider this your last warning! The field trip buses depart in thirty minutes!"

STATION LIMINUS

"THIRTY DAYS! EARTH WILL SELF-DESTRUCT IN T-MINUS THIRTY days," the robotic AI voice announced loudly.

A hologram of the planet glowed above a thirteen-sided table, around which twelve of the Multiverse Allied Council's delegates were seated. The group was gathered in the diplomatic wing of Station Liminus, a megastructure that served as the central meeting place within the liminal zone between dimensions.

The image of Earth rotated. Swathes of red and orange pulsed across the distressed planet's surface, indicating areas of extreme warming, pollutant concentration, resource depletion, and more.

Secretary Ignatia Leapkeene pressed a button on her wristlet and the hologram disappeared. Her indigo robes swirled around her and the small, corkscrewed horns that rose from her temples darkened from ivory to deep violet, as they always did when she was faced with a difficult decision.

"Esteemed members of the Multiverse Allied Council, thank you for gathering for this critical meeting. As you can see, planetary collapse within Dimension14 is imminent. For this reason, I seek your sage counsel." Ignatia regarded each delegate, trying to gauge their reactions.

The faces of the council were great and varied—humanoid, alien, and even cyborgian. Exoskeletal, radially symmetrical, scaled, furred, ancient, young, and more, representing a diverse array of intelligent life-forms from across the multiverse.

Ignatia stopped last at the face of a human male of middle age, the most recent addition to their group. His hair was an unnatural shade of blond that bordered on fluorescent yellow, slicked back aggressively with a veneer of shellac. He wore what struck Ignatia as a rather gaudy pinstriped suit, but then again, Earthling fashion was a bit of an enigma to her. He appeared to be sweating profusely in spite of the Station's superior ductworks, which pumped a steady stream of fresh, oxygenated air into the geodesic-domed meeting chamber.

"As the newest member of our great council, I had hoped that our inaugural meeting with Mr. Salvido Finto, representative from Earth of Dim14, would be under more auspicious terms. But alas, here we are." Ignatia exhaled and gestured ceremoniously to Mr. Finto.

He rose to his feet and dabbed sweat from his brow. "Thank you, Secretary Leapkeene. I'm very pleased to meet you all." He looked around. "Beautiful place you got here.

Impressive architecture. First-class finishes. Not as nice as my private villa in the Maldives, but pretty close." He waited for laughter but none came. He cleared his throat.

"Let me tell you, it's an honor to be chosen by the great people of Earth to represent the great planet of Earth. I understand from my advisor that your little club has been around for a while, and it might seem like Earth is late to the party." He grinned, his teeth abnormally white. "But let me tell you, you've saved the best for last. It's true. You're lucky to have us. Our planet has never been better. We are, quite simply, the best." He smacked his lips with satisfaction, as though he'd practiced that last bit.

The other delegates blinked, their faces blank.

"Did you not understand the earlier transmission?" Ignatia asked, perplexed by the man's unwarranted bravado.

"Perhaps his translator is broken?" Bo'lar, the Minister of Jelingor, said quietly, turning to General Shro, the delegate from Hasz, seated to her left.

"No, I think his translator is in fine working order," Shro replied.

Quirg, a doughy, four-armed delegate from Quomo of Dim5, leaned over and whispered, "Perhaps the trip across the Threshold compromised his brain functionality?"

Ignatia struck the table with a ruby gavel, silencing the chatter. "Mr. Finto, we just informed you that your planet is on the brink of destruction."

"Hogwash!" the man replied, shaking his head vehemently.

"Pardon?" Ignatia asked.

"I run one of the top energy operations in the world. EnerCor's profits have never been higher. Earth is in great condition."

"On the contrary. Scientists from across the multiverse have reviewed the data and they all concur: Your planet is in dire condition. If no action is taken, your *great* planet and all its *great* life-forms will perish. Is this clear?" Ignatia asked, her horns darkening with concern.

"I don't like what you're implying," Finto shot back, growing agitated.

"I should think not."

He began to lose his composure. Spittle flew from his mouth. "You can't just spring something like this on me! On us. Out of nowhere!"

"Oh, please," Bo'lar replied. "You must have known that this outcome was inevitable. Treat a planet as you have—filling your seas with plastic, burning noxious fuel, roasting your ice caps like marshmallows, felling your forests—what did you expect?"

"Bo'lar is right. It is hard to have sympathy for you and your fellow Earthlings, Councilor Finto." Governor Neel, a humanoid man of modest stature with pale blue skin and antennae extending from the top of his head, spoke clearly. "While the inhabitants of Earth only recently discovered how to cross the Threshold and connect with the broader multiverse, the rest of us have followed your civilization from afar for quite some time. I recall the efforts of many activists: Thunberg, Copeny, Bastida, Hirsi, Patel, Margolin,

Nazar, and others. They all raised concerns about environmental degradation, protesting and pleading for change. Sadly, their efforts were largely ignored. By politicians, lobbyists, and businesspeople such as yourself."

"How dare you!" Finto said, clenching his diminutive hands into fists.

"In their defense, the situation in Dim14 has escalated faster than anyone initially calculated. Exponentially so," said Duna, a young, nonbinary delegate from Mertanya of Dim10, with frilled ears and green-tinted hair. "I believe there is much worth protecting on this planet."

"Oh, really? Enlighten us, Duna. Have you truly amassed such vast stores of knowledge in your minor years?" Xol, a beetle-like creature, glared.

Duna looked up. "Do not patronize me. Even as the youngest member of the council, my voice—and vote—carries as much weight as yours. In my dimension, the opinions of our youth are as valid and respected as those of old crones."

Xol's face pinched into a scowl. He said no more.

"Earth has produced wondrous flora and fauna." Duna glanced at Finto, trying to convey solidarity. "Even its humans, flawed as they may be, deserve our attention and care. Their history should not be lost, nor should their future."

Finto sopped sweat from his neck and nodded gratefully.

"Do you propose we aid Dimension14 in some way?" asked Ignatia.

Shro scratched his chin. "Are reparative measures even feasible at this late phase?"

Ignatia considered this. The data projections were concerning. Still, she held on to a shred of hope that something could be done. Extinction was not a topic she took lightly.

"Hope is a very human thing, isn't it?" Xol said, reading his colleague's thoughts, plucking them from her mind, uninvited. Ignatia hated that Vermaskians could do this. "Stop immediately, or risk expulsion from the council," she ordered. He slunk back in his chair, clacking his jaw defensively.

"We could assist with evacuation and resettlement. Terraforming efforts on Ebvar's fourth moon have been largely successful. I'm sure we could engineer something suitable to human life. A little water, some oxygen, gravity, temperature regulations. Simple enough," Shro offered. Ignatia was surprised but encouraged by the typically stern general's tone.

"Perhaps if we ramp up our efforts, it will be fully inhabitable in a decade or so," Governor Neel said.

"We have thirty days. Not a decade," Duna reminded them all.

"Besides, only a handful of Gates exist linking Dim14 to the Station," Quirg responded. "It would be impossible to move a population of billions across the multiverse in such a short time." He turned in his chair. "What do you suggest, Mr. Finto?"

Finto's mouth drooped like an angry child about to have a tantrum. When an agent from the World Intelligence

Agency approached him about the highly confidential MAC gig a few weeks ago, he had been flattered. He accepted the diplomatic post thinking it would involve swanky inter-dimensional dinner parties, luxe soirees, and lucrative busi-ness opportunities. He hadn't anticipated actual diplomacy or hard work of any kind.

An advisor had briefed him before he traveled to the Station, but she kept going on and on about the most bor-ing details and he lost interest quickly. Instead of studying the binders of critical information she had prepared for him, he opted to play golf on his private course with a few of his closest billionaire buddies.

"Mr. Finto?" Secretary Leapkeene asked, her horns turn-ing a disconcerting orange color.

Salvido Finto swallowed, but a lump remained in his throat. He was woefully unprepared. Rather than admit his shortcomings to himself or anyone else, he looked around the room for someone to blame for his own incompetence. That was how he had ascended through the ranks at Ener-Cor, after all. And, he knew, it was exactly how many great politicians operated on Earth. Surely, it would work well for him here, too.

4

EARTH

"YOU'VE GOT THIS," TESSA SAID TO HERSELF UNDER HER breath as she boarded the bus for the field trip. She clutched Zoey's clarinet case. It was both reassuring and frustrating that no one had figured out her true identity yet, and crazy how something as simple as a layer of clothing could sway people's perceptions.

She wasn't thrilled to be going on a boring tour of NASA, but on the upside, she was getting out of a dreaded algebra quiz. Even better, her brainiac twin would have to take the quiz in her place, which would definitely boost Tessa's less-than-stellar average for the term.

"G'morning, Zoey!" a chaperone called from his seat behind the bus driver. He was stocky and bald, wearing chinos, an emerald green and yellow Conroy Cadets windbreaker, and a whistle on a lanyard around his neck. Tessa recognized him as the band coach. What was his name again? She knew it started with a *B*. Or was it *D*? Ugh. Better to just smile and nod.

"Excited for practice later today?" he asked. "We'll be working on some really fun formations."

"That sounds . . . empyrean!" Tessa imitated her sister's typical cheeriness and annoying vocabulary. She was bringing her A-game to this swap because the stakes were high. If she got busted as an imposter, she would be forced to join the band—as a *baton twirler*. That would be a nightmare. Not only because her injured left wrist had a limited range of motion, but mostly because joining the band would mean wearing a uniform. As a rule, Tessa didn't do polyester, especially metallic, ill-fitting, head-to-toe polyester with some feathery hat on top. She shuddered thinking about how ridiculous she would look. She wouldn't lose this bet. She couldn't.

"Hurry up, loser. You're taking forever-ever-ever-ever . . ." Gage huffed a few feet behind, practically kicking Dev, who had stopped in the aisle to tie his shoelaces. Dev quickly slid into the open seat behind Tessa, his face burning with shame. All he wanted was to make it through the day invisible and unscathed. As Gage passed, he dropped a string of cruel comments under his breath.

Tessa shot him a look of disgust. "You can't say those things," she snapped, in Dev's defense. Zoey always spoke up in the face of injustice. Normally, Tessa was too shy to use her voice that way, but something about pretending to be her sister freed her from all that. She rose to her feet.

Gage squared his shoulders, lowered his voice so the teachers couldn't hear. "What're you going to do about it? Tell your popular, prettier sister? Or call your mommy, Mrs. Mayor? Everyone knows she has no real power. My parents own half the businesses and real estate in Conroy. With reelection coming up, your mom's going to need all the help she can get. Chances are, she'll come begging for my family's endorsement."

"That doesn't mean you get to speak to people the way you just did," Tessa said, disgusted.

Dev looked up at her, incredulous. She defied all his rules for surviving middle school. Although this scared him a little, he also respected her for it.

"But it does," Gage spat. "I can pretty much do whatever I want." He turned and stalked toward the back of the bus, kids parting like the sea around him.

Lewis climbed on board and flopped down next to Dev. "Hey, man. Why the sad face?"

"Gage," Dev replied. One word said enough. He peered over the seat back sheepishly. "Thanks for sticking up for me, Zoey. You didn't have to do that."

"Sure I did." Tessa's heart was still hammering from the heated exchange. "Someone needs to put that punk in his place." She couldn't believe she had ever had a crush on Gage. Ugh. The thought made her want to puke.

"Seriously. Wanna prank him?" Lewis got a wicked glint in his eyes.

Blake stopped in her tracks, clearly mistaking the look for flirtation. "Oh, hi, Lew." She batted her eyelashes.

Hailey sidled up next to her. "When's your next race?" she asked, tossing her long chestnut hair over her shoulder. "We can't wait to cheer you on."

Lewis glanced sideways uncomfortably. "Um, I'm actually going to skip the next race. It conflicts with band practice."

The girls' faces scrunched up, like they smelled something rotten. "Really? What does your dad think about that?"

"Dad's cool with it. Mom too." This was a complete lie; Lewis hadn't told his parents that he'd rather focus on music than sports. Besides, they were preoccupied with yoga classes, golf outings, and his brothers' athletic achievements. Maybe they wouldn't even notice if he quit the track team entirely?

Hailey and Blake moved on, whispering and giggling behind their hands.

Maeve boarded the bus last. She scanned the rows, trying and failing to make eye contact with someone, anyone, who might share their seat. Her cheeks grew hot, but she kept grinning. A star performer always stayed in character.

The bus lurched forward. "Finally! Thank you!" she said as a boy named Caleb moved reluctantly to make room for her. Maeve sat down—to the unmistakable *tblllttt* of a whoopee cushion. The bus exploded with laughter.

Gage and his bully friends, Thaddeus and Lee, howled. "Play *that* on your flute!"

It's not a flute, it's an oboe, Maeve thought furiously. Aloud, she mused, "That would be a hard note to hit." Her perky smile remained fixed in place. She spotted Lewis and Dev diagonally across the aisle. She reached out and tapped Lewis's shoulder. "Was this your handiwork?"

He gave her an innocent *Who, me?* look.

She rolled her eyes. "Flatulence is a very natural occurrence, you know. Basic bodily functions are the lowest forms of humor."

Lewis guffawed. "You insult me again, Maeve Greene. Whoopee cushions are a totally novice move. Like I told you earlier, I am an artiste." He gave a chef's kiss.

Someone made an armpit fart. The bus erupted with laughter again.

"All right! Settle down!" the bus driver hollered, turning onto the highway.

"We'll arrive at our destination in half an hour," added Mrs. Minuzzi, one of the trip chaperones. "I encourage you to engage in quiet and respectful conversation with your peers during this time. You may also choose to brainstorm thought-provoking questions to ask our tour guides later."

A few seats behind Maeve, Isaiah slunk down low. He had plenty of unanswered questions. He pulled the Journal of Strange Occurrences out of his backpack and pretended not to overhear everything that was going on around him. Dev might've wished he could be invisible, but Isaiah was actually good at it. Ever since his uncle's funeral, most people tiptoed around him, kids and teachers alike. He guessed it was better than being picked on, but some days he wished someone—anyone—would check in. Usually that was Zoey, except she'd ignored him all morning. Had he done something to upset her?

He spotted her reflection in the bus window. She was seated several rows ahead of him, next to a girl named Jamila who played trombone in the band. The silver cuff bracelet on Zoey's left wrist glinted in the sunlight that was beginning to break through the rain clouds. Isaiah squinted. Wait a minute. Aside from a purple smartwatch, Zoey never wore jewelry. This was certainly a Strange Occurrence. He scribbled a note in his journal. He squinted. And was that mascara on her eyelashes? As he studied his friend more carefully, he realized Zoey wasn't Zoey. She was Tessa, *dressed* as Zoey. He inhaled sharply.

His mind raced. Why hadn't Zoey mentioned this plan to him? She'd been looking forward to the NASA field trip. Why would she willingly opt out? He supposed she could still go with the Monday group, but that would mean switching places with her sister *again*. Something was up, and Isaiah was determined to figure it out. But he wasn't about to ruin the ruse. If the Hawthorne-Scott twins were up to something, he'd play along.

5

STATION LIMINUS

THE MEETING AT STATION LIMINUS WAS NOT GOING WELL. IN fact, it was bordering on chaos. Ignatia rapped her ruby gavel, trying to regain some semblance of order and decorum.

"Earth does not deserve our assistance!" Xol cried.

Bo'lar sneered. "Agreed. Your people have brought this upon themselves. Let us not cause discord amongst the council. The Earthlings' dilemma is not ours to fret over. Let their planet self-destruct."

Cirzin's three pale eyes flickered in his ancient oval face. "My fear is that the problems facing the inhabitants of Dim14 could affect the integrity of the multiverse, including *our* dimensions. These things can catch, you know."

Shro's body grew rigid, the muscles in his angular jaw taut.

"Don't be ridiculous," Xol said with a huff. "Stupidity, greed, and complacency are not contagious."

Admiral Snortwraithe shot a look at Finto. "That is debatable. However, cataclysmic environmental collapse is never a fully isolated phenomenon. Let us not forget that a long time ago, a similar event produced ripples, tears, and anomalies in the space-time continuum. Some of us, like myself, lived through it."

Cirzin nodded slowly. "The fabric of our great multiverse has become increasingly volatile and interconnected in recent years."

The room fell quiet. Finto scratched his head dully.

"What course of action do you propose, Cirzin?" Ignatia asked, hoping to move toward resolution.

He exhaled slowly. "A targeted compactification would minimize dimensional membrane damage."

"What? You want to blow up Earth?" Duna said, slapping a hand onto the onyx table.

Cirzin shook his head. "Not blow up. Implode."

"How is that different?" Duna asked.

"Compactification is a controlled procedure. To be clear, I do not wish to pursue this option, but it *is* an option."

"No, no, no!" Finto shook his fists angrily. Being a delegate was no fun. At all.

Duna sat up taller. "I suggest we enact emergency restoration measures, like a bandage, to keep the ailing planet functioning for at least one year. During that time, we invite a small group of Earthlings to visit Station Liminus. We train them in sustainable strategies, educate them about the multiverse, give them tools to succeed, then return them to their dimension to heal their planet."

Quirg arched a spiked eyebrow.

Bo'lar grumbled. "You give them far too much credit. The Earthlings only recently managed to cross the Threshold. Most of them cannot even comprehend the possibility, let alone the sheer complexity, of the multiverse." She set her six eyes on Finto. "Clearly, their intelligence levels are inferior. They will provide us with nothing but an interdimensional headache."

"What if they offered us something in return? Something that would make the hassle worthwhile," Shro suggested.

"As in?" Ignatia asked.

Shro regarded Mr. Finto. "I understand Earthlings possess certain technologies and skills that may prove valuable to the rest of our dimensions. Mr. Finto, you are an executive at a successful mining corporation, correct?"

He nodded proudly.

Shro turned to the council. "Perhaps the elusive regenerex ores on each of your planets could be extracted with his assistance?"

Secretary Leapkeene glanced at the empty chair to her left, reserved for Eryna, the powerful queen of Klapproth. She remained in quarantine on Dim2 since the silvox plague struck, rendering the entire population incommunicado. No one knew if, or when, Eryna would return to her post within the council.

"Good plan," Finto said, as though he had been the one to suggest it. "Now that you mention it, I believe my advisor has already tapped a group of investors, er, candidates, for this sort of thing. Highly skilled technicians and brilliant thinkers. The best. The brightest. Hand-picked from across the globe."

"How soon could they arrive on Station Liminus?" Ignatia asked.

Finto tugged at the collar of his button-down shirt, trying to remember what his advisor had said. "Our Conroy operative should be ready any day now."

At this, the table grew quiet, each delegate deep in thought.

"We must act. And to do so, we must vote," Ignatia announced.

Key pads flickered to life on the table's surface. Each council member entered their votes. Ignatia assessed the responses.

"It is not unanimous, but it is decided. Using regenerative therapies from our various dimensions, Earth will be put on temporary life support. If the selected Earthlings survive the trip across the Threshold, if they can make a compelling case for saving their planet, and if they prove that they can contribute in meaningful ways to the multiverse, we will consider additional aid. However, if justification for resuscitating Earth cannot be exhibited, we will pursue a targeted compactification."

Bo'lar and Snortwraithe groused. Duna breathed a sigh of relief.

"Mr. Finto, you will return to your dimension at once and mobilize your envoys," Ignatia instructed.

Salvido Finto stood and straightened his jacket. He desperately wanted to get out of the stuffy meeting chamber and back to Earth. "Thank you," he said.

"Quirg, please escort the councilor to Gate Hall," Ignatia said, rising to her feet. "Prepare to initiate a Transfer."

The Klapprothi child hid in a forgotten corner of Station Liminus. Queen Eryna had given clear instructions: Gather information but stay out of sight. Stay out of trouble. Stay alive. She hadn't said anything specifically about staying within the cramped capsule's quarters. Virri was restless, bored, hungry. She would need to find her way back to Kor soon.

She climbed a bench, scaled the wall nimbly as a lizard. From there, she reached up, prodding the ceiling panels, careful not to scrape her sensitive fingertips on the sharp edges. She located the metal grate of a ventilation duct and used her three long, dexterous fingers to unscrew the bolts holding it in place. They came free easily. This made Virri smile. Escape routes were usually much more treacherous.

With almost liquid movement, she pulled herself up into the opening, her small size betraying impressive strength. She pressed her hands and sensory ports to the duct. She shivered. Not because the metal was cold to the touch, but because the vibrations from afar told her the emergency MAC meeting was not a calm one.

She needed to learn more. She crept silently through the duct system, winding deeper into the Station's twisting innards. Without an illumabeam to guide her, the tunnels were as black as the darkspace beyond the Station's outer walls. Virri navigated using touch alone.

She came to a ventilation chute. Somewhere far below, a mechanism clicked and rumbled. Suddenly, a valve opened, blowing scalding, acrid air into her face. She fell backward, her sensory ports stinging. She rubbed her face and hands, humming to heal the pain, until the burning sensation dulled.

She continued on, careful to avoid other release valves and gas lines. She traversed a split in the ductwork. Which way? She felt for a signal, then began to scale the vertical shaft overhead, secreting a sticky film from her palms that allowed her to climb without slipping.

Finally, she reached another juncture and pulled herself into a spacious tunnel. There, she paused, mapping the route in her mind's eye, committing the labyrinthine ducts to memory. Left. Right. Down. Across. Up. Left again.

She stopped at the edge of a large polygonal grate, with louvers that opened and closed like gills. Below, twelve delegates debated loudly. Despite the rising volume, the Klapprothi child heard nothing. Like the others of her planet, she had lost her ability to hear after the plague.

The argument below grew louder; the sound vibrations unsettled Virri. She could not discern their exact meaning, but she knew there was nothing peaceful or harmonious about them. Instinctively, she curled herself into a tight knot, her retractable carapace hardening in a protective shell around her body.

EARTH

"WE'RE HERE!" COACH DIAZ ANNOUNCED AS THE BUS PULLED up to a sprawling complex of hangars, research pods, administrative buildings, domed telescopes, radio towers, and more. The central structure was made of concrete, steel, and glass, its angled roof emblazoned with the NASA logo. For a moment, Dev glowed with pride. His dad worked here, and this place was cool.

Mrs. Minuzzi addressed the students. "Before we disembark, I would like to remind you that you are ambassadors for our school. Your words and actions are reflections of Conroy Middle School. Please conduct your-selves accordingly."

"Attending field trips like this is a privilege, not a right!" Coach Diaz added, giving his whistle a toot.

"Yes. We expect your best behavior. Understood?" Mrs. Minuzzi asked.

A chorus of *uh-huhs, yups,* and *sure, whatevers* rumbled down the aisle.

Maeve stood and responded in an irritatingly chipper voice, "Yes, ma'am! Thank you, Mrs. Minuzzi, for your leadership and service! And thank you, Coach Diaz and Miss Panos, for chaperoning as well. We will make you proud."

"What a suck-up," Jamila muttered.

"Seriously," Tessa responded, forgetting to act like Zoey.

Jamila quirked an eyebrow. "Sounds like someone's still harboring feelings about the drum major title . . ."

"I don't know what you're talking about," Tessa replied, trying to regain her composure. Truthfully, she *didn't* understand the dynamic between Zoey and Maeve. Ever since starting middle school, the twins had grown apart, sharing less and less, arguing more and more. Maybe swapping places for a few hours would give Tessa a chance to reconnect with Zoey in some way.

Dev picked up his saxophone case. "Why couldn't I have chosen to play a smaller, lighter instrument, like, say, the piccolo?"

"You think that's bad? I have to haul this around!" a ginger-haired boy named Nolan said, heaving a tuba off the bus.

One by one, the students made their way toward the main entrance. As Isaiah was about to exit the bus with his trumpet in hand, he stopped to thank the driver. The driver stared back at Isaiah. His right eye twitched, his expression shifted. In a gravelly voice he said, "May your journey be a bold one. May you find the answers you seek."

"Uh, thanks?" Isaiah shrugged and stepped off the bus, trying to play it cool. Inside, he was jittery.

"What was that all about?" Dev asked.

"The bus driver told me to have a bold journey. Bizarro!" Isaiah laughed nervously. He'd record this Strange Occurrence in his journal as soon as they got inside.

"Huh. He told me to confront my darkest fears," Dev said. "Which is extra weird because my mom said something very similar this morning."

"That's pretty heavy for a field trip."

"Given my current circumstances, it actually makes sense. My dad works here." He pointed to the building they were about to enter. "And I'm afraid he's going to embarrass the pants off me."

"That's assuming you even have pants to embarrass off after Gage delivers that supersonic-atomic-bubonic wedgie he promised," Lewis said.

"Not funny!" Dev jabbed Lewis with his elbow.

"Are you guys talking about Benni?" Maeve butted in. "He's been driving Conroy buses since our parents were kids, back when they still ran on gas instead of solar energy. Can you imagine?"

"Yuck. No wonder the city had a smog problem."

"Seriously. Gramps even claims Benni drove the bus back when *his* grandfather went to school, which can't be possible. The guy would be like a hundred and fifty years old. Still, Benni's been around a long time. Probably knows a few things. Maybe you should think long and hard about whatever he told you."

"Well, what did he say to you?" Lewis asked.

Maeve tossed her shoulders back. "He said, 'Choose truth over theater. Unless theater is your truth.' Which is, like, the most perfect thing for a performer like me." She fanned her hands out dramatically. "He could clearly see I was born for the stage, the limelight."

"Sorry to burst your bubble, but marching band isn't exactly Hollywood."

She huffed. "Obviously. But it's a stepping-stone to greater things. A foundation of music and choreography. I mean, drama practically oozes from my pores." She struck a pose.

"Are you sure whatever's oozing isn't actually leftover slime from that spack-attack?"

She narrowed her eyes at Isaiah. He closed his mouth quickly.

Lewis frowned. "All Benni said to me was, 'Don't touch anything, dimple-boy.'"

"See? Told you the guy was wise." Maeve gave a satisfied nod. She turned on her heels and marched toward the entrance.

"Is it just me, or is that girl more annoying than usual today?" Lewis asked.

Dev shrugged. Maeve didn't bother him that much. He actually sort of admired her gumption. Like Zoey, she wasn't afraid to speak up. Maybe that explained why she and Zoey often butted heads. It was also probably one of the reasons Maeve was a regular victim of locker spack-attacks.

Nearby, Tessa was quiet, listening to the others. The bus driver had spoken to her, too. His dark blue eyes had bored into hers, like he was seeing *beyond* her. It sent a shiver down her spine. He had said, "May you embrace your true identity and find your voice." Which meant she was probably doing a sucky job impersonating her sister. She would really need to up her game if she was going to pull off this whole imposter gig.

"Hurry along, everyone! Time waits for no one!" Mrs. Minuzzi beckoned the class toward a set of gleaming double doors.

STATION LIMINUS

"WE RECEIVED WORD THAT MR. FINTO TRANSFERRED SAFELY back to Earth and is resting at home in Milan," Shro informed Ignatia.

A small group of councilors had gathered in the Station's diplomatic salon for refreshments before an afternoon packed with judiciary hearings. Each of the thirteen dimensions was more or less autonomous, governing themselves however their dominant life-forms deemed fit and fair. However, cross-dimensional crimes and legal issues that arose on the neutral Station headquarters itself were tried by the MAC, under terms set forth in the Multiverse Accord.

"Resting?" Ignatia shook her head, sending a cascade of hair over her angular shoulders. "Shouldn't he be assembling the envoys and debriefing them? His planet is on the verge of ruin and he decides to take a nap?" She sighed forlornly. "I fear I will never understand Earthlings..."

"It seems Finto did not tolerate Transfer well," Shro

explained. "He reported many side effects . . . stomach pains, intense headaches, warped vision, pixelated extremities."

Ignatia set down her steaming mug of tartea. "What was that last one?"

"Apparently Mr. Finto claims that he cannot *see* or *use* his arms at this time. He says he can *feel* them, but his cellular realignments seem to be glitching."

Quirg grumbled, "If they cannot handle Transfer, they should not participate in council matters. Simple enough."

"Well," Duna interjected, "each species reacts differently. Mertanyans such as myself cannot Transfer without severe molecular damage after the age of nineteen. That is why delegates from my dimension are always young, like me."

Xol leaned back, picking his pincers with a sharpened claw. "Does this mean Finto will not be accompanying the selected Earthlings to the Station?"

"It is a possibility." Shro stirred his tartea and added an extra cube of sweet succrolein.

"The Earthlings still have much to prove. I hope they do not waste this opportunity, for our sake and theirs." Ignatia rose from her chair, her indigo robes moving liquidly around her. "I seem to have lost my appetite. I think I will take a brief walk through the Station to stretch my legs before our next session commences."

Whenever she could shirk her governing duties for a few precious minutes, Ignatia liked to wander the Menagerie, the Arboretum, and Gate Hall, remarking on the beauty and variety of their great multiverse. It helped clear her head. Lately, she'd been more stressed than ever. The council had grown increasingly divided, with the tenor shifting from harmony to discord. It troubled her. She longed to confide in her longtime colleague and dear friend, Queen Eryna. But the quarantine was still under effect. For the time being, Ignatia was unable to send or receive transmissions to anyone on Klapproth.

She took a deep breath and walked briskly. She paused at the Arboretum's large glass entryway. This time of year, the greenhouse was a riot of color—each ziffel, dahlia, and rosewhip blossom more extraordinary than the next, competing for pollinators' attention. At night, the bioluminescent lichens were dazzling, as were the carnivorous rat-catchers, massive succulents that fed on nocturnal pests. She was grateful that Duna had proposed the initiative, and she hoped to expand the impressive collection of plants in the coming months.

In the Menagerie, Ignatia enjoyed watching golden eels writhe in tanks of slick mud, and hook-beak preybirds tending nests of feathered hatchlings. She couldn't resist a quick visit to the playful poleers, who preened their checkered coats while chittering happily from cactus tops.

She turned and strode in the direction of Gate Hall, encountering Quirg, worrying over a red brick portal. As custodian of the Gates, Quirg was responsible for monitoring the Station's entry and exit points. It was an important job; the MAC wouldn't tolerate strange beasts or invasive species wandering into their headquarters, unchecked.

Permanent Gates were reserved for dimensional constituents who traveled to and from Station Liminus on a regular basis. Other portals came and went, shifting frequently, representing vernacular building techniques from across the multiverse. There were doors made of ancient stone, sleek carbonile cables, gleaming alloys, durable plastene. Some openings were built from wood, mud, and thatched straw. From time to time, brass-rimmed glass portholes appeared, offering glimpses of sparkling turquoise water and extraordinary aquatic creatures. Quirg liked those very much, but they made a mess when opened incorrectly.

The naturally occurring Gates, known as Rips, were the most troublesome. These arose with little warning, cleaving walls apart, their blackened edges raw and flashing with quantum lightning. Sometimes they closed moments after opening; others lingered for days, or years, like seeping wounds that wouldn't heal.

"Do we know where the Earthlings will exit?" Ignatia asked, pausing to peer through a door at the landscape beyond, with black sand deserts, ice-capped mountains, and floating islands.

"Not yet," Quirg replied, waddling to keep pace with long-limbed Ignatia, whose strides outmatched him by two. "Once Finto's team initiates the transfer sequence, we should receive portal coordinates," he said. "You will be notified immediately."

Ignatia nodded her approval. "Thank you, Quirg." With that, she turned to leave, eyeing the vast array of doors that led into and out of various dimensions.

Sometimes, when time allowed, she would linger and open a mossy door just to breathe in humid, orchid-scented jungle air, or feel the warmth of Ornstav's sun on her face. Of course, not all dimensions contained such beauty and wonder. Danger, darkness, and terrible monsters lurked behind some doors. These remained locked, forbidden. Not even mighty Ignatia dared to go near them. As she departed Gate Hall, she hoped opening up the Station to the inhabitants of Earth was not a mistake.

8

EARTH

"WELCOME TO THE GWEN RESEARCH CENTER!" A CHEERY GUIDE named Ari greeted the Conroy students. She wore a cobalt-blue NASA-issued jumpsuit, a wide smile, and a silver nose ring. "We are one of ten NASA field stations in the United States."

"That we know about," mumbled Isaiah under his breath.

"Must you have a conspiracy theory about everything?" Maeve whispered back.

"I am a truth-seeker, okay?" He cast a sidelong glance at Tessa, who still hadn't spoken to him.

Dev was looking in the same direction, praying his father was too busy unscrambling the mysteries of the cosmos to make a surprise appearance and embarrass him in front of his crush.

"We're excited to teach you about the groundbreaking and important work we do here," Ari said. She gestured to an X-ray machine and metal detector. "Before the tour officially begins, you'll each need to clear security. Standard procedure, like at an airport. Just to make sure no one is smuggling in any alien life-forms." She winked and the chaperones chuckled.

"What's the point of looking for aliens when we've already got plenty of freaks in our midst?" Gage murmured, just loud enough that Maeve and a few others could hear. "Did you enjoy your little locker redecoration this morning, Greene?"

Maeve's upper lip quivered, then went ridged as she fought off tears. No matter how hard she tried, her pale skin betrayed her in moments like this, flushing deep red.

Isaiah watched out of the corner of his eye, his vision blurring at the edges as his anger grew. He homed in on Gage; Maeve was to his right, Nolan to his left. His eyes trailed Nolan's arm, stopping at the huge tuba case, his thick fingers struggling against the weight. A few inches below was Gage's foot. Tuba. Foot. Tuba. Foot. And then, as though Isaiah were willing it to happen, Nolan's grip slipped and the huge case landed with a satisfying *thunk!*

"OOUCHHH!" Gage cried, jumping up and down, clutching his smashed toes.

"What is the matter?" Mrs. Minuzzi demanded as the boy flailed.

Gage pointed at Nolan. "He dropped that enormous . . . dorkwhistle on my foot!"

The class burst into laughter. Dev relished the fact that he wasn't the source of their glee for once.

Coach Diaz cleared his throat. "I believe the correct term is *tuba*, Mr. Rawley."

"It's not funny! I think my toe's broken!" Gage bellowed.

"It was an accident! I swear," Nolan said, studying his own hand, perplexed.

Isaiah drifted to the perimeter of the room, rubbing his eyes until his vision cleared. He hadn't actually made Nolan drop the tuba, had he? No. Ridiculous, impossible. That would require an act of telekinesis, and even *he* didn't believe in that. Still, something felt...different. He wondered whether, if he spent some time training, he might be able to harness the feeling. He shook his head. That was just plain silly. It's not like he'd been bitten by some mutant spider and suddenly acquired a superpower. *Although that would be pretty cool...*

"Gage, follow Miss Panos. She'll take you to the infirmary." Mrs. Minuzzi smoothed her floral blouse. "We haven't even begun the official tour, and I feel the need to remind you all of our earlier conversation. You are ambassadors. Please act accordingly."

Coach Diaz scanned the crowd. "As for my band kids, I expect a flawless performance, if you catch my drift. Keep a tight grip on those 'dorkwhistles,' folks." His mustache twitched as he tried to keep a straight face. "Now let's get moving. Aten-hut! For the non-band members among us, that means, let's go!"

One by one, the students moved through security,

emptying their pockets of loose change and electronics. Backpacks and instrument cases slid through the X-ray scanners.

"All phones must be left in secure cubbies during the tour. Not only are these devices distracting, but they can disrupt our network transmissions. And we can't have you sharing photos of our top secret technology," Ari said half-jokingly. She eyed Nolan's foot-flattening tuba. "There's an unoccupied lab down the hall where you can store your instruments for the duration of the visit."

"Awesome," Dev said, eager to ditch his saxophone as quickly as possible.

Ari waved them to the left. "This way."

She led the band kids down a corridor. She entered a code and an unmarked gray door swung open. Half of the room was crowded with cardboard boxes and overstuffed file cabinets. Rolls of yellowed mechanical diagrams and elaborately detailed blueprints were strewn haphazardly across stainless steel tables. The other half of the room was cordoned off with sliding white panels, behind which some defunct machines were likely gathering dust. Ari motioned to an empty table. "You can leave your instruments there."

"What was this lab used for?" Isaiah asked, setting down his trumpet.

"Quantum collision experiments." Ari paused, like she couldn't decide if she should share more. Then she spotted a big, red *Declassified* stamp on the cardboard boxes and shrugged. "A team of scientists wanted to construct a collider that could smash tiny particles together, in order to transform and relocate them."

"As in...teleportation?" Isaiah asked, his voice cracking embarrassingly.

"I suppose you could say that. But I heard it was a total dead end," Ari said dismissively. She tapped her watch. "Let's hurry and rejoin the group so we can get to the more interesting parts of the tour!"

The cadets exited, but Isaiah lingered. He found this room plenty interesting. His uncle had mentioned a quantum collider once, a few months before he disappeared. He reached into his backpack to retrieve his Journal of Strange Occurrences, but it wasn't there.

"Huh?" He spilled the contents of his backpack onto a nearby table. "Aw, man!" He must have left the journal on the bus. He kicked the table leg angrily. Pasted to the back cover of his journal was a large envelope were Isaiah kept Ming's postcards and letters.

They were all he had left of his uncle. He closed his eyes and tried to remember the curve of his uncle's handwriting, the numbers and diagrams. But he couldn't recall the specifics. The thought of the journal getting lost, or falling into the hands of someone like Gage, made his stomach ache.

He had turned to leave when something caught his eye. Printed in blue ink on the side of a cardboard box was a thirteen-pointed symbol with an inner weaving of geometric shapes and curved lines. His eyes traveled across the room, landing on a wall-mounted plaque. The same symbol was etched onto the metal surface.

His breath hitched. He might not be able to remember any specific details about colliders from Ming's letters, but he had seen *that* before. A few times, in fact. On the back of a postcard from Manila. Hand-drawn on an index card with burned edges, postmarked from the Iberian Peninsula. His head swam. This was the sort of connection he had been searching for, hoping for—a single bread crumb in a trail of clues he believed, now more than ever, that his uncle had left for him.

"Isaiah!" Maeve called from the hallway. "What are you doing in there? Stop dawdling!"

"Coming," he replied, stealing one last look at the room. He needed more time. He had to find his way back to this place.

"Eye-say-yah!" Maeve said, chopping his name into three parts.

He followed the group back to the lobby, but not before discreetly lodging a pencil into the door hinge of the storage room, preventing it from locking behind him.

STATION LIMINUS

Dearest Mother,
I have arrived safely on Station Liminus. As you
instructed, I remain hidden. Kor cares for me as
much as she can, sharing her rations and offering
refuge inside her collapsible capsule. I am able to
escape the holding cell thanks to my climbing and
camouflage skills, but Kor is not.

Using items in Kor's bag or tools I could acquire
from the Station's repairworks, I could probably
help break her out, but she says we must wait until
the moment is right. I don't always understand her
logic. I think she should come and hide with me in
the ducts, but she says she learns valuable intel from
hanging around with criminals in the Station's main
holding cell.

Not sure what she plans to learn from them,
other than how to curse in about fifty-nine

different languages and the need for more potent interdimensional deodorants. Have you ever smelled an angry Oolg? I hope you never have to! My sensory ports are still recovering.

Whenever I doubt Kor or question her, she gets this glint in her eyes. She says, "You never know who might wander in. Or what they might be willing to trade." You told me to trust her, so I do. But I'm not always sure that's a good idea. Sometimes when I hide deep inside her capsule bag, I find things that don't belong in there. Things that should maybe be returned to their rightful owners.

Speaking of trust, thank you, Mother, for entrusting me with this task. I will not let you or the people of Klapproth down. I think I have found a potential ally that I can trust, a young delegate from Mertanya, the orange-skied planet of many moons. I will approach this delegate when the time seems right. Until then, I wait . . .

A galaxy of love,
Virri

Virri stared at the note, written with cryo ink in looping Klapprothi script. She crumpled up the pixel paper. Why did she even bother to write? There was no way to send the message back to her home planet.

She had broken into the Station's mainframe, but all of the communication channels with her dimension were blocked. All of Klapproth had been placed under a seemingly impenetrable interdiction.

She walked in circles around the robotics vault, tapping her carapace with her three long fingers, trying to come up with a solution. There had to be some way to transmit a message home. She just had to figure out how ...

STATION LIMINUS

"AN INTRUDER HAS BEEN DETECTED!" THE STATION'S CENTRAL AI announced loudly.

Quirg hurried down the hall. As he rounded the bend, he groaned, "Not again."

"MOOOOOO!" said a black-and-white four-legged creature.

Shro appeared, looking anxiously from side to side. When he spotted the creature, he threw his hands up. "For goodness' sake, Quirg! What is that beast doing here?"

Quirg clenched his spiked teeth. "I don't know how it got in, but I will deal with it."

"You'd better. If the secretary finds out . . ."

As if on cue, Ignatia's voice echoed down the hall, her boots clacking as she hurried in their direction. She stopped, stared. "Oh, my!"

"MOOOOOO!"

"Your Eminence." Shro moved beside her. "Please. You

should return to the judicial chambers. I know how busy you are in these times of discord. So many criminals compromising the security and prosperity of the multiverse."

Quirg nodded. "Yes, I will reroute this creature, which seems to have strayed from—"

"From Dimension7," Shro interrupted, his voice sharp.

Ignatia frowned, her horns changing color. "I've traveled to Dim7 multiple times and never encountered one of these. What is it?" She stepped closer.

"I haven't the slightest clue." Quirg feigned ignorance.

"I believe it's a bovinius lactosis. I implore you to distance yourself, Your Eminence. I hear they are quite dangerous. Vicious temper, infrared eye beams, or some such. See that hanging sack of poison?" Shro pointed at the cow's udder. "I've heard it explodes when the beast is agitated, releasing a lethal toxin."

Ignatia gasped. "How awful!"

"Indeed. Best to let Quirg handle this. As custodian, it is his job after all." Shro shot Quirg a loaded look.

"Right." Ignatia paused. "Although . . . do you think we should maybe . . . keep it? In the Menagerie, perhaps?"

"Absolutely not. We already have two of them."

"We do? I hadn't noticed. In that case, maybe we should move them into a more visible enclosure. There's an empty habitat next to the colossadon. It howls all day long. Poor thing must be lonely."

"Of course the colossadon is lonely! It ate every last one of its kind!"

"Well, yes. But even deadly beasts require some company, I'd imagine." Ignatia stared at the cow. The cow stared back, blinking chocolate-brown eyes sweetly. "This one doesn't look too threatening to me."

"Looks can be deceiving, Your Eminence. You haven't forgotten about the floofling incident, have you?" Flooflings looked like bunnies with soft lavender fur but bit like vipers. A litter had once devoured half the commissary's fuelcell rations and chewed through some highly valuable data cables before anyone recognized what a menace they were.

"Such a shame. They were cute though, weren't they?" Ignatia didn't mention that she had kept a pair in her private chamber—carefully secured within a gnaw-proof tank. She fed them old electronics.

"You can never trust the cute ones, I say," said Quirg. "They skew your judgment." The cow batted her long lashes. Her tail swished from side to side. "See what I mean? Calculated manipulation!"

In reality, he knew that the creature was a harmless dairy cow that had slipped through a bothersome dimensional rip he hadn't yet mended. But admitting that to the secretary could cost him his job. And he had thirty-nine children back on his home planet of Quomo to feed.

Ignatia's wristlet buzzed. She glanced down. "I'm needed in the courtroom."

"Go," said Shro. "We have everything under control."

"Thank you both. I appreciate your help." She departed, leaving Quirg and Shro alone in Gate Hall.

"Was she serious about the Menagerie?" Quirg asked.

"Does it really matter? Get rid of that thing as quickly as possible," Shro hissed, before marching away, the muscles in his hunched back rippling beneath his rust-colored suiting.

Quirg scowled. He led the cow toward a large barn door. He slid the red painted panel aside, revealing a lush green landscape with rolling hills covered in sweet, fragrant clover. Eight moons winked in the tangerine sky. "Off you go. I hear Mertanya is lovely this time of year. Safe travels," he said, giving the cow a pat on the rump.

"MOOOOO!" the cow replied, trotting happily across the Threshold, her bell clanging softly as she disappeared.

11

EARTH

GLITTERING CONSTELLATIONS DANCED ACROSS A SIMULATED night sky. Chins tilted upward, mouths agape, the students of Conroy Middle School gazed at the auditorium's curved ceiling as galaxies materialized, swirling and bursting with color and light. A recording narrated a cosmic journey, zipping between solar systems, orbiting burning balls of gas, dodging errant asteroids. The projection slowed, zoomed in.

A single planet came into focus: green and blue, capped with white poles and downy cloud wisps. Earth, the way it had looked before. Now, of course, the sapphire blues were muddled, the ice mostly gone, the clouds polluted and gray, the emerald greens pale and anemic, replaced in many places by barren browns. Maeve felt a pang in her chest; she wanted to know *that* version of Earth. She wanted to live *there*.

The lights came on; the nostalgic image disappeared. A microphone crackled and hummed over the speaker system.

"Greetings, Earthlings!"

Dev cringed. He knew that voice. To his horror, his father appeared, entering the stage backward, wiggling and shuffling, attempting the world's most awkward moonwalk. Everyone cracked up. Everyone except Dev.

"Hello! Hello! What better way to enter NASA than with a moonwalk, am I right?" His eyebrows waggled. "My name is Dr. Mohan Khatri, head of the Quantum Studies department here at the Gwen Research Center. I'm happy to report that I am a much better physicist than dancer." He busted a goofy move, making the kids laugh again.

Wait, were his classmates actually enjoying this? Dev sat up, listening carefully. The laughter sounded good-natured, not cruel or taunting. He'd heard the latter version enough times to recognize the difference. He started to relax. Maybe this wouldn't be such an awful day after all.

"Since that animation was made, our planet has undergone major changes at a rapid pace," Dr. Khatri said. "Sort of like puberty, which most of you are probably familiar with."

Dev cringed. Had his dad really just said *puberty*? Gross.

"While unwelcome blemishes and funky body odor can be unpleasant, they are nothing compared to the challenges currently facing our planet. Here at NASA, our work is more critical than ever. We send probes into space to study far-reaching solar systems, and we develop innovative solutions to improve life here on Earth. Our satellites track weather patterns, tectonic activity, and more. We've sent humans to the moon and Mars. Although that last trip didn't end according to plan, but that's a story for another day..."

Dev shifted uncomfortably in his chair.

"So, are you an astronaut, or what?" Thaddeus asked, growing bored.

"Alas, I am not. My work focuses on a very unique field called *catastro-physics*, which means I study the way space, time, and matter react under calamitous or catastrophic conditions."

"That sounds doomy," Isaiah said quietly, wishing he could take notes in his journal.

"Do you get to blow stuff up?" Gage asked.

"As a general rule, I try not to," Dr. Khatri replied. "In fact, I aim to do the opposite. Currently, my team is developing a range of exciting prototypes, including a Syntropitron."

"A what?" Isaiah asked, perking up.

"Imagine reverse dynamite."

"I hear that stuff is the bomb," Lewis mused.

"Exactly!" Dr. Khatri said. "Instead of entropy—the chaos and disorder that occur when energy pushes particles apart—our patented syntropification process pulls mass, time, and space together. In theory, we could use the Syntropitron to rebuild and reconfigure individual atoms, repairing planetary damage at various scales." An image appeared on the screen behind him.

"Here's a demo video to illustrate the concept." A glass vase sat on a table. A scientist wearing safety goggles smashed the vase with a hammer. Then, the scientist returned with a tubular contraption. She aimed the tapered edge at the broken vase. The machine shook, and a burst of fluorescent light leaped out in a searing arc. In the blink of an eye, shards of shattered glass re-composed themselves, as though someone had pressed rewind. The scientist stepped back and revealed the vase, wholly intact, sitting on the table in its original location.

Maeve clapped enthusiastically from the front row.

"Thank you," Dr. Khatri said. "My goal is to make our world better for future generations—which means you." He gazed out at the crowd. "Because we are all stewards of this special place we call home."

"Give me a break! That video was just a magic trick with some crummy special effects," Gage said skeptically.

"You may think so, but what you witnessed was real. At this stage, our prototype is only capable of minor syntropification, but we hope to expand and improve the invention. Imagine if we could repair holes in the ozone, rebuild eroded shorelines, restore rainforest habitats. The possibilities are infinite."

"What's stopping you?"

"Our biggest challenge is finding a sustainable fuel source capable of powering larger prototypes," Dr. Khatri replied.

"Are you sure you're not an astronaut?" Jamila asked hopefully.

"Again, I am not an astronaut." Dr. Khatri sighed. "My jobs here at NASA include physicist, inventor, team leader, and occasional late-night tea-brewer. However, my favorite job is being a father. And, lucky me, my firstborn is here today! You may know him as Dev, but he'll always be my little Dev-i-doodle."

Dev froze. His mouth went dry. Everyone turned to stare. He wondered if it was scientifically possible to die from embarrassment. Like actually drop dead. Because he was feeling pretty close. He spotted Zoey looking at him across the auditorium. His face flushed Mars red. His skin felt approximately the same temperature as the surface of the sun. He ducked his head, wishing with all his might that a portal to an alternate dimension would suddenly open, offering an escape from this torture.

Thankfully, before his dad could do more damage, a woman in a charcoal suit and crisp white lab coat strode onto the stage, drawing everyone's gaze. Her dark brown hair was swept into an elegant chignon. Her smile dazzled.

"Hello!" she said. "I'm sorry to keep you waiting. I hope my esteemed colleague kept you entertained and engaged. His moonwalking skills are unparalleled!" She smiled pleasantly. "And at NASA, we take moon walks of all sorts very seriously."

This drew a small laugh from the crowd. Dev exhaled, grateful for the diversion.

"My name is Dr. Genevieve Scopes and this is Professor Ian McGillum." A stout, gray-haired man scuttled onstage, holding a clipboard with one hand and waving with the other. "Together with Dr. Khatri, we collaborate on some exciting projects. Would anyone like to get a special, behind-the-scenes tour?"

Dozens of hands shot into the air. "Great! I love your enthusiasm. I believe your chaperones divided you into two groups. Orange group, please follow Professor McGillum. Purple group, please come with Dr. Khatri and me."

Dev looked down at a big purple dot on the nametag stuck to his shirt. From his place onstage, his dad flashed a dorky double thumbs-up. Dev couldn't believe his terrible luck.

EARTH

DEV SHUFFLED TOWARD THE CLUMP OF OTHER PURPLE-DOT kids. He was grateful that Lewis was in his group, and Zoey, too. Even if she made his heart race and his palms clammy.

His father opened his arms as he approached. "What? You're not going to hug your dear old dad?" Despite Dev's protests, he pulled him into a bear hug, mussing his hair.

"Dad! Please. You can't do that. I'm not five years old!" he said, mortified.

Dr. Khatri buttoned his lab coat. "Right. You're nearly a teenager now. Allergic to hugs. Fine. I understand. Maybe you're too cool to try the antigravity simulator, then?"

"What? That sounds amazing! We have to try that!" Lewis said. "Is it like virtual reality?"

"Even better. It's *real* reality," Dr. Khatri replied.

"Whoa."

Dr. Khatri extended his hand to Lewis. "What is your name, young man?"

"Lew, sir!" he said brightly.

"Loser?" Dr. Khatri scratched his head. "What an unconventional moniker."

Lewis shrugged. "Lewiston Wynner, to be precise. Dev and I are in marching band together."

"A fellow musician? Brilliant!" His face lit up. "Did you know music and physics are closely related? Kepler, Newton, Sagan, and others were fascinated by the connections between the two. Modern string theory posits that the subatomic particles that make up our universe are similar to the notes one can play on an instrument, like a symphony of vibrating strings."

"Really?" said Lewis, genuinely intrigued.

"And saxophonist John Coltrane was inspired by Einstein and incorporated physics and geometry into his musical compositions. Right, Dad?" Dev added, happy they could find some unembarrassing common ground.

"Yes! His *Interstellar Space* album will transport you to new dimensions."

"It will?" Isaiah asked, leaning closer.

Dr. Khatri smiled. "Not literally, of course. But emotionally, musically, maybe even spiritually."

"My dad loves Coltrane, too," Zoey said, joining the conversation. "Nice tie, by the way." She pointed to the purple-and-black silk tie with a giant pi symbol above an image of a cherry pie.

Dev was dumbstruck. Had Zoey Hawthorne-Scott actually complimented his father's horrendously nerdy accessories? Maybe he *had* slipped into some alternate dimension.

"Ah-ha! See, Dev? I knew your friends would appreciate my style. I've even got matching socks!" He lifted his pant leg as proof.

"Okay, time to go. This way, please!" Dr. Scopes sang, leading the group out of the auditorium and down the hall.

As they walked, Isaiah asked Maeve, "Do you notice anything odd about her face?"

"Who? Zoey?" Something about her former best friend was different today, but Maeve couldn't put her finger on it.

Isaiah shook his head. "No, Dr. Scopes. Does she look blurry to you?"

"I think you need new glasses," Maeve replied.

"I don't wear glasses."

"Maybe you should get some. She looks fine to me. Pretty, even."

Isaiah blinked. Dr. Scopes's face lacked contrast, like she was airbrushed. Too smooth, too soft. He blinked again. She returned to normal. Maybe Maeve was right about the glasses . . .

A few minutes later, they entered a bright, busy laboratory. Scientists sat at long benches, piping liquids into trays, scanning slides, and dissecting dishes of gelatinous goo.

"Are those blobs . . . alien life-forms?" Tessa asked.

Dr. Scopes chuckled. "No, but close. This team is studying physarum polycephalum, also known as slime mold, found right here on Earth."

"Yeah, pretty sure I found some of that stuff smeared across my locker this morning," Maeve mumbled.

"Slime mold is a brainless, neuron-less superorganism with high intelligence levels," Dr. Scopes explained.

"Sounds like my older brothers, minus the intelligence part," said Lewis.

"What do you do with it?" Jamila asked, grimacing at the sight of a particularly gooey blob.

Dr. Khatri smiled. "For a while, we believed mimicking the human brain was the optimal way to create artificial intelligence systems. But there is a vast array of nonhuman life worthy of emulation. The ingenuity of our biological brethren is astounding."

The tour moved on, stopping next at a sound lab with textured walls, computer screens, microphones, and speakers as big as trucks. Two technicians wore black headphones and worked at a massive mixing console.

"This is where we listen to our radio telescopes, scanning for sound patterns that may indicate the presence of life beyond our solar system," Dr. Scopes told them.

"It's also where we record our monthly *Houston, We Have a Podcast* shows," Dr. Khatri added, grinning.

"Like the Arecibo message of 1974 and the Voyager Golden Records, our team transmits interstellar radio signals across a universal beta channel. Our transmissions carry basic information about humanity and Earth, in the hopes that extraterrestrial intelligence might one day receive them," Dr. Scopes explained, pointing at the various buttons on the mixing stations.

"How would you access the beta channel?" Nolan asked.

"It's actually quite simple. Any radio tuned to transmit signals near the 145 megahertz frequency will be picked up."

Isaiah seemed intrigued by the idea. "So, could I send you a message from my living room in Conroy?"

"If you constructed an operable transceiver, then yes, you could." Dr. Khatri nodded.

Dr. Scopes stepped in. "But you could also just get in touch through our website, or the direct phone line. Much easier than building a radio of your own."

"What happens if you do hear from aliens one day?" Jamila asked.

Dr. Khatri's eyes lit up. "Well, in the event we do make contact with sentient species in the future, our linguistics team is working hard to develop a universal sonic language that would allow us communicate with other life-forms. That's also where some of our AI research will come in handy. Discovery is a wonderfully collaborative process!"

Dev rolled his eyes. His dad was geeking out, hardcore.

Isaiah raised his hand. "What about extra-*dimensional* communication?"

Dr. Scopes's forehead crinkled. "I'm sorry, I don't understand the question."

Isaiah felt the eyes of his peers on him. He wasn't

one to speak up in class; most of his classmates tended to forget he existed at all. He cleared his throat. "You're talking about contacting planets in other solar systems. But what about beyond the Milky Way? What about separate universes?"

Dr. Scopes's face shifted. She looked at Dr. Khatri uncomfortably. "At one time, people postulated that other dimensions might exist within a broader multiverse of sorts. I know movies and books romanticize this concept, but parallel universe theories have been discredited by the scientific community."

His uncle's face flashed in his mind's eye. "What if someone disappeared into thin air?" Isaiah asked, his gray eyes eager. "How could you explain *that*?"

"That sounds more like a question for a forensics team than for NASA scientists." She let out a hearty chuckle. The class laughed along with her.

"No, I'm serious. What if there were signs that the universe had holes, or tears? Places where one dimension intersected with another. Could something like that be possible?"

"Well, anything is possible," said Dev's father.

"Dr. Khatri, with all due respect, we can't entertain such outlandish hypotheses. It would be reckless to fill these kids' heads with untested science. Don't you think?" Dr. Scopes gave a mauve-lipped smile.

Dev's father shook his head. "On the contrary, in the words of Professor Tegmark, 'If we dismiss theories because they seem weird, we risk missing true breakthroughs.'

Dimensional plurality and liminality are fascinating concepts worthy of consideration."

"What do you mean by liminality?" Isaiah asked.

"It refers to the in-between zones along dimensional borders. As you said, places where someone or something might slip through, from one world to another."

The group was quiet, listening intently. Dr. Khatri continued, "Ever since the Big Bang, our universe has been slowly expanding. Space-stretching, as predicted by Einstein's general theory of relativity, could eventually result in dimensional tears. I believe there may be regions of space-time beyond what we can see."

Dr. Scopes let out a soft sigh and patted Dr. Khatri on the shoulder. "My colleague is humoring you. In reality, nothing of the sort could exist. The laws of physics won't allow for it. Now, who wants to sample some freeze-dried space ice cream?"

The kids cheered, all except Isaiah, who wasn't satisfied with the answer. As his classmates filed out of the room, he lingered, searching for signs of the thirteen-pointed symbol he'd seen earlier.

Out in the hallway, Dr. Khatri pulled Dev and Lewis to the side. "Remember the antigravity simulator I mentioned?" he said quietly, watching as Dr. Scopes led the others toward the Milky Way Café. "How would you and your friends like a special demo?"

"Really?" Dev asked.

"I'm in!" Lewis said.

"In for what?" Maeve said, nosily.

"Dev's dad is going to take us someplace top secret and extra cool."

"Sounds fun. I'll join you," Maeve replied, even though she hadn't exactly been invited.

"You can come, too. If you want," Dev said shyly to Zoey, who was hanging back, looking a little lost.

"Sure, okay," Tessa said, figuring this was probably what the real Zoey would do.

Dr. Khatri clapped his hands. "Fantastic. I think you four will enjoy this detour." His eyes twinkled. "We can meet up with Dr. Scopes later. Besides, space ice cream tastes like chalk. Highly overrated, in my opinion."

As they descended a back stairwell, Maeve asked, "Where's Isaiah?"

Tessa shrugged. "He must have gone to the café or something."

"Too bad for him. He's going to miss all the fun."

Isaiah slunk along the corridor, ducking into doorways whenever someone in a blue NASA jumpsuit or white lab coat approached. If anyone asked, he'd say he was a field tripper who'd lost his way looking for the bathroom. Innocent enough. Believable too, he hoped.

He climbed a staircase made of glass and steel, spiraling like a double-helix. He rounded the corner and jogged past the auditorium where he and his classmates had watched the introduction video. His heart beat quickly as he ducked under yellow caution tape, passing through an area marked *Restricted Access*. He thought about his uncle, going under-cover in harrowing circumstances, taking risks to expose the truth with his camera in hand. Maybe sneaking around NASA wasn't exactly the same, but Isaiah felt like his uncle Ming would understand. His mother, on the other hand? Not so much.

He tiptoed silently. Motion-sensor surveillance cameras swiveled as he passed. He was too preoccupied to notice their blinking lights. Time was running out. He needed to get back inside the collider room before anyone noticed he was missing.

13

EARTH

"PREPARE TO BE AMAZED . . ." DR. KHATRI SWIPED AN ID CARD, pressed his thumb to a scanpad, and entered a ten-digit passcode. Huge silver doors opened with a hiss. He led the cadets inside. "This way."

Dev, Lewis, Maeve, and Tessa stepped into a tall cylindrical tower. Clad in shining aluminum panels, the structure rose several stories high with a massive fan spinning at the top. A control center with at least a thousand switches adorned the lower wall. Dr. Khatri began to prepare the demonstration. He opened a cabinet to gather a few supplies.

"This looks like the inside of my grandfather's silo, only much cleaner. With more gadgets and less corn," Maeve said, transfixed.

"Your grandfather has a farm?" Lewis asked. Aside from Miss Mary's Dairy, not many private farms existed in the area anymore. Most food was grown in high-density greenhouses that were managed by MegaAg.

"He used to. Before blight ruined his crops, and practically everyone else's." Maeve remembered running through the fields with Gramps and her mom. How long ago had it been? Seven years, maybe eight? She had been young, but the memories were vivid. She missed those carefree days with the sun on her face, dirt under her nails, and grass stains on her knees.

Then things took a turn for the worse. After the farm went under, they moved from the cozy farmhouse to a cramped trailer on the outskirts of the city. Her mom's moods shifted, darkened. Everything changed so fast. Not only the situation at home, but everywhere. *Precipitous*, the newscasters said. Warming, melting, rising tides, drought. One thing led to another. The snowball effect, everyone called it. To Maeve, it felt more like an avalanche.

"My grandmother had a farm once, too," Tessa said, although her memories were less fond. She instinctively touched the cuff bracelet hiding her scar from the tractor accident.

"Yeah, I know, Zo. We've talked about this before. Remember?" Maeve gave her a probing look.

"Right, sorry," Tessa said, trying to cover up the mistake. "I must have forgotten."

"Forgotten, or never listened in the first place?" Maeve replied, her cheeks pinking.

Tessa stared, unsure how Zoey would respond to the loaded question. Thankfully, Dr. Khatri appeared, presenting them with an armful of strange garments. "Time to suit up."

"There is no way we'll fit into those, Dad," Dev said, eyeing the hefty silver, black, and green outfits.

"Ah, but you will. Because our textile specialists engineered these with responsive self-sizing modulation fibers."

"So, like, fancy spandex?" Tessa ventured.

"Sort of. But more high-tech. And shinier!" Dr. Khatri grinned. "Could I have a volunteer?"

"Oh! Me! Me!" Lewis jumped up, nearly crashing into Maeve.

"Lewiston. Thank you. Here you are." Lewis stepped into a voluminous suit. It hung like an elephant's skin around him. "Watch this." Dr. Khatri pressed an orange button on the suit's shoulder seam. The material shifted, adjusting in mere seconds to every inch of Lewis's body, as though the cloth had been custom-tailored to fit his long, skinny legs and gangly arms.

"This could revolutionize the fashion industry," Tessa gushed.

"Indeed." Dr. Khatri nodded. "The potential is immeasurable. No pun intended."

Once everyone was dressed, Dr. Khatri talked them through the flight procedure. "And now, we fly. Or float, rather. Ready?"

"Yes!" they shouted excitedly.

Dev was shocked. First, he had no idea his father had access to such amazing technology. Second, his friends genuinely seemed to think his dad was great. Which he was (when he wasn't terrifically embarrassing). The day had taken a wonderful, unexpected turn.

But it got even better when his father activated the Zero-Grav sequence. A gust of cool air ruffled their hair. With a *whoosh!* their feet lifted off the floor. The kids rose higher and higher, somersaulting and swimming through the air, incredulous and delighted.

Maeve dipped and whirled, singing the school motto loudly, "We are Conroy Cadets, hear us roar! Look to the sky—watch us SOAR!" She began leading the others through some weightless marching band choreography. Tessa didn't know the moves, but she improvised and followed along pretty well, surprising herself by actually having fun. For once, she wasn't obsessing about whether she looked dorky or whether the other kids were judging her.

Laughter echoed off the flight chamber walls. Below, Dev saw his father gazing up at them from the control panel. Dev smiled and mouthed the words *thank you.*

His dad waved and nodded.

"This is the absolute best day!" Lewis said, floating by, doing the funky chicken dance.

"You're so much more graceful in antigravity conditions," Maeve said, giggling, feeling lighter and happier than she had in months. She didn't ever want to come down.

"I think that's the first compliment you've ever given me, Maeve Greene," Lewis said.

"Enjoy it, Wynner, 'cause it'll probably be the last."

A small smile cracked her serious face and they both started laughing.

After a few minutes of blissful weightlessness, a buzzer sounded. "Time's up," Dr. Khatri announced. "Untrained bodies should only experience limited intervals of Zero-Grav."

The kids landed softly, their shoes bouncing on impact.

"That was better than any ride at the amusement park," Lewis said, grinning from ear to ear. "Seriously. Thank you, Dr. Khatri."

"You're really lucky," Maeve said to Dev. "Your dad is total hashtag-dadgoals."

"Thanks. I agree." He paused. "I'm sure your dad is pretty great, too."

She looked at Dev, her blue eyes steely. She'd never met her father, but she wasn't about to ruin this moment thinking about him.

"I hope you kids feel inspired by the possibilities of science. Now, let's join Dr. Scopes in the jet propulsion center. I think you'll find it equally fascinating."

Before they could continue, a deep, muffled sound—like a distant explosion—boomed. The bass reverberated in their chests. The metal walls groaned.

"Is that part of the demo?" Tessa asked before a violent jolt knocked her off her feet. The floor shook, juddering and grinding. The room plunged into darkness. A second later, the emergency lights flared on.

"Everything's fine," Dr. Khatri managed to say, just

before the Zero-Grav regulators glitched out, lifting the kids a few inches off the ground, then slamming them back down. Up, and down again.

"Dad! Make it stop!" Dev cried.

"Grab on to something!" Dr. Khatri shouted, suspended in a semi-weightless state, clawing his way toward the control panel. He flipped open a small plexiglass box and pressed a red override button. Gravity was restored, and the vibrations stopped. The kids dropped in a heap onto the floor. Lewis tumbled into Tessa.

"Sorry!" Lewis said, standing and offering Tessa his hand. "Are you okay?"

"Yeah, I'm fine," she said, blushing.

Dev watched, a twinge of jealousy twisting his stomach.

"Anyone injured?" Dr. Khatri asked, helping the others to their feet. Aside from minor bruising and frayed nerves, everybody was intact.

"What happened? Was that a quiver, or something else?" Dev asked.

"I'm not sure," his father replied, brows furrowed. "This structure's foundation is built on pendu-rollers, which minimize the impact of seismic activity. Standard quivers don't typically impact our top-priority labs. Whatever just occurred was more intense than anything I've felt in here before." He rebooted a computer and studied the data pouring across the screen.

Just then, a blue light pulsed on the control panel, followed by a high-pitched alarm.

Bwoop! Bwoop!

"What now?" Maeve yelled, covering her ears.

Dr. Khatri picked up a headset. "Code Vero? Passcode nine-seven-H-four-B. Are you sure? How is that possible? Yes. Has the reactor been compromised? Good. And the samples in Omega Lab V? Any destabilization? Of course. I'll be right there." His tan skin paled.

"Kids, I apologize. There's been a...disruption... in one of our other laboratories. Until we understand the extent of the damage, all non-affected rooms must be secured. I'm hopeful this is just a false alarm, but I need to investigate." He ran his hands nervously through his salt-and-pepper hair, making it stand up wildly like Einstein's. "I will retrieve you as soon as the situation is under control. Until then, Dev, I'm putting you in charge. Look out for your classmates."

"Dad! You're leaving us here? Alone? With an anti-gravity simulator?" Dev sputtered.

His father cringed. "Right! Can't do that. No, no, no. Far too risky." Dr. Khatri's eyes darted back and forth. "This way. Hurry! You must shelter in place. Now!" Dr. Khatri rushed across the room and pushed a tall server unit aside, revealing a hidden door. "You'll be safe in here until we figure out what's going on." He wrenched the door open and turned on the light. "If you get hungry or thirsty, there are snacks and beverages in your suits." He was uncharacteristically harried as he shuffled the kids into the room.

"Wait! What is going on?" Dev cried over the shrieking alarm.

"Don't worry. Everything will be fine!" The door shut. His father was gone.

Dev yanked the handle. "We're locked in."

14

EARTH

DEV WASN'T SURE WHAT WAS SCARIER, THE WAILING SIREN IN the simulator or the eerie quiet of the soundproof room they were stuck inside now. What if something happened to his dad? What if a full-blown earthquake had struck? Were his mom and Sejal safe? Dev banged the door with his fist. Would anyone be able to hear them call for help?

"Where are we?" Tessa asked, her voice quiet and unsteady.

"Looks like some old equipment repair area," Maeve said, poking around.

The room was small and cramped, loaded with boxes and rusting tools. A single dim fluorescent bulb hummed. Tessa prayed it wouldn't go out. Claustrophobia was making it hard to breathe. "Is there enough air in here?" she asked, tugging the collar of her suit.

"I think there's more space this way." Lewis moved a wooden crate aside, clearing a path. The others followed.

"For a guy who studies catastrophes and chaos theory for a living, your dad seemed pretty freaked out," Maeve said, gingerly stepping over broken machine parts.

"I know," said Dev. "I hope everything is okay."

"Me too. I want to get out of here as soon as possible," said Tessa.

"What did your dad mean when he said there's food and drinks in our suits?" Lewis asked, padding his hands across his chest, looking for hidden snack pockets.

"I don't have a clue. But we've got more pressing things to worry about right now. Shhh! Listen."

Behind a wall of boxes, they heard a scraping sound, a sharp tick, rustling.

"What is that?" Tessa whispered.

"Someone, or something, is in here with us," Maeve said, her voice barely audible. "I'm going to investigate." She lifted her chin bravely. Before anyone could convince her otherwise, Maeve slipped around the corner. She yanked a cord, flooding the room with light.

"AHHHH!" A boy with spiky black hair leaped back.

Maeve squinted. "Isaiah?"

"What are *you* doing in here?" he sputtered, his heart pounding.

"We could ask you the same question," Maeve said, not missing a beat. The other kids stepped into the light.

Isaiah gave a shy wave. "Hey, guys. I was just headed to the bathroom when an alarm went off. All these NASA dudes came charging down the hall in hazmat suits. I got spooked and ducked into the first room I could find."

Maeve didn't buy his story. There was definitely something he wasn't telling them.

Lewis sidled up and flung his arm around Isaiah's shoulder. "Well, looks like we've got the band back together again."

Isaiah inched away. "Hold on, what are you guys wearing?"

Tessa tugged self-consciously on her silver-and-green mesh suit.

"Didn't you hear? These are our new band uniforms. Cosmic, right?" Lewis gave a wiggle.

"He's joking," Maeve said. "Dev's dad let us try this anti-gravity simulator. Which was incredible. But right as we finished flying, the whole place went berserk. We didn't have time to change before we got trapped in here."

"We're not trapped," Isaiah said. "I propped open the door." He turned, just as the pencil rolled across the floor. "Scratch that. We're doomed."

"Wait a minute," Dev said, swiveling around. "This is the room where we stashed our instruments at the beginning of the field trip."

"It is?" said Isaiah, feigning surprise.

"Look!" Dev pointed to the table in the corner. His saxophone, Maeve's oboe, Lewis's drumsticks, Zoey's clarinet, and Isaiah's trumpet were all there.

"Sweet! I propose an impromptu jam session," Lewis said, grabbing his sticks and tapping them on the table.

Maeve shrugged. "I rarely agree with Lewis, but it's not

a bad idea. Who knows how long we'll be stuck in here? We need all the practice we can get before regionals."

"Fine, but this better not take too long. I have to pee," Tessa said, angling for a way out of playing her sister's instrument.

"Technically speaking, the suit can accommodate that," Dev replied.

"What?"

He pointed to a series of buttons running along the suit's left sleeve, from shoulder to elbow. "It looks like you can activate built-in fluid absorbers that are basically high-tech space diapers."

Tessa made a disgusted face. "There is no way you are going to convince me to willingly pee my pants."

Dev immediately regretted the embarrassing blunder. Lewis examined his own suit. "What do you think this one does?" He pushed a button with a hamburger symbol on it. Out of the sleeve popped a flattened, crinkly sustenance packet. Lewis tore it open and sniffed the contents. "It's definitely not a burger, but it smells edible." He took a taste. "Hmm, not bad. Sort of like freeze-dried soup flakes." He emptied the rest of the packet into his mouth and licked his lips.

"These are certainly an improvement over our band uniforms," Maeve said, impressed. "Speaking of which, Zoey, did you talk to your sister about redesigning them?"

Tessa bit her lip, confused. "Um, no. Remind me what that was about?"

"Seriously? It was your idea!" Maeve shot her a frustrated look. "You were going to ask Tessa to spruce up the uniforms before regionals, since she's really talented at design and has an eye for fashion. At least that's what *you* said. But based on what she was wearing this morning, I'm not so sure."

"What? That ensemble was a total lewk!" She stopped short. "Er, I mean, yeah, it was a hot mess. And yes, she's totally on board with redesigning the uniforms."

Maeve eyed her. "Something is up with you today."

"Sorry, I think that antigravity flight messed with my brain a little." Tessa turned, worrying her face would give her true identity away. Truthfully, she was touched that her sister had advocated for her. Especially since Zoey usually teased her about her interest in fashion. But why hadn't Zoey brought it up yet? Maybe she would have, if they hadn't spent the morning bickering. She felt a stab of guilt. She would make things right tonight when she got home from the field trip.

"So, where should we practice? It's kind of cramped over here," Isaiah said. If the others got distracted playing, maybe he could sneak back and check for more evidence of that strange symbol . . .

"Let's see if there's more space over here." Maeve led them toward the white panels in the far corner. She slid one aside. Behind it hung a thick black curtain. They ducked beneath it.

"Check this out!" Lewis said, stepping into a glittering cylindrical structure. It was slightly larger than a minivan and open on both ends, lying lengthwise like a tunnel. Along one side, wide screens curved above what appeared to be a mixing console. Four flat circular discs were mounted to a narrow rectangular platform, like turntables. "It's a DJ booth!"

"Huh?" Dev stepped into the structure and inspected the walls flanked with metal scales and laced with thick bundles of colored cables. "A DJ booth would be cool, but I think this might be the abandoned quantum-collider Ari mentioned."

"Abandoned, or hidden?" said Isaiah. "There's no dust in here. Someone has been using this . . . thing. And fairly recently." If he hadn't left his journal on the bus, he definitely would have written this observation down.

"He's right." Lewis ran a finger along the top of the console. "Not a speck of dust. Clean as a whistle." A screen blinked on.

"I don't think we should touch anything. Especially you, Wynner. Remember Benni's advice on the bus?" Maeve said.

"But this is so rad! I bet the scientists come here to party after work. Look! There's even a disco ball." Overhead, a crystalline sphere rotated slowly.

"DJ booth or not, the acoustics are surprisingly good," Maeve said, after practicing a few notes on her oboe.

Lewis ignored her advice and spun the circular discs

with his fingertips, singing, "Chickity-check, one-two! Yeah, that's right, I'm DJ Lewsy Lew. In the house, spinning tunes. All the way from NASA to Neptune!"

A kaleidoscope of colored light pulsed from the crystal sphere as it began to rotate.

"Aten-hut," Maeve said, getting into the spirit and assuming her role as drum major. Normally, the others would have found this annoying, but in the moment, it was actually kind of fun. They grabbed their instruments and began to play. All except Tessa, who fiddled with her sister's clarinet, pretending to clean it. She wasn't about to give up her true identity now. As much as she wanted to win the bet with Zoey, she was also starting to enjoy the company of these band geeks. If she told them she'd been lying all this time, what would they think?

"System activated." No one heard the robotic voice over the peal of Lewis's drum beat and the honk of Dev's saxophone. "Commencing Transfer sequence . . ."

15

STATION LIMINUS

"PORTAL AJCO5I7 LOCATED IN CONROY, OHIO, HAS BEEN ACTI-vated," Quirg announced to the delegates gathered in the diplomatic salon. "It appears the Earthling envoys are preparing for Transfer."

Ignatia nodded, her horns brightening to a vibrant yellow. "Good. That was faster than I expected. They are clearly motivated."

"If my planet was on the brink of destruction, I'd evacuate quickly too," said Bo'lar.

"Based on the bioscan feedback," Quirg said, "the Transfer pod appears to contain five adolescent humans."

"Five? That can't be right." Shro looked perturbed. "Finto said his team had pre-selected seven adult humans. Best and brightest. Unparalleled skill sets."

"Perhaps the others didn't make the final cut?" Xol said.

"Or perhaps once they learned about the hazards of interdimensional travel, they aborted the mission. Crossing the Threshold is not for the faint of heart," Governor Neel added.

"Or stomach," muttered Cirzin, who dreaded the trips between dimensions. Some species tolerated Transfer better than others. Unfortunately, tender-bellied Nharlites weren't among them.

"True. I doubt Earthlings travel well. They seem rather . . . mushy. So very . . . delicate." Xol hissed, his thick beetle-like exoskeleton creaking as he shifted in his seat.

Ignatia wrung her hands. "Yes, Councilor Finto did report feeling quite unwell following his return journey. I'm hopeful he will travel via the Luciana portal and meet his colleagues here at the Station, though I have not received an affirmative response."

She was unnerved by Finto's lack of communication, but he was a rather odd little man. She wondered how and why the citizens of Earth had elected such a person to represent them. She kept this thought to herself; she did not wish to instill doubt or stoke further ire in her fellow delegates.

"Shro, please notify the rest of the council of the Earthlings' imminent arrival," Ignatia said, regaining her focus. "Duna, you will be responsible for the Earthlings' orientation. The Station can be an overwhelming place for new visitors."

"Of course." Duna nodded. "I am grateful for the opportunity, Secretary Leapkeene."

Nestled in a duct high overhead, the Klapprothi child felt the voice vibrations. There was an eagerness, an excitement to the sound pattern. Something was about to happen. Good or bad, Virri couldn't decide.

16

EARTH

RIFFING AND JAMMING, THE KIDS WERE LOST IN THE JOY AND energy of the music. Lewis, carried away, started drumming his sticks wildly on three large cylinders that rumbled like timpani.

"Lewis! Cut it out," Maeve snapped.

"No way, Mae! Can't you see I'm in the groove? Dropping these beats!" A deep boom echoed through the room. A shiver of energy blew their hair back.

Lewis's hands stilled; everyone fell silent. With an ear-splitting *zing!* red lasers shot out from the crystal disco ball, forming a web of light like a cage around the kids.

"Transfer: Initiated," a robotic voice said. "Gate Materialization: Initiated."

"Uhhh . . . What's happening?" Lewis asked, wide-eyed.

"Destination: Station Liminus."

"No one move," Dev said, his heart hammering his ribs.

"Are you nuts? I'm getting out of here before this thing

blows up." Isaiah tried to exit the structure but the lasers formed an invisible, impenetrable force field. "I can *see* through it, but I can't *move* through it!" He held his palms up, like a mime.

"Get me out of here! I do not do well in confined spaces!" Tessa banged her good hand against the wall.

"Dev, your dad works here. You must know how to deactivate this thing," Isaiah said. "If you don't, we're totally—"

"Don't say it!" Maeve warned.

Beads of sweat ran down Dev's face. This was like stage fright, but worse. Everyone watching him, waiting to see what he would do. He bit his lip. "Maybe I can figure it out . . ."

"I'll help you. I'm an ace at video games," Lewis said. "How different could this be?"

He and Lewis started hitting buttons, their fingers flying across keys, looking for a power switch, an eject button, anything.

"All of you, relax. I'm sure Dr. Khatri will be back soon. He'll get us out of here. In the meantime, quit messing with technology you clearly don't understand before you do more damage, okay?" Maeve was surprisingly calm. She'd been in much higher-stress situations at home. She knew when to sit tight and wait for the worst to be over.

A high-pitched wail, like a kettle left to boil, ruptured the quiet. A floor valve opened, blasting them with frigid air. The crystal sphere began spinning faster and faster, glowing brighter and brighter, until the light burned and blinded their eyes. The five kids huddled together, shivering, covering their ears and squeezing their eyes shut. Tessa reached out instinctively and gripped the nearest hand, which happened to be Dev's. For a fleeting moment, he forgot they were all probably about to die.

The collider shuddered, chattering their tooth, shaking their bones. Intense pressure crushed and pulled them apart at the same time. Isaiah tucked his knees to his chest, feeling like his body was splitting into a million tiny pieces. When he looked down at his hands, he was terrified to see they were gone, fading and flashing in pixelated patches.

Someone cried for help, but the deafening noise swallowed the words.

Sparks flew; the walls buckled and warped. The collider's circular opening flashed with scenes of gray stone walls, jagged ice-tipped mountains, lush green moss, and finally the cavernous, pitch black of a starless night.

"Hang on!" Dev shouted as they were pulled toward the opening.

The kids tumbled, spiraling, screaming for help.

There was a static roar, the deep bass of an earth-rending explosion.

Then nothing but deafening silence.

17

STATION LIMINUS

THE SPINNING SLOWED. THE CRUSHING PRESSURE RELENTED.
The air popped and crackled. The cadets stumbled to their feet, dizzy and nauseous, ears ringing, eyes red-rimmed. Pinpricks of warm light flickered at the edges of their vision.

"What happened?" Tessa rasped, her throat raw from screaming.

"I don't know, but I feel like someone put us inside a blender and made a smoothie," Dev moaned.

Isaiah looked down at his hands. They were shaking, but he was relieved to see they were back to normal. Well, mostly. His skin had an odd coppery sheen, but maybe that was the reflection from the walls around them, which gleamed like a shined penny. "Wait, where are we?" he asked.

Maeve touched the sides of the copper pod they were encased within. There were no control panels or screens. No visible seams, no doors, windows, or escape hatches.

Lewis shook his head. "We're not in Kansas anymore, and we're not inside the DJ booth either."

"We were never in Kansas or a DJ booth," Maeve replied.

"The good news is I can confirm our spacesuits *do* have fully functioning pee-eradication systems." Lewis grinned sheepishly.

"Ew." Maeve stuck out her tongue. "That is definitely TMI."

A voice thundered, "Greetings, Earthlings!"

"Phew!" Isaiah let out a strained laugh. "For a minute, I thought we were actually doomed! But it's just your dad, playing a prank on us."

"I knew it. I totally called it." Lewis thumped Dev on the back.

"You did not."

"Did so. I just didn't say it out loud."

Maeve rolled her eyes.

Just then, the copper capsule peeled open, unfolding like a lotus blossom, floating in pure white nothingness. A crooked concrete path appeared at their feet, leading to a door partially obscured by thick fog. The capsule trembled, sparking and fizzing at the edges.

"What's happening now?" Tessa said, steadying herself.

"I don't know, but we'd better get moving." Maeve stepped forward, testing the stability of the path. It creaked but seemed stable enough to cross. "Come on. Single file. Aten-hut."

The others followed, moving quickly but carefully.

"How are you so chill right now?" Tessa asked Maeve, wishing there was a railing to hold on to.

"One of us needs to keep a clear head," Maeve said, gingerly putting one foot in front of the other. "And you know what I have to put up with at home. In some ways, this is easier."

Tessa wasn't sure how to respond. There was a lot more to Maeve than she'd realized. She felt bad about all the times she'd teased her behind her back.

Isaiah was the last one to step out of the capsule. No sooner did his feet touch the walkway than it began to shake and crumble.

"Uh, guys?" Isaiah called out, nudging Dev in front of him. "I'm not trying to exaggerate or anything, but if you don't speed it up a little, we're doomed. Like, for real this time."

Dev looked back and saw the path disintegrating behind them. "You heard the man! Move! Move!" he shouted.

One by one, the kids ran and dove through the open door, just as the walkway gave out, crashing soundlessly into the white oblivion. Lewis kicked the door shut behind them. The second it closed, it carbonized and cracked down the middle. A blackened rot spread outward from the crack, swallowing up the door and the surrounding wall.

"Maybe this isn't a prank after all," Lewis said, rising to his feet.

"Ya think?" Tessa snorted.

"It's more like a nightmare." Isaiah had experienced

that sensation before—the terror of diving through a door in the nick of time as your world collapses around you. He had been dreaming it, night after night, ever since his uncle's funeral.

Dev was about to offer his hand to help Tessa, but she was already up, dusting off her silver suit. In spite of back-to-back near-death experiences, her hazel eyes were bright, her dark skin radiant. "Where to from here?" she asked, giving him a tentative smile that weakened his already wobbly knees.

"Um, that way?" Dev pointed. To the left stretched a seemingly endless hallway, adorned with every sort of door imaginable. None of them were black and smoldering like the one the cadets had just exited, however.

Suddenly two figures swept into view, gliding along the hall. From a distance, they appeared to be a woman and a teenager, but as they got closer it was clear they were not fully human. One towered nearly seven feet tall and had two small horns protruding from her temples. The other was about Lewis's height with green-tinged hair and frilled ears.

The tall woman regarded the kids with piercing violet eyes. Her silver hair moved like water, plaited in elaborate whorls and eddies, framing her angular face. She wore dramatic indigo robes. Fashion-obsessed Tessa gawked; the luminous cloth looked as though it was woven from actual galaxies, with glimmering starlight captured between the folds.

Lewis's jaw dropped. Maeve delivered a discreet elbow

to his ribs, and he clamped his mouth shut and swallowed hard.

"Welcome," the woman said, extending her arms ceremoniously. "You have successfully crossed the Threshold and reached Station Liminus, the official Multiverse Allied Council headquarters and critical nexus point within the fabric of our great multiverse. I am Ignatia Leapkeene, Secretary of the—"

A wave of nausea hit Isaiah. He gripped his stomach. "I don't feel so good," he said, falling to his knees.

EARTH

DR. KHATRI BURST THROUGH THE DOORS. SPRINKLERS DOUSED the halls with a spray of water, tamping out any chance of fire. Emergency lights strobed, illuminating a path through the empty corridors of the Gwen Research Center. Everyone else had evacuated and was awaiting further instruction at the muster point on the perimeter of the complex.

In spite of whatever hazards the earlier energy disruption may have unleashed, Dr. Khatri refused to leave the building. He wasn't exactly athletic, but now he ran faster than he ever had. Dr. Scopes followed, her perfectly coiffed chignon disheveled.

"The children are in *there*?" she asked, panic rising in her voice as she realized where they were headed. All the other field trippers were safely aboard the school bus with Benni and the other teachers, preparing to depart. "You left a group of middle schoolers alone with an antigravity simulator?"

"Of course not! I'm no fool, Dr. Scopes. I secured them within the adjacent equipment room."

"Which room exactly?" she panted, trying to keep up. Running in heels was harder than it looked.

"The one that connects to the defunct collider lab."

Her face blanched. "There are valuable assets and documents stored in there. We need to make sure the equipment is intact!"

Dr. Khatri wheeled around and leveled a look at his colleague. "Equipment and files can be replaced, Dr. Scopes. The children are irreplaceable."

"Absolutely. That's what I meant." She nodded, looking frazzled. "I'm sorry. Of course the safety and well-being of your son and his friends are our top priority." She smoothed her hair, damp from the spitting sprinklers. "They must be terrified, poor things."

Across town, Zoey and her classmates crouched under their desks at Conroy Middle School. The lights flicked off and on a few times. The ground shook. A few books fell from the shelves. No one was really freaking out; they were all pretty used to the quiver drills at this point, although this particular quiver felt a lot stronger than recent ones. Some kids used the time under their desks to pass notes back and forth, others used it as a chance to nab a quick nap or play games on their phones, which were normally forbidden during class.

Zoey tapped her smartwatch and typed a text message to Isaiah. *Feel that quiver over at NASA? It was a big one this time, right?! Make sure you note it in your journal!* she typed. *Is it just me, or does Conroy seem more, I don't know, weird lately?* But then she quickly deleted the entire text before hitting send, remembering that she was pretending to be her sister, and that "Zoey" was currently at NASA with Isaiah.

Instead, she typed a quick message to Tessa to see if she was okay, but Tessa didn't respond. Typical. She was the queen of ghosting lately—too cool for everyone, her own sister especially. Zoey hated to admit how much this actually stung. She pushed the feeling away.

She wondered if Isaiah had figured out Tessa's true identity yet. He probably had. Not much got past him. She liked that he saw connections between things that other people missed. He'd been like that ever since she could remember, and they'd been friends since kindergarten. Maybe that's why his uncle had left him all those cryptic notes? She just wished she could help him put the pieces together somehow. Whatever Ming was trying to tell Isaiah before he disappeared seemed important, but neither she nor Isaiah could figure out what it was all about.

The floor beneath her jolted. The furniture vibrated. The room went dark. Zoey looked down at her watch, hoping a message from Tessa would illuminate its screen, but it remained blank.

After a few seconds, the shaking ground stilled, the lights and overhead fans turned back on, and everything returned to normal. The school's emergency alert system instructed them that it was safe to return to regular activities. Mr. Kimpton told everyone to put their phones away and return to their seats.

Zoey crawled out from beneath her desk and straightened Tessa's jean jacket, the one that apparently complemented the purple leopard print skirt and embellished V-neck tank she was wearing. She couldn't wait to shed the whole ensemble and return to her own comfortable clothing and her own normal identity.

STATION LIMINUS

"WE NEED A MEDIC!" MAEVE SAID, KNEELING BESIDE ISAIAH. "Something's wrong with him."

Isaiah retched and gagged, convulsing in pain. His friends tried to comfort him, but he waved them away. He knelt and closed his eyes, hoping the waves of nausea would subside.

The secretary pressed some sort of device on her wrist and a scuttling team of small, spherical robots collected around the kids. They cleaned up the vomit on the floor and circled the cadets, scanning them with ticklish orange laser beams.

"What are these things?" Tessa said, trying not to giggle. This was most definitely not a time to giggle.

"They are called biobots," the younger figure with greenish hair replied brightly. "Semi-sentient devices that help keep our Station running shipshape."

Lewis turned to Maeve and whispered, "Do you have any idea what is happening right now?"

She shook her head, trying to hide her shock, but her game face was failing her. The commotion of their arrival had attracted a crowd, each newcomer more curious-looking than the next. There were short, furry creatures walking upright in white lab coats; armored, beetle-like creatures as tall as Lewis; round, amorphous creatures with ancient-looking faces; and a variety of human-esque figures with a rainbow of hair and skin tones. The cadets gaped and blinked and rubbed their eyes.

Isaiah, beginning to feel better, slowly stood up, only to find himself face-to-face with a caterpillar the size of a bathtub. He wobbled woozily again. Dev reached out to grab his arm and steady his friend. Dev pushed a button on his silver mesh suit that had a blue droplet icon. A small packet of fresh water emerged from the sleeve. He offered it to Isaiah, who accepted the water gratefully, taking slow sips.

The caterpillar creature continued to slide past, its lime green underbelly dotted with hundreds of tiny suction cups, which it used to scale the curved wall nearby. It stopped halfway up, its dozens of eyes watching the kids from above.

Maeve, channeling her inner performer, forced a cheery smile onto her face. She tapped Lewis gently on the shoulder. "It's rude to stare, you know."

"He's staring at us! They all are."

She huffed. "You act like you've never seen a gigantic alien caterpillar before, or a . . ." She didn't even know what to call the others.

Lewis's eyes grew wide. "I never have! Have you?"

"Well, um, no," she stammered. "But I have manners. We only have one shot to make a good first impression."

Isaiah moaned, doubling over again. The biobots buzzed with irritation and continued mopping.

"Too late for that," Lewis mumbled.

"All of you, please give us some privacy!" the tall, authoritative secretary commanded. The creatures dashed, scurried, and slid away. She turned and looked down at Isaiah, who was wearing a Conroy Cadets T-shirt, black zip-up hoodie, and jeans instead of a NASA Zero-Grav suit like the others. "Minor bodily trauma and cellular disruptions are normal side effects of interdimensional travel," she assured him. "Your innards should be mostly fine . . . once you finish rearranging them."

"Did she say *mostly fine?*" Tessa asked, horrified, touching her own stomach, wondering what sort of invisible damage their journey may have caused, and hoping her suit may have protected her in some way.

"Uh, did she say *interdimensional travel?*" Lewis sputtered. "Because I'm positive my parents did not sign a permission slip for *that.*"

Isaiah looked up. His eyes were bloodshot, his voice barely above a whisper. "What did you do to us?" he asked. His head felt like it had been crushed in a vise.

A doughy, four-armed creature appeared beside the secretary. "What did we do to *you?* What did you do to your Transfer portal?" He gestured angrily at the wall behind the cadets, which had corroded into a smoldering hole. "The entire Gate collapsed in your wake! The adjacent openings are damaged as well!"

He barked orders in an alien language. A squad of larger biobots arrived and immediately began cordoning off the area with a combination of high-tech electrode ropes and rudimentary orange traffic cones. A separate squad attempted to board up the damaged doorway with thick metal sheets and welding torches.

"Earthlings of Dim14, this is Quirg," explained Secretary Leapkeene. "He is a delegate in our council, hailing from Quomo in Dim5. He also serves as custodian of the gates, which is why your rather dramatic arrival is causing him consternation."

"Dramatic? More like destructive!" Quirg grumbled.

The secretary craned her neck and peered down the hall. "Ah, yes, and here comes General Shro."

A broad-backed man marched down the hall, his gait purposeful, his sliver-tipped boots clicking loudly on the polished moonstone floor. He wore a rust-colored jacket made from the tanned hides of some sort of spacebeast. "I came as soon as I could. So nice to finally meet—" He stopped, staring at the children, sizing them up with slate-gray eyes. His carmine skin was pulled taut across his angular jaw. "Where is—?" He stopped before saying more.

Isaiah's stomach churned.

A thousand questions hung in the air.

20

EARTH

"KIDS!" DR. KHATRI SHOUTED. "WE'RE COMING. DON'T WORRY!" He wrenched the simulator door open, coughing as he inhaled a plume of acrid fumes. "Dev? Lewis? Answer me! Please."

Inside the storage room, smoke dissipated, revealing a mess of toppled bins and shelves. Cardboard boxes were singed, their contents scattered across the floor, blackened with an oily residue. Broken machine parts and tools glowed an angry shade of orange, the metal molten hot.

Dr. Khatri called out again, his voice frantic. "Dev?" He pushed aside crates and stepped over debris. It looked as though a bomb had exploded. "Maeve? Zoey?" His heart pounded, fearing what he might see as he slid a half-melted plastene panel aside.

Dr. Scopes followed, covering her mouth and nose with the collar of her lab coat. The children were nowhere to be found. A cracked crystal globe dangled from the ceiling, slashing the room with beams of red light.

"Is this...the quantum collider?" Dr. Khatri stepped closer. "Our designs never advanced beyond basic calculations and rudimentary models. The construction was too costly, plus the team agreed the apparatus was too dangerous. All research was halted." He rubbed his temples where an intense headache was brewing. "Has someone been building this behind our backs?"

Dr. Scopes swallowed solemnly. "It appears our colleague Professor McGillum is not who he seems."

He wheeled around. "What do you mean?"

"I received the manifest from the muster point. Ian McGillum never checked in. The rescue squad is sweeping the other buildings, but so far, no sign of him." She placed a gentle hand on Dr. Khatri's elbow. "I'm so sorry, Mohan. I believe he was secretly working on the collider and activated it somehow. He's either with the children, or he fled the scene after causing today's energy disruption."

"With the children? But where? Where could they have gone?" He eyed the destroyed control console. "Do you really suppose they broke through a dimensional membrane?"

She sighed. "I know I've been a skeptic about your many worlds theories in the past, but I don't know how else to describe whatever happened here. I suppose it's possible the children crossed into an alternate universe." Dr. Scopes gestured forlornly to the damaged equipment. "If only we could fix the collider, we could follow them...wherever the collider may have transported them, that is."

"We can!" Dr. Khatri said, struck with a lightning bolt of

an idea. "We could use the Syntropitron, my reverse dynamite invention! It was specifically designed to repair catastrophic damage. With a few modifications, I bet it could realign and restore the dispersed collider particles and reconstruct the machine. It could work!"

Dr. Scopes hung her head. "The Syntropitron is also missing."

"Missing?"

"I took an inventory of our critical equipment following today's energy disruption and noticed it was gone. Professor McGillum must have stolen it." Her face twisted with disappointment. "Who knows the extent of his deception?"

"This ... this ... is an act of mutiny!" Dr. Khatri squeezed his eyes shut, furious. "Four innocent kids disappeared into thin air thanks to that man's recklessness!"

"Actually, five." She winced. "A boy named Isaiah Yoon is also missing from the school's manifest. Security footage shows him approaching the defunct lab before the evacuation."

Dr. Khatri hung his head. "How am I supposed to explain this to their families?"

"We'll find them. I promise."

"Where could they be?" Dr. Khatri asked the ceiling, a note of desperation slipping into his voice. He looked down. A wide, oval patch was charred into the tile floor. In the center, a single, splintered drumstick spun, round and round, until it finally slowed to a stop.

STATION LIMINUS

DEV DIDN'T HAVE A HEADACHE LIKE ISAIAH, BUT HIS MIND WAS spinning as he tried to make sense of everything that was happening, everything they were seeing. He studied the three unusual faces before them. "I'm sorry, but where are we, exactly?" The field trip had definitely veered off course. Waaaay off course.

Shro cocked his head. "Station Liminus, of course. Did Finto not debrief you?"

"I don't know who that person is, but I'd really like to speak with Dr. Mohan Khatri," Dev said, trying his best to sound assertive. Something told him his rules for surviving middle school didn't apply here. Wherever *here* was.

"Who?" Quirg waddled closer, a look of disdain creasing his face.

"My father," Dev said, his pulse thrumming. "Catastrophysicist and head of Quantum Studies at NASA. I need to speak with him. Now." Dev swallowed. "Please?" he added.

"I've never heard of such a person," Shro said apologetically. "Have you, Your Eminence?"

The secretary shook her head, her silver hair glinting in the bright Station lights.

Isaiah's eyes landed on Shro's lapel. A pewter pin in the shape of a thirteen-pointed star gleamed. He gasped. "Wait . . . who are you?"

"Ah, how rude. In my excitement, I failed to properly introduce myself." Shro bowed, displaying his muscular, slightly hunched back. "I am General Shro. My realm, Hasz, exists within Dim3. I lead the Dimensional Defense Department here on the Station. To ensure the safety and liberty of all." He thumped a fist to his chest proudly.

"Right, that clears up a lot," Tessa muttered.

Shro stepped aside. "And I assume you've met our youngest delegate, Duna of Mertanya from Dim10?"

The cadets smiled politely. "Sort of."

Shro nodded. "And of course, Her Eminence, Ignatia Leapkeene, who hails from L'oress of Dimension 1. She is secretary of the Multiverse Allied Council, also known as the MAC."

"So, she's, like, the Big MAC?" Lewis asked, trying not to chuckle at his own joke.

Maeve gave him a withering glare.

Ignatia regarded the children as though they were exotic

animals in the Menagerie. "Where are your supplies?" she asked. "We were told you would be bringing state-of-the-art equipment."

"Equipment?" Dev replied. "Our instruments are right here." He lifted his saxophone.

Lewis waved his drumstick. He had only one now. The other must have gotten lost during their journey.

Ignatia leaned down to get a better view. "And those will aid in plastocyrene terraforming efforts?"

"Probably not, but they help us play a wicked version of Queen's 'We Will Rock You,'" Lewis said. "Does that count?"

"Queen who? Do you refer to the silent monarch of Klapproth?" Ignatia asked, her horns flashing a vivid cerulean.

"Um, no. The band."

Ignatia inspected her necklace. "Is my translator scrambled?" She tapped the tiny, multifaceted blue stone that hung from a delicate chain around her neck. "I cannot understand a single thing these Earthlings are saying."

Shro shook his head. "I believe our translators are working just fine. However, there does appear to be some confusion. Are you the Earthling envoys, or not?"

"Maybe?" Dev offered. "Our teacher Mrs. Minuzzi said we should be ambassadors during our field trip. Is that the same?"

Ignatia shook her head, mystified. "Are you skilled in

essential knowledge spheres, able to make valuable contributions to the multiverse?"

"We floss flawlessly in formation during our half-time routine. So, yeah, I'd say we're pretty skilled." Lewis demonstrated the dance move, then served up his signature smile, dimples and all. That always helped in situations like this.

"I knew this was a bad idea . . ." Quirg muttered, exhaling sharply through the six nostrils that ran in two rows down the middle of his plump face.

"Quiet!" Ignatia commanded. "If I require your counsel, I will request it. Until then, please keep all unsolicited feedback to yourself."

"Yes, Your Eminence." Quirg nodded meekly.

Ignatia's horns darkened to a deep wine hue. She was clearly losing her patience. "Duna! This exchange is becoming rather vexing. Please orient these small humans. It appears that even Earth's 'best and brightest' require a refresher course in Multiverse 101."

She turned to Shro and Quirg. "I have pressing matters to attend to. As I'm sure the rest of you do as well. Please return to your regular posts." She directed a pointed look at the cadets. "If you'll excuse me, I will see you all later at the official hearing."

"The hearing?" Dev asked, scratching his head.

"Do not worry, Your Eminence," Duna said assuredly. "I will bring the Earthlings up to speed. I'm sure they are well aware of their duties while visitors on the Station." Duna gave Tessa and the others a kind smile. "It will just take a little while for them to adjust."

"Fine." The secretary nodded curtly. "But remember, their time here is not infinite."

Lewis scuffed his boot on the shiny floor. "And I thought Coach Diaz gave lousy pep talks..."

22

EARTH

"**THIS FIELD TRIP IS A COMPLETE DISASTER!**" COACH DIAZ declared.

Mrs. Minuzzi whimpered in agreement. She wrung her hands and shuffled anxiously back and forth along the sidewalk behind the Gwen Research Center's parking lot.

"Mrs. Minuzzi, Coach Diaz, please calm down," Dr. Khatri said, speaking to the chaperones in a hushed voice outside the muster point. The buses hadn't been authorized to leave until all students were accounted for. Benni, one of the drivers, had led his bus in some meditation and mindfulness exercises, but after waiting nearly an hour, the kids were growing rowdy and bored in their seats. A paper airplane flew out the bus window, whizzing by Dr. Khatri's head.

"I assure you we are doing everything in our power to locate the missing students," Dr. Scopes said.

"Missing? Did you say missing?" Mrs. Minuzzi almost fainted.

"Perhaps I used the wrong word. They are here, some-where. The Gwen Research Center is a large facility. The quiver and subsequent energy surge caused a lot of disruption. The students were likely just frightened and sought cover. We have a team sweeping each building," Dr. Khatri said.

"You should both join Miss Panos on the bus and return to school with the children. We will notify Principal Brant and apprise her of the situation," Dr. Scopes added.

"This better get resolved quickly. We have a very important band practice this afternoon," Coach Diaz said, tugging at the whistle hanging around his neck. "Regional championships are right around the corner. If we're going to have a shot at winning, we need our best musicians. Including your son."

"I understand." Dr. Khatri nodded, feeling an ache in his chest as he thought of Dev. "Locating the children is our top priority."

Dr. Khatri's assistant hurried across the parking lot, looking frazzled. "Sorry to interrupt. There's a call for you on line one." She held up a cell phone.

"Pamela, please take a message," Dr. Khatri said. "I'm in the middle of something right now."

"Sir, the mayor is on the phone."

"How did she find out her daughter is missing?" Dr. Khatri shook his head.

"She doesn't know that Zoey is missing, sir. Not yet," Pamela said quietly. "Apparently, whatever happened this afternoon was not limited to the Center. The entire city of Conroy is going haywire. Even the surrounding counties have reported outages and extended flickers."

"Really?" Dr. Scopes asked.

Pamela tucked her hair nervously behind her ears. "The mayor's team suspects that the massive energy surge that followed today's quiver may have originated from our facility. She's . . . not happy."

It was possible that the quantum collider, once activated, could have caused the surge. Rupturing a dimensional membrane was bound to have some ripple effects. Dr. Khatri sighed. Things were worse than he thought, but he couldn't lose his head now. His son and now an entire city were depending on him.

"Thank you, Pamela. Dr. Scopes, please escort Coach Diaz and Mrs. Minuzzi back to the buses. They should return to the school at once. I will take care of everything else."

Pamela nodded and handed him the phone.

Dr. Khatri cleared his throat and pressed the button for line one. "Mayor Hawthorne, to what do I owe such a—"

Before he could continue, Valerie Hawthorne barked, "I need answers!"

STATION LIMINUS

AS SOON AS SECRETARY LEAPKEENE DEPARTED FROM GATE Hall with Shro and Quirg, Duna turned to the kids. "Since this is your first journey across the Threshold, I am sure you have many questions. And I am here to answer them."

Duna had a warm demeanor and a confidence that Tessa found reassuring. She felt the anxiety that had been building in her chest slowly dissipate.

"You'll come to see that the multiverse is astoundingly, wonderfully diverse. As Shro mentioned, I hail from an Earth-like variant known as Mertanya, located in Dim10. Most Mertanyan people, such as myself, identify as nonbinary, meaning not exclusively male or female. Therefore, we use the pronouns *they/them*."

Maeve nodded. She knew a few kids at school who used gender-neutral pronouns; she would make sure to use Duna's correctly.

"I'm fifteen years old and proud to serve my dimension as the youngest delegate in the MAC," Duna continued. "When I'm not on duty here at the Station, I enjoy racing hoverdiscs, reading holographic novels, playing AstroBlasters, and cooking enparillos with my ninth grandparent, Nooni."

"Ooh, tell us more about enparillos!" Lewis said, giving his rumbling stomach a pat.

"Enparillos are crescent-shaped pastries filled with minced riverbeast meat and lots of spices," Duna replied with a wide smile. "Nooni's are the best in the multiverse."

"I don't know what a riverbeast is, but that sounds pretty delicious to me."

"Everything sounds delicious to you," Maeve said.

Lewis grinned. "You're not wrong."

Tessa regarded Duna. Aside from frilled ears and closely-cropped green-tinted hair, they looked like a typical human teenager. A small blue translator dangled from a chain around their neck, alongside a collection of other necklaces with hammered silver tags. They wore a white shirt adorned with dozens of important-looking badges, putty-colored jodhpur-style pants, and the raddest high-top sneakers Tessa had ever seen. She instantly liked Duna's style.

"And now I would like to get to know all of you." Duna asked each of them their names and listened intently as they replied. Tessa almost revealed her true identity, but caught herself before she slipped. She knew she'd have to tell them all the truth at some point, but this didn't feel like the right moment.

Shortly after they'd finished their introductions, a device on Duna's wrist buzzed. "Ah! Time to go. This way!"

The cadets picked up their instruments and followed, eager for more information.

"The Station can be disorienting and overwhelming at first," Duna said as they walked.

"That's the understatement of the year . . ." Dev replied, looking around the breathtaking building in awe, wishing his father were there to see it, too. The pearly white floors shone. The ceilings soared, curving and faceted with interlocking panels that glowed with simulated sunlight.

"Why are there so many doors? And where do they go?" Dev asked, pointing down the hall.

"They lead into and out of each dimension, of course," Duna said, as though it were the most obvious fact. "Most dimensions have multiple access points, which is why there are so many doors."

Tessa bit her lip and stopped walking. "I feel like we need to back things up a bit. What are these dimensions everyone keeps mentioning?"

Maeve paused too, nodding in agreement. Generally, she didn't like to admit that she didn't know everything about everything. But she felt like they needed to understand the full scope of their situation. "And the multiverse?" she added. "What is that all about?"

Duna came to a halt. They looked surprised, but not

disgusted or flustered like Ignatia and Quirg had. "You really don't know about the multiverse?"

The cadets stared at Duna blankly.

"My dad has talked about 'many worlds' theories before," Dev said, "but I thought he was just geeking out."

"Plus, during our tour of NASA, Dr. Scopes denied anything of the sort could exist," Isaiah added, still irked by the way she had dismissed his clearly valid question.

Duna shrugged coolly, looking undeterred. "Okay, well, I guess we have more to cover than I thought. Gather round." They pulled a small circular device from their pocket and tapped the illuminated glass surface. "This is called a lynk. It's like a more sophisticated version of the smartphones I've heard you use on Earth."

"Which none of us have at the moment, because we left them at NASA," Lewis lamented.

"I'll use it to demonstrate some of the basics." Duna scrolled and tapped the lynk a few times. An image sprang to life. "Picture if you will a balloon, like this one." They held up the screen for the kids to see. "You have these on Earth, right?"

Tessa nodded. "Yup. They're used for special occasions, like birthdays or parties."

"Exactly. Now imagine there are thirteen balloons, all different colors. Each one represents a different dimension, or verse. Together, they represent the multiverse. The balloons formed, or were inflated let's say, in the wake of a major astronomic event. I believe you call it the Big Bang." Duna checked to make sure they were following.

"The balloons all contain the same basic foundational particles, but each one developed slightly differently, forming the unique worlds in which you and I live."

Tessa thought about Zoey. She and her sister were identical twins with the same DNA, but with each passing year, they became more and more different.

Duna continued their explanation. "Because of their shared origins, the planets within each balloon abide by roughly the same laws of physics and exist within similar solar systems, but each has varied atmospheric conditions, temperatures, landforms, and so on. For example, Klapproth is primarily aquatic. Jelingor in Dim12 has three moons. My home planet has an orange-hued sky. Calweh in Dim11 is highly gaseous."

"Just like you, Lew," Maeve said.

"Har har. Very funny."

"Over the course of the last few billion years, these differing characteristics caused diverse life-forms to evolve and flourish in each dimension. Which is why delegates like Quirg and Xol look dissimilar from myself."

"It reminds me of themes and variations in music," Dev said. "If you take a core group of musical notes, then arrange and play them differently, you'll get a variety of related melodies."

Duna's russet eyes sparkled. "I am not well-acquainted

with Earthling musical theory, but the concept seems correct. Each dimension is a variation on a theme."

Duna tapped their lynk and another image appeared. "Now imagine that each of the thirteen balloons we just described has a string attached to it. These strings all connect at one central point, where they are tied into a knot of sorts. This knot is Station Liminus, the place we're standing now. It's the only juncture where all thirteen verses meet, and that makes it quite special."

Dev looked down at his feet and the floor below in awe. The ideas Duna was describing were slowly crystallizing in his mind. He was giddy with the possibilities, in awe of the sheer vastness of the multiverse. He was also startled and unsettled by how quickly his entire understanding of the world could be dismantled and reconstructed. It took his breath away a little.

"Most dimensions access the Station through a network of constructed portals or gates, like the one you traveled through today," Duna said. "However, the balloons—or dimensions—are floating in space, in the center of a mirrored room of sorts. Even though they are tied together, the balloons sometimes drift and bump up against each other. Where they touch, additional gateways can form, linking one dimension to another, though usually only for a limited time. We refer to these as Rips."

Isaiah was instantly reminded of Uncle Ming. He had always suspected that his uncle had accidentally slipped from their world and into another. His pulse raced. Maybe he had been right all along...

Duna looked thoughtfully at the group. "I would advise you not to travel through Rips, due to their volatile nature."

"What would happen if we did?" Lewis asked.

"You could end up somewhere rather inhospitable with no clear path home. And you might suffer more extreme cellular mutation and degradation."

"Did you say 'mutation'?" Tessa asked, fidgeting with her mesh suit, hoping her body hadn't grown something like snakeskin during their accidental journey.

"Anytime you move from one dimensional boundary into another, you cross the Threshold, which is a highly charged field of quantum energy. We call this process *Transfer*. Not all species are adversely affected. Some tolerate it well, while others... less so." Duna turned to Isaiah. "Which reminds me, how are you feeling?"

Isaiah lifted his chin, his face flush with color. "Much better, thanks."

"I vomited for a full hour after my first Transfer, so I can commiserate. You'll get used to it eventually," Duna said. "The effects usually fade."

"Usually?" Isaiah grimaced.

Duna's lynk pinged. They glanced down at the device. "We still have much to discuss, but we have some intake procedures to complete before you can meet the council."

A second later, a round hoverdisc, like a giant floating

yellow doughnut, arrived. A set of steps materialized. "Come on up," Duna said, boarding the craft. The bandmates climbed in.

A shimmering image appeared in the craft's open center. "This is a 3-D holomap of Station Liminus." Duna enlarged the hologram with their fingertips. "We're here." They pointed to an area shaped like an infinity symbol. "Gate Hall not only contains the Station's primary entries and exits, but it also forms the kinetic core of the Station. As you can see, it resembles an ouroboros, constantly moving and changing, never static. Our gravity simulators are tied to its movement."

"If the core stopped rotating, would we become weightless?" Dev asked, remembering the freeing feeling of the Zero-Grav flight back at NASA.

"Most likely. But the core was designed with highly advanced perpetual motion technology. The likelihood of it failing is next to none." They gestured to the hologram. Additional dome-shaped structures radiated out from the core, stacked like barnacles on the hull of a ship.

"The purple areas of the holomap represent the Station's primary function nodes: diplomatic, judicial, security, research, and enrichment. The smaller areas represent the necessary support spaces."

"What are those?" Maeve asked, pointing to hundreds of threadlike connectors that snaked between each space.

"A complex web of ducts," Duna explained, "carrying fresh air, power, magnetizer channels, data cables, water, gas lines, and more. They run under the floors, through the ceilings, and between the walls. This infrastructure allows for easy expansion and flexibility. Handy, if we need to repurpose a room, for example, or construct a new node. In fact, the MAC recently voted to expand the Station in exciting ways."

They tapped a control panel near their seat, adding a layer of information to the holomap. "The blue represents our future plans. Of course, there are some kinks to work out, but we hope to build a vibrant hub between our great dimensions. Right now, the Station is only open to delegates such as myself, dimensional constituents, defense personnel, sanctioned traders, researchers, and inventioneers. But in the next few years, we may open Station Liminus up to tourists and students, too. I think it could be a great way to strengthen interdimensional bonds."

"Wow. Imagine coming here for a class field trip?" Lewis said, wide-eyed.

"Um. We sort of did. Unintentionally," Tessa reminded him.

EARTH

THE PHONE CALL BACK ON EARTH WAS GETTING MORE HEATED by the minute.

"I'm going to need you to explain this in a lot more detail, Dr. Khatri!"

"Mayor Hawthorne, I assure you, we will fix this."

"You'd better," she said firmly. "Or NASA will no longer enjoy the generous funding streams or zoning liberties you've grown accustomed to."

"I understand," Dr. Khatri said, pacing across the parking lot outside the Gwen Research Center. The field trip buses were set to depart any minute.

Valerie Hawthorne took a deep breath. When she spoke again, it wasn't as a mayor but as a mom. "I would like to speak with my daughter Zoey."

Dr. Khatri coughed. "Yes, right. About that . . ."

"Where is my daughter? Please put her on the phone."

"She's here, but not . . . *here*."

Mayor Hawthorne snorted. "What does that mean?"

"A group of five students, including your daughter and my son, may have inadvertently accessed a top secret portal capable of connecting our dimension to the larger multiverse."

Mayor Hawthorne let out a hearty laugh. "Good one! Now tell me what's really going on."

The line was silent.

"Dr. Khatri, you must be joking," she said, her voice unusually shaky.

"I wish I were."

"How could something like that even happen?" she cried.

"We have reason to believe that one of our colleagues, Ian McGillum, went rogue and constructed a functioning quantum collider secretly within the NASA facility."

"And this colleague? Where is he now?" Mayor Hawthorne demanded.

"We have not been able to locate him. We don't know if he's on the run or if he was in the portal with the children when they disappeared." Even as he spoke the words, he found them hard to believe. "We think he may also have stolen a very important piece of equipment, a device called a Syntropitron."

"Is it some sort of weapon?"

"No, thankfully. It's used to repair broken particle structures. We don't know why Professor McGillum took it or what he plans to do with it. Dr. Scopes is leading an investigation into his whereabouts, and I'm working to establish a communication channel between us and the children, wherever they may be."

Mayor Hawthorne was quiet for a moment. "Tell Dr. Scopes I can have a citywide search team mobilized within the hour. We'll set up checkpoints along all major access roads into and out of Conroy."

"Thank you, that would be helpful," Dr. Khatri replied gratefully.

"And the children?" Mayor Hawthorne pressed, clearly racked with worry. "How can I help you find them?"

Dr. Khatri proceeded to talk the mayor through various rescue scenarios. He breezed over some of the finer details of catastrophysics, not because he doubted the mayor's intellect but because he himself still hadn't figured it all out.

She let out a long breath. "This is worse than I thought." But there was no time to wallow. They needed to act quickly, to set a plan in motion.

"I will issue a press release regarding today's quiver," she said. "As for the children, I think it's best if we don't alert the public to their absence just yet. I would like you to coordinate with school leadership. Have them contact each family and inform them that their children were selected to participate in a special overnight sleep study. Tell the parents and guardians it was a highly competitive process and that their kids are Conroy's best and brightest. They'll likely be too proud to overthink or second-guess."

"Very well," Dr. Khatri said.

"If the media gets wind of the true story, it will cause panic. Discretion is key," Mayor Hawthorne added.

"Agreed."

"Good. I'm depending on you to bring our children home, safe and sound."

25

STATION LIMINUS

"YOU HAVE ARRIVED AT YOUR DESTINATION," A SOOTHING AI VOICE said as the yellow hoverdisc slowed to a stop.

The cadets unbuckled their safety harnesses and climbed down. Duna led them through a set of massive silver doors. "Before you can begin your important work with the council, you must be processed and scanned." They looked at them kindly. "Don't worry, it sounds worse than it is. This way . . ."

The cadets followed silently, taking in the sights and sounds. The Station's main intake area was as big as their school's gymnasium. Colorful flags representing each dimension in the multiverse hung from elaborate ceiling trusses high overhead. The kids had never seen their dimension's flag before but instantly recognized the blue-and-green planet—the way Earth had looked in better days—set on a black background scattered with small white stars.

Up ahead, sentient creatures of all shapes and sizes

filtered through rectangular booths that scanned them with beams of yellow light. Their belongings underwent a similar process, riding ribbons of floating conveyor belts as teams of biobots inspected capsules and trunks for prohibited materials. After retrieving their belongings, the travel-weary creatures moved on to a second row of booths, where they presented chip cards and holodocs to bored-looking Station agents who either approved or denied their entry and exit requests.

"We'll be here for days at this rate," Dev said, eyeing the serpentine queue.

"Ah, not to worry." Duna guided the kids toward an expedited service line. "Only the best for our Earthling envoys!"

Once they had all passed muster, Duna escorted them to a small antechamber. Compared to the sweeping and sterile intake area, the octagonal room was almost cozy, with rich red-and-gold lacquered paneling and warm light winking from asymmetrical crystalline chandeliers. Several tables were arranged within the space, each looking as though it had been carved from an asteroid, with jagged veins of metallic minerals. Arrayed around the tables were elegant wingback chairs, made from the actual wings of some very unusual feathered creatures. Right away, Lewis noticed large refreshment carts filled with carafes of steaming beverages and trays of thin, hexagonal crackers.

"This is the diplomatic salon," Duna explained, taking a seat. "Make yourselves comfortable. Enjoy a cup of tartea, a specialty of Dimension11." The kids joined them at the table, feeling slightly out of place, like they'd snuck into the teachers' lounge at school.

Tessa selected a mug, which was heavier than it looked, forged from some dense space alloy. She tipped a carafe to pour herself some tea, but the liquid moved as slowly as molasses. She lifted the mug to her lips. It tasted like licorice, peat moss, and sesame. She couldn't decide if the combination was gross or sort of delicious. She took another sip, pinky out, hoping she looked sophisticated.

Dev sniffed the tea but decided against it. The thick, viscous liquid rivaled his mother's awful smoothie for the title of universe's nastiest beverage.

"Duna, earlier you told us there were thirteen dimensions. But I counted fourteen flags in the intake terminal," Maeve said. "And Ignatia referred to our dimension as Dim14. What's that about?"

"Ah, yes. We still include Dim8 in the flag array and numerical nomenclature, lest anyone forget."

"Forget what?" Isaiah asked, taking a bite of an oddly shaped cracker. It dissolved in his mouth and tasted like salty chalk. He tried not to gag. "What happened to Dim8?"

Duna frowned. "I had not anticipated sharing this piece of our history with you all so soon, but it is important to understand the past, for it guides the future." They set their cup carefully on its saucer. "In the earliest days, before the Station was built, the dimensions—or balloons—were all floating freely. Dim1 bumped into Dim2. They shared information and technology. They traded goods. They coexisted peacefully. In time, they encountered a third dimension. Then a fourth and fifth.

"These relatively peaceful encounters continued until contact was made with the eighth dimension. Dim8 contained a harsh, barely hospitable planet called Empyria with an even harsher ruler. It was discovered that the Empyrean One was exploiting a nearby ninth dimension, draining the planet of its resources and enslaving the gentle Nharlite people.

"The original seven dimensions refused to stand idly by and watch one dimension overpower another. They intervened and drew the ire of the Empyrean One. What followed was the bloodiest interdimensional battle the multiverse has ever known. Millions of lives were lost."

"But it was seven against one," Lewis said, stuffing his face with crackers and guzzling sludgy tartea. "It should have been easy!"

"Should have been, yes. But it wasn't. The leader of Empyria was ruthless, conniving, greedy. Everyone underestimated the power she possessed, the cruelty and capabilities of her weaponry. The original seven dimensions formed an alliance—the original Multiverse Allied Council—and planned to retaliate with a collective strike on the Empyrean One.

"Before they could launch their attack, a massive cosmic disruption occurred within Dim8. A black hole formed, swallowing Empyria and everything around it. In order to save the rest of the multiverse from being sucked into the black hole's ravenous nothingness, the newly formed MAC untethered Dim8, essentially cutting it off from the rest of us forever."

Dev wished so badly that he could take notes or record everything Duna was saying so that he could share it with his dad.

"What was the cosmic disruption?" Isaiah asked, equal parts intrigued and terrified.

Duna shook their head. "No one knows exactly. Many believe the Empyrean One herself created it, choosing to sacrifice the lives of everyone and everything on her own planet, rather than surrender."

Isaiah's gray eyes widened. "So, could Dim8 still be out there somewhere, a lone balloon just floating around? Could the Empyrean One be hiding within the folds of interdimensional darkspace, licking her wounds, awaiting an opportunity to reemerge?"

"Geez, Isaiah!" Maeve huffed, throwing her hands in the air. "Way to bring the doom!"

Duna frowned, as though the idea was deeply unnerving. "My understanding is that the untethering was successful. That balloon has popped and its string has been cut, so to speak. The demise of Dim8 may be part of our shared past, but thankfully Empyria is not a threat to our future."

Isaiah nodded, but he couldn't shake the twinge of doubt he felt deep in his chest.

Duna touched a finger to their pewter pin, a thirteen-pointed star Isaiah had noticed Shro also wearing. "I am proud to serve on a council that fights for justice. We were unified through hardship, and it made us stronger."

"What happened after the war?" Tessa asked.

"It took centuries for the multiverse to recover. Since then, the MAC has been cautious about the inclusion of new dimensions into the council. I suppose that is why so many delegates have been reticent to accept Dim14, your home dimension, with open arms. Especially since it took Earthlings so long to cross the Threshold." Duna sat up a little taller and inspected their lynk. "Which reminds me, when do you expect Mr. Finto to join us?"

Maeve scowled. "Who is this Finto guy anyway? That's the second time someone's mentioned him, but I have no idea who he is."

"Me neither," Dev added.

Duna nearly spit out their tartea. "He is the delegate from Earth, of course! Just as I am the delegate from Mertanya. We all report to Station Liminus for a few days each month to address a variety of multiverse issues. We vote on expansion plans, negotiate trade partnerships, share vital information, and oversee cross-dimensional judiciary matters. Some delegates have more permanent leadership posts within the Station, such as Quirg, who acts as custodian of the Gates, and Ignatia, who presides over the entire council."

Maeve frowned. "So, where's Mr. Finto now?"

"Back on Earth, I presume," Duna said. "Though I'm hopeful he'll arrive at the Station soon."

"What I want to know is who put him in charge?" Tessa

said, growing annoyed. "My mother is a politician, and if Earth picked someone to represent *all* of us, we should have had some say in the matter."

"That is not my area of expertise," Duna replied. "How each planet chooses to govern their populations is not something the MAC gets involved with, for the most part. Ignatia believes each dimension should remain relatively autonomous. So long as they play nice in the interdimensional sandbox, that is. I don't know how Salvido Finto was selected, but he did seem woefully unprepared for the task at hand. Which is why you five were summoned."

"Summoned to do what exactly?" Maeve asked, treading carefully. "I'm still unclear on that part . . ."

Duna blinked. "To use your high-level skills to aid in terraforming efforts, and assist with regenerex mining, among other things."

"Sorry, what?" Lewis said, scratching his head.

"To help save your planet, of course," Duna replied as though this were the most obvious thing.

Isaiah startled. "Wait, why does our planet need saving?" He remembered the visions he'd been having more frequently, apocalyptic landscapes that flashed before his eyes during quivers, then disappeared just as quickly.

Duna's brow furrowed. "You really don't know?"

"Know what, Duna?" Dev said, growing concerned.

Duna scrubbed a hand across their forehead. "I didn't expect to have to deliver this news, too. I'm sorry, Earthlings, but your home is on the brink of collapse."

EARTH

ZOEY WAITED OUTSIDE THE GIRLS' LOCKER ROOM. SHE GLANCED up at the clock on the wall. Where was Tessa? Band practice was about to start and her sister was totally MIA. She typed an irritated message into her eChron watch and waited for Tessa to send some snarky reply, but nothing happened. Zoey had assumed Tessa would be itching to change back into her normal clothes and return to her regular, much cooler identity, but she was nowhere to be found. Maybe the field trip had run late? Maybe the quiver had caused some traffic delays?

Then Zoey spotted Gage and Blake coming down the hallway. "Hey! Guys!" she called out, giving a wave, remembering that they were friends with Tessa and had gone to NASA today, too.

"OMG, that was the worst field trip ever!" Blake said dramatically. "I missed you, girl!" She gave Zoey a hug, which was super weird because popular girls like Blake never gave her the time of day. Except when she was disguised in her sister's designer clothes, apparently.

"What was so bad about it?" Zoey asked, trying to get back in character and act like Tessa. Cool and aloof, a note of boredom perpetually woven into her voice, like she always had something better to do. Like she was granting you some sort of favor by giving you the smallest ounce of her attention.

"I mean it was suuuuuper boring. So, like, sciencey. Eww." Blake pretended to gag. "And then that quiver hit and spooked everyone. It was total pandemonium. Not chill at all."

"Was anyone hurt?" Zoey asked, growing a little more concerned.

"I don't think so," Blake said, opening a compact to fix her lip gloss in the small mirror. "Except Hailey chipped a nail, I think. Tragic, right?"

"Uh, did you forget about my injury?" Gage said, lifting up his foot.

"It looks fine to me," Zoey said. "What happened to it?"

"That nerdy ginger kid happened, that's what."

"Who? Nolan?"

"Oh my gosh, Tessa, I can't believe you actually know his name. You are hysterical," Blake cackled, and gave her a playful swat.

Gage scowled. "Yeah, I guess that's him. He dropped his giant dorkwhistle on me. And I'm pretty sure he did it on purpose."

Zoey knew Nolan well; that kid didn't have a mean bone in his body. But she honestly wouldn't have blamed Nolan if he *had* dropped his tuba on Gage's foot intentionally.

"He's lucky my foot's not broken. My dad definitely would have sued!"

Blake rolled her eyes. "Okaaay, Gage. Don't be dramatic."

"I was so mad that I swiped it!" He lifted up a huge black case. "See? Gonna teach that loser a lesson. It was chaos when we evacuated the building, so I don't even think he noticed I'd taken it. He's probably gonna freak when he realizes it's missing." He laughed meanly. "Sucker."

"You have to give that back," Zoey snapped, her face flushing with anger. Gage locked eyes with her, surprised by her tone. She swallowed and tried to soften her voice so she sounded more like the real Tessa. "Why don't you give it to me, Gage? Please? I'll return it to Nolan. I wouldn't want you to get in trouble." She knew Gage and her sister had some history, and she suspected he still had a crush on her, so she batted her eyelashes, hoping it might help.

"Fine," Gage relented. He handed over the case. "I don't really want to be seen carrying it around anyway. Might damage my rep, ya know?"

"Hey, have either of you seen my sister anywhere?" Zoey asked, setting the case on the ground. She'd lifted a tuba before, but this felt much heavier.

"No," Gage said, leaning on the nearby locker, uncomfortably close to Zoey. "And I still can't believe you're related to a band geek."

Zoey fumed. She had to clench her teeth just to keep from biting his head off. Once she regained some small bit of composure she said, "Don't talk about my sister like that." She glared. "And you'll never be half as cool as those band geeks." She delivered a swift stomp to his already sore foot before storming off, lugging Nolan's tuba case awkwardly.

"Ouch! What the heck?" Gage yelled, but she refused to turn and look back.

She hurried down the hall and exited the building, wondering if Tessa might be waiting for her at Baxter Field, where band practice was supposed to start in just a few minutes. She was about to cross the parking lot when a big blue electric bus pulled up to the curb, its roof glittering with solar panels and electricity conversion cables. It had been retrofitted from its earlier days as a gas-guzzler, and you could still see patches of its old yellow paint beneath the new coat of blue. Benni, the driver, stepped down.

"Just the girl I was looking for," he said with a warm smile.

"Hey, Benni," she said, setting the tuba case on the side-walk and shaking out her arm. "You drove to the field trip today, right?"

He nodded.

"Was Tess, uhhh, I mean, Zoey on your bus? I can't find her anywhere." She tried to hide the frustration in her voice.

He looked at Zoey carefully. His left eye twitched. "I think you will find the answers you seek in here," he said cryptically, handing her a notebook.

She stared down at Isaiah's Journal of Strange Occurrences. "Where did you find this?" she asked. But when she looked up, Benni and the blue bus were gone.

STATION LIMINUS

BACK IN THE DIPLOMATIC SALON, DUNA HAD JUST DESCRIBED the severity of Earth's situation to the cadets. They sat in silence for several minutes, baffled, upset, and frustrated. Tessa felt like she might burst into tears; Dev was so overwhelmed that his face and hands went numb; Lewis gaped, open-mouthed like a fish out of water.

"It troubles me to see you this way, Earthlings," Duna said gently. "Do not fret, please. Remember, the MAC agreed to aid Earth for a full year. In that time, you will be trained to heal your ailing planet. You will be heroes."

"Heroes? There's a new title!" Maeve snorted. "Normally, everyone just calls us band geeks, freaks, or space cadets."

"I refuse to believe it," Duna scoffed. "As Earth's most intelligent, competent, and resilient humans, *you* are the most qualified individuals for the job. That is why you are here."

"The collider..." Dev said, putting together the pieces.

"I think there was some sort of mix-up. We're not elite, advanced, or even that coordinated."

"Hey, speak for yourself," Lewis snorted. "I'm a great dancer."

"What I mean is, we're only kids," Dev said.

"Only kids? How can you say that?" Duna wagged a finger. "If you want the council to respect you, you must respect yourselves." They thumped a fist to their chest proudly. "Keep in mind, I am fifteen, only a few years older than you. In my dimension, youthful voices are embraced and celebrated. Do not diminish the value of motivated minds and hearts!"

"Right. I totally agree. Except this whole thing was an accident." Dev looked at the others apologetically. "And it's my fault, because it was my dad who—"

"Stop." Duna raised a hand, their face clouded with conflicting emotion. Even though the kids and Duna were alone in the room, Duna leaned forward and lowered their voice. "By denying that you are the selected Earthlings, you may incriminate yourselves in a number of crimes. Not to mention compromise your planet's only shot at an already fragile aid package."

"Crimes?" they all said in unison, gulping.

Duna looked distraught. "This is just the sort of thing the council will seize upon," they said seriously. "They'll make an example of you. Or worse. You must show them you are up to the task at hand."

"Listen, Duna. I appreciate your faith in us. I really do,"

Maeve replied. "But this is too big for us to take on. In any other circumstance, I would totally be on board with the *fake it 'til you make it* approach, but if we mess this up, lives may be at stake."

"Don't you get it?" Isaiah hissed. "They already are!"

Maeve bit her lip. "We need to get home as quickly as possible and make sure the right people speak to the council. If Earth is truly in such bad shape, we can't risk it."

"I agree with Maeve," Lewis said, "and that rarely happens."

Duna sighed. "I understand your reasoning. But..." They paused, looking at each cadet, one at a time. "I wonder if maybe you *are* the people meant to fix this."

Dev shook his head despondently. "We told you, this was a mistake, a misunderstanding."

Duna clasped their hands together. "Perhaps. However, the multiverse works in strange ways. On Mertanya we're taught to trust in coincidence." They looked down at the chains around their neck, at the rectangular silver tags that bore scripts and symbols the cadets could not understand. "You have something called *fate* in your world, correct? Occurrences that are preordained or destined to happen in a particular way?"

"Yes." Maeve nodded. "In ancient Greece, the Fates were three goddesses who presided over people's destinies by spinning, measuring, and cutting threads associated with each person's life."

"Exactly," Duna said. "Sometimes callings are woven into our futures, into the very fabric of history, long before we are even born. In my language, we call it *th'ahnai*, an ineluctable outcome. It is often represented by a ring intersected by a dot, demonstrating that all outcomes will eventually return to their point of origin."

"You don't actually believe that, do you?" Tessa said.

Maeve elbowed Tessa. "Stop it. You're being rude."

Duna waved a hand. "No, no. It's fine. I understand your reluctance. But I hope you might consider the possibility that you five may be destined for something bigger."

The cadets let Duna's words sink in. For Maeve's whole life, she'd been told she wasn't good enough, that she'd never amount to anything. That her future in Conroy was a dead end. She had refused to believe it, always searching for a way out. And now someone was telling her she might be bound for greatness. The idea was exhilarating, intoxicating. And terrifying.

Dev's mind was racing. "What happens if we can't convince the council to save Earth? What if the terraforming or mining, or whatever else they expect us to do, isn't successful?"

"Aw, buddy," Lewis said, giving Dev a friendly pat on the back. "Remember what Mrs. Minuzzi always says: Mistakes are part of learning."

Duna sucked in a breath. "On the contrary, if you fail, the council will compactify Earth."

Lewis blinked. "Do what now?"

"Without getting into the complex laws of physics, it's essentially putting a celestial body into a trash compactor and squeezing it down to the size of a marble, then flicking it away," Duna explained.

"Rude." Tessa scowled.

"I agree. Which is why I voted against such actions. But the council worries that if your planet self-destructs, there may be ripples throughout the multiverse. When Dim8 vanished, neighboring dimensions suffered adverse effects, like warped magnetic fields, atmospheric degradation, et cetera. Luckily, most planets recovered, but the council is wary of exposing the broader multiverse to harm."

"I can't say I blame them," said Dev glumly.

Maeve huffed. "So, you're telling me that humans have not only nearly destroyed our own planet, but we've also put the entire multiverse in danger?" She was disgusted and dismayed by the entire mess.

Duna shrugged. "Essentially, yes."

"Geez. No wonder Ignatia and Quirg dislike us so much," Tessa said.

"Ignatia may seem stern and intimidating, but she is fair. And Quirg's not as bad as he looks. Somewhere deep beneath that grouchy exterior, he actually has a heart. Technically, three of them. All Quomions do."

"And Shro? What about him?" Isaiah asked.

Before Duna could answer, a sentry appeared in the doorway. He summoned Duna, and they conversed quietly in an alien language the kids could not understand.

After a few minutes, Duna returned, their face serious.

"The council has assembled for your official hearing. It is time to go."

"Ugh. I didn't sign up for this," Isaiah moaned.

Duna's russet eyes flickered with an idea. "You're musicians, right?" They pointed at Maeve's oboe.

The kids nodded. Thankfully, all their instruments had passed inspection at intake.

"Then you're going to need to improvise."

Maeve set her jaw. She was a performer, darn it. And this disaster could be her greatest achievement. These kids, her school, heck, the entire planet was counting on her.

"I have to go now," Duna said. "One of our Station guides will arrive shortly and escort you to the meeting chamber." They looked at the kids. "Good luck. I'm rooting for you. The council desperately needs fresh voices, new perspective. I will do what I can to help, but the rest is up to you."

"So, like, no pressure, right?" Lewis said, smiling goofily to mask his nerves.

EARTH

GIL GREENE SAT UP IN HIS RECLINER. HIS HEARTBURN WAS worse than normal. Maybe it was the chili dog he'd eaten for lunch, or maybe it was the fact that his granddaughter hadn't come home yet. Maeve often stayed at school after band practice, or stopped by the library to do her homework before returning to the trailer, but today she was later than normal. He couldn't blame the poor kid for making herself scarce. The last few years had been rough on all of them. He wished he could change the past, but no good came from thinking like that.

He surfed aimlessly through the television channels, grateful the power had been restored after the day's freak quiver and energy surges. He stopped at one of the local stations.

"Breaking news!" the reporter said. "Miss Mary's Dairy Farm reports another missing cow!"

The video cut to a farmer named Ray Harkis, the owner

of the dairy, and one of Gil Greene's longtime pals. Ray was holding a pitchfork and shouting, "I blame those MegaAg folks! Every year, they come knocking, making me offers, trying to convince me to give up my land and my livelihood." He scowled. "Well, that's never gonna happen! I told 'em to get lost. But folks like that don't take no for an answer. Instead, they come sneaking round, trespassing on my land. Kidnapping my cows, trying to intimidate me." His voice grew louder. "If they keep this up, they've got another thing coming!" Ray shook his fist angrily.

Gil watched the rest of the segment. In the distance, on the screen, he caught a glimpse of an old silo with the faded letters *G-R-E-E-N-E* painted on the side. His corn and soy fields had once been adjacent to Ray's dairy. Something deep inside Gil's chest softened. He missed that place terribly. He missed the life they had had there. He knew his granddaughter and daughter did, too.

He pulled himself out of the recliner. He was tired of feeling useless. He would stop by Miss Mary's Dairy for a visit. He would help an old friend, in case any hooligans came snooping around, looking for another cow to kidnap. At the very least, he could bring Ray a chili dog to fill his stomach.

Gil Greene grabbed his shotgun from the locked cabinet in the den, hobbled out to the pickup truck parked in the yard, climbed in, and drove to the outskirts of town.

STATION LIMINUS

A COMPLEX SILVER DUCT SYSTEM PUMPED FRESH OXYGEN INTO Station Liminus, but the air felt thick and tense. The cadets had been moved from the lavish diplomatic salon into a cold, white waiting room with uncomfortable metal benches. The typically boisterous group was quiet, awaiting an audience with the council. Each of them was full of uncertainty and nervous energy.

Lewis drummed his fingers on his knees incessantly, his shaggy, sandy-colored hair falling over his eyes. Maeve was meditating on her bench with her eyes closed, getting into character. Dev sat nearby, watching Tessa fidget with her silver bracelet.

"Psst! Hey! Earth to Zoey," Dev hissed, sliding along the bench near her.

Tessa snapped her head to the side. "Huh?"

"I've been calling your name for, like, five minutes."

"You have?" She'd been so deep in her own thoughts,

it took a second before she realized he'd been calling her sister's name, not hers. If she was going to keep up this ruse, she needed to be more careful.

"Anything you want to talk about? I know it's been a rough day, but you seem . . . different." In the past, he'd been too shy to say more than a handful of words to Zoey, but the day's events had helped him feel a little braver.

She stared blankly back. "Um, no?"

His crooked grin drooped.

"It's just, I don't think this is the best place to chat." She gestured around the room. Cameras blinked from each corner, recording their every move, and armored guards stood at attention along the perimeter.

Dev looked disappointed but nodded.

"I'm fine. Really," she lied. "It's probably just hyperspace jet lag or something." Unintended teleportation was draining enough, but pretending to be her sister was becoming exhausting.

"Here." He shook a bag of sour gummies. "I know candy helps calm your nerves before a big performance. Remember, we're in this together."

Tessa felt bad that she didn't know anything about her sister's preperformance butterflies, or her candy-eating ritual. She vowed to take greater interest in Zoey's band performances when they returned home. "Where'd you get those?" she asked Dev, holding her palm open.

"Lewis bought, like, fifty packs at the Milky Way Café during the field trip. I stashed a bag in my pocket before we tried the Zero-Grav simulator. Somehow it survived the trip." He shook some gummies into her hand. Without thinking, she popped a pineapple one into her mouth. Dev watched her curiously.

"Mmm, yum," she said. She ate another pineapple gummy, then another. "I feel better already. Thanks."

"No problem." Dev flashed a soft smile. He didn't call her out, but in that moment, he knew the girl sitting beside him was definitely *not* Zoey Hawthorne-Scott. He'd been crushing on the real Zoey since the day they'd met at band auditions, and he knew she despised all things pineapple. He felt confused, and a little deceived. He turned away.

"Cheer up, dude," said Lewis, noticing Dev's change of mood. He scooted beside his friend and grabbed a fistful of gummies. He'd already eaten his own remaining pack of licorice twists. "It could be worse. At least your parents don't think you're at track practice. They'd lose their minds if they knew I quit sports so I could focus on the band," Lewis said, chewing thoughtfully.

Tessa's eyes grew wide, listening. Apparently she wasn't the only one with a secret.

"You didn't tell me you quit," said Dev, surprised.

"I just decided," Lewis said. "If today's multiple near-death experiences have taught me anything, it's that life's too short."

"That is surprisingly deep," Dev said.

"My family thinks music is artsy-fartsy. Everything is a competition to them." Lewis sighed and ate another gummy.

"I just wish I didn't have to hide the thing I love." He started tapping a soulful beat on the seat with his single drumstick. "I wish I could show them ..."

"Seventy-six percent chance we're doomed!" Isaiah announced loudly as he flopped onto a nearby bench. After Duna left, he'd started calculating their (steadily declining) odds of survival.

"Optimism, Isaiah," Maeve shot back, opening one eye. "The word of the day is *optimism*." She went back to her meditations.

A young woman with a pierced nose and a cobalt-blue jumpsuit entered the room. She looked identical to the guide who had first welcomed them to the Gwen Research Center.

"The secretary will see you now," she said.

"Ari?" Dev jumped to his feet and ran to her, relieved to finally see a familiar face.

She leaned back suspiciously. "Have we met?"

"Yes! You greeted us at NASA today. During our field trip!"

Her face was blank.

"You helped us store our instruments in the old collider room." He held up his saxophone. "Remember?"

"I am sorry, Earthling. You are sorely mistaken." She pointed to a nametag pinned to her lapel. It contained a lengthy string of symbols and letters in an alien language. Below that, it read in English: *Ira*. "*Not Ari*, now, am I?"

Dev shook his head despondently. Was anyone who

they seemed? He cast a long look over his shoulder at Tessa. She was undeniably pretty, but his heart didn't skip a beat like it usually did. Now that he knew she wasn't really Zoey, something in his heart changed.

"You must have met one of my doppelgängers," Ira explained.

"Your what?" Dev refocused on the guide standing in front of him.

"A sort of twin," she said. "Someone who looks almost exactly like you but is entirely different. We often have doppelgängers in parallel dimensions, but I wouldn't suggest seeking them out. If you cross paths with your doppelgänger in a parallel dimension, you can disrupt the space-time continuum, which can get rather . . . messy. Definitely not recommended."

"No, I'm sure it was you. It had to be!" Lewis said, butting in.

Ira frowned. "It is quite possible you saw someone who *looked* like me, but I can guarantee it was not the same me who is talking to you at this very moment." As she turned, Lewis spotted a long, spiked tail protruding from the back of her jumpsuit.

"Oh. Never mind," he mumbled.

"Hurry. The council awaits. Please follow me," Ira said. "They do not like to be kept waiting."

After her meditations, Maeve was feeling focused and centered. She rallied the group. "Let's go. Aten-hut! And don't forget your instruments." She strode forward, back straight, just as she had led the middle school marching band into the Southern Ohio stadium not so long ago for the Soy Blossom Bowl. She held her chin high to give an air of confidence, but deep down she didn't have the best feeling about confronting the council.

Dev stepped forward on shaky legs, while Lewis shuffled and tapped his feet in a nervous rhythm.

"Eighty-three percent," Isaiah muttered under his breath, clutching his trumpet.

Tessa lagged behind, unsure where Zoey would fit into all this. Maeve shot her a puzzled look but kept marching ahead. Tessa gripped her sister's clarinet, feeling grateful for its weight, for having something solid to hold on to.

The lobby doors split open with a hydraulic hiss. Two massive guards with eight legs and six beefy arms between them led a creature out of the vestibule. It struggled against electromagnetic shackles and made an angry, gargling sound. It spit green goo at the guards. One blob flew in Dev's direction; he ducked just in time. If being a band geek had taught him anything, it was how to dodge spitballs, thanks to bullies like Gage who liked to use the back of his head for target practice during lunch. Turned out the skill set was just as useful when it came to goo-slinging aliens.

"That Oolg lied about embezzling a shipment of thornmelon seeds," Ira explained. "He will serve a ten-year sentence in the Praxalis Penitentiary in Dim6. A fair punishment, in my opinion."

Isaiah's eyes grew wide. "He's going to jail for stealing some seeds?"

"While the Station itself is a prosperous place, many planets across the multiverse are struggling. Famine, drought, and blight are becoming more widespread. Only a few crops can grow in increasingly harsh climatic conditions. You Earthlings should understand this as well as any."

Maeve nodded, thinking wistfully of their old farm.

Ira continued, "The theft is bad in itself. What's worse is that he lied about it. Members of the MAC take a solemn truth oath; our partnerships are built on trust. Honesty is a critical component of diplomacy. Especially in these uncertain times."

Tessa felt as though the words were directed to her. A hard lump formed in her throat.

"Please excuse me for a moment," Ira said. She crossed the room and began entering a code into a wall-mounted console.

Isaiah turned to his friends, panic smeared across his face. "If that's the punishment for swiping some seeds, what do you think they'll do to us? We stole a freaking rocket ship!"

"Calm down," Maeve whispered. "It wasn't a rocket. And we didn't steal anything. We accidentally accessed a top secret quantum collider and initiated a cross-dimensional Transfer. That's all."

"Yeah." Isaiah rolled his eyes. "'Cause that sounds a whole lot better."

Dev bit his lip and looked around. "I'm not sure the whole *fake it 'til we make it* thing is going to work so well after all. If the councilors start questioning us, we should be on the same page."

"Good point. We'll tell the truth: It was all Lewis's fault," Maeve said.

"Hey!"

"You are the one who got us into this mess," Maeve replied, anger welling up.

"I did not!" Lewis scoffed.

"Did too!" Maeve stomped her foot, losing her cool. "You were, like, 'Come this way. There's an epic DJ booth with a disco ball!'"

Lewis threw his hands up. "Well, there was a disco ball, wasn't there?"

"Sure, one that shot lasers and nearly obliterated us!" Maeve snapped. So much for her peaceful meditations.

Isaiah shrugged. "She has a point."

Just then, a loud beep sounded and a set of doors parted. The cadets were shuttled into a large vaulted chamber with carved moonstone walls and thousands of interlocking triangular screens arching overhead. Each panel glowed, shifting from color to color before settling on a warm, pearly hue. A few larger panels were transparent. Through these, the kids caught glimpses of the sky beyond. For a moment, Maeve half expected to see the Conroy skyline, or the cornfields of her old family farm. Instead, the view was an endless expanse of the emptiest, blackest black. Unlike normal windows on Earth that tended to let light *in*, these seemed to suck all light *out*.

A varied assortment of alien, cyborgian, and humanoid creatures sat in rows of high-backed metal chairs that curved around a circular pedestal, atop which sat Ignatia in her indigo robes and the other delegates. The kids recognized Shro and Quirg, and of course Duna.

"Enter, Earthlings!" Ignatia's voice echoed off the walls. Floor lights flickered, illuminating an aisle leading from the entry to the central podium.

The cadets were frozen, clumped in the doorway, stunned by the array of faces in the crowd.

Ira leaned in and whispered kindly, "Go ahead. The secretary doesn't bite." She gave them a gentle nudge. "But the Vermaskians and Izoxis most definitely do. Steer clear."

"And I thought getting called into the principal's office was bad." Lewis hunched his shoulders.

The secretary rose to her feet, the corkscrewed horns protruding from her temples turning from ivory to sapphire. She looked the children up and down.

"I am relieved to see that you are feeling better and that you have recovered from your inaugural Transfer. Now, we invite you to take the stage and present your case to the council and constituents from across the multiverse."

Maeve was torn, her head spinning with the enormity of the task at hand. Lie or tell the truth? Lie or tell the truth? Benni's advice popped into her head: *Choose truth over theater. Unless theater is your truth.* She never shied away from a chance to shine, but this felt too big, even for the most seasoned performer. Even though she wanted to believe what Duna had said about fate...

She stepped forward. "Your Eminence, thank you for welcoming us onto Station Liminus. I speak on behalf of all my fellow bandmates, er, Earthlings, when I say how totally amazing it is. We really, um, respect what you're all doing here. Our planet could learn a lot from the peaceful diplomacy and spirit of collaboration you've got going on."

She took a deep breath and stole a look at the others. Lewis flashed a big thumbs-up. "You're killing it!" he whispered encouragingly. Clearly, he had already moved past their spat. She smiled back. She straightened her shoulders. Her nerves were settling. She could do this.

"While we are grateful for this opportunity, and for your hospitality, we need to tell you all something."

Duna shook their head ever so slightly, as though trying to discourage Maeve from the misstep she was about to take.

"I regret to inform the council that my peers and I traveled here today by mistake."

A hush fell over the crowd. "Mistake?" Quirg asked, cocking his head to the side. "Or false pretense?"

"I promise you, we meant no harm. None at all. I don't even fully understand how this happened, but it seems we arrived here in error," Maeve said, smoothing her mesh suit and exhaling.

Murmurs and agitated chatter erupted throughout the chamber.

"Silence!" Ignatia boomed. "Why did you not say something sooner?" She leaned forward, her violet eyes flashing with intensity as though she were seeing the cadets in a new light.

"We sort of tried to, but we were so overwhelmed and confused. We didn't even realize what was happening with the collider until it was too late."

"Too late?" Quirg scratched his chin. "Too late indeed."

"We thought about playing along, but Ira told us how much the MAC values honesty, so we felt it only right to—"

"I have heard enough." Xol hissed angrily. "These Earthlings are deceitful! They mock our protocols. They insult our intelligence. They waste our time!"

"No! Can't you see? She was trying to do the opposite!" Tessa pleaded in Maeve's defense. Maeve shot her a grateful but worried look.

Ignatia moved across the raised platform, her heels clacking a sharp rhythm on the floor. "I had hoped your first encounter with the council would proceed in a very different manner. I am deeply disappointed in your conduct."

"This sounds a lot like the lecture my dad gave me when I didn't make the lacrosse team last season," Lewis grumbled, looking down at the ground.

"The MAC will need to review your case, but based on

your confession, your actions appear to be in direct violation of numerous interdimensional laws." Ignatia proceeded
to recite a dizzying list. "How do you plead?"

"We're innocent," Maeve replied. "I told you, we made
an honest mistake."

"Mistake or not, you have jeopardized the integrity of a
highly critical operation and wasted valuable resources, not
to mention the time and energy of our esteemed council
members, as Xol pointed out," Ignatia said.

Maeve used her most mature voice, projecting loud
enough for all to hear. "We sincerely apologize. I'm sure we
can fix this."

"Not likely." The secretary pursed her lips. "Unless you
possess a cache of regenerex ores?"

Maeve frowned, her veneer cracking. "Um, no."

"Can you reconfigure an eight-cylinder celestial cer-
aboard terracraft?" Ignatia probed.

"I don't even know what that is," Isaiah said.

"Can you cultivate lunvar seeds in arid pegolith soil?"

Dev gulped. "Not likely." He thought about his mother's backyard greenhouse. She'd let him grow pea sprouts
in there once, but they'd all died. He hadn't inherited her
green thumb, that was for sure.

Ignatia pressed on. "Can you calculate the algorithms
necessary for—"

"You lost me at algorithm. I'm flunking out of seventh-
grade geometry," Lewis replied.

"Is there anything useful you *can* do?" a six-limbed member of the council asked.

"Well, yeah," Lewis said brightly. "Like we told you before, we can play music and dance at the same time. It takes real skill. In fact, we recently took second place in the annual Southern Ohio Soy Blossom Bowl marching band competition!"

"Second place? Impressive," Shro said mildly, steepling his slender fingers.

"Let us show you," Lewis offered, sporting a wide, proud smile. "We'll have this place moving and grooving in no time."

Tessa felt panic rise up and wash over her like a wave. There was no way she could play Zoey's clarinet. She would be discovered as an imposter . . . and then what?

Thankfully, the secretary replied, "That won't be necessary."

"Ninety-four percent chance we're doomed," Isaiah whimpered under his breath.

"Fine, then just send us home," Lewis said, feeling dejected. He was tired. He was hungry. He wanted to play some video games and sleep in his own bed and wake up to the smell of bacon frying in the kitchen. Even a smackdown from his older brothers would be better than this.

Maeve regained her composure. "Exactly. We'll gladly go back, and the special, super talented Earthling grown-ups can come in our place to help save planet Earth."

Lewis offered Maeve a fist bump. "Boom! Problem solved."

The secretary's expression curdled. "While I appreciate your honesty, that cannot happen."

"What? Why not?"

"Unfortunately, the portal you triggered was damaged during your Transfer, rendering a return journey impossible."

The cadets glanced at one another. They *had* pressed quite a few buttons trying to override whatever autopilot sequence they'd accidentally activated.

"We can take a different portal, then. We don't mind. Even if it's the scenic route, or whatever," Tessa replied.

"Do you really think it's that simple?" Quirg sneered.

"Your actions disabled all of our communication lines with Dim14. And only a handful of portals exist linking your planet to the Station. All of them appear to be inactive at this time. Councilor Finto himself was unable to join you for this reason."

Dev blurted out, "We'll help repair them!"

"With what? A flaxophone?" said Bo'lar, gesturing to Dev's instrument.

"No, but I'm pretty good with electronics. And Zoey knows how to code. Maeve's a natural leader. And Isaiah takes really detailed notes. And Lewis, well, Lewis provides lots of entertainment."

"Dang right I do."

"We could work together..." Dev's voice trailed off as

he realized how silly it all sounded. How insignificant their contributions would be.

"I vote to get rid of them as soon as possible. They've seen too much of the Station and our proprietary technology!" an angry council member said. "How do we know they're not spies? Shape-shifters have attempted to infiltrate the Station before. Remember?"

"I do. And I understand your concerns, but we had the Earthlings scanned earlier," Shro responded with a dismissive wave of his hand. "They are nothing but regular, non-modified human Earthlings. Harmless. Completely ordinary and unremarkable in every way."

"Exactly," Lewis agreed. "We are completely—hey, wait a minute . . ."

"I vote to Release them!" a council member barked.

"Yes!" Maeve nodded. "That's a great idea. Release us! I feel like this conversation has come full circle." She took a deep breath. "Fantastic. So, we're all in agreement?"

Ignatia arched an eyebrow. "We do not take decisions of this magnitude lightly. I call for an official vote." She scanned the rows of agitated council members before settling a pitying gaze on the cadets. "Guards! Lead the Earthlings to the central holding cell until further notice."

30

EARTH

FOLLOWING CAREFUL INSTRUCTIONS FROM DR. KHATRI, MRS. Minuzzi made the first phone call to the families of the missing children.

"I didn't give Isaiah permission to stay overnight," Sylvie Yoon said, trying to keep her panic at bay. "This activity is not a good idea for someone like my son. Please, could you put him on the line. I'd like to make sure he understands what a sleep study entails."

"I'm sorry, Mrs. Yoon. But Isaiah is currently in the middle of, um, an orientation meeting."

"You don't understand. He has ... nightmares. Night terrors, actually. I worry that if he is in the company of others, his dreams could cause a disturbance. I just don't feel this is the right choice for my child."

"We understand your concerns. But please think of this as a learning opportunity for him." Mrs. Minuzzi went on to read the script Dr. Khatri had provided.

After a few more minutes, Sylvie hung up the phone. She had agreed to let Isaiah participate in the study, but she was uneasy. Was Isaiah angry at her for calling the grief counselor? Was this an act of tween rebellion? She and her son hadn't been apart for a single night since last September. She knew he was probably in good hands, but her heart was heavy with worry.

Lewis's mother, Elise Wynner, got the next call.

After a brief discussion, she said, "Thank you for calling, Mrs. Minuzzi." She hung up the phone feeling quite pleased.

"Who was that?" Kingston asked, shoveling a forkful of meatloaf into his mouth.

"Your brother's teacher. Lewiston was invited to participate in a sleep study at NASA. He'll even get extra credit."

"Huh? He gets extra credit for sleeping? No fair!"

"Apparently it was an honor to be selected. Your father will be so proud." She beamed. "It seems Lewiston actually won the field trip after all."

As soon as their mother left the room, Kingston turned to Winston. "Let's raid baby brother's room while he's gone." Kingston grinned wickedly. "I bet he's got a bunch of money saved in that piggy bank of his."

"Totally," chuckled Winston. "I think he's hiding a stash of leftover Halloween candy up there, too."

Little did either of them know that Lewis's ultimate Brute Brothers Takedown prank was still armed and ready.

Kingston cracked his knuckles. "What a sucker. Come on. Let's go!"

"Sorry Lew," Winston mocked. "You snooze, you lose."

Two minutes later they were staring at each other, dumbstruck, covered from head to toe in maple syrup, shaving cream, feathers, little suction cup darts, and the most dreaded of all weaponry—glitter bombs.

STATION LIMINUS

THE HOLDING CELL WAS AN OCTAGONAL POD SIMILAR TO THE diplomatic lounge, but this one had too-bright lights, uncomfortable chairs, and no refreshments. Each cadet was shackled with electromagnetic tethers that flared bright blue and sent a warning shock through their ankles if they struggled against them. The goo-slinging Oolg they'd seen earlier occupied a far corner. A trio of hairy, waist-height inmates occupied another bench, swatting each other and occasionally biting one another with sharp yellow teeth, chittering like angry, oversized squirrels.

Closest to Tessa sat a scruffy humanoid kid in a tattered maroon jumpsuit with a large capsule bag slung over her shoulder. Her skin was scattered with amber-colored freckles. Her half-shaved hair was pure white, as were her irises.

"Well, well. Look what the prison guards dragged in. Let me guess—Earthlings?" the girl asked in a lilting accent. The blue translator around her neck was a slightly different shape and color than the ones the council members wore.

"How could you tell?" Lewis asked.

"No gills. Two legs, walking upright. Warm-blooded. Bilateral symmetry. Nike sneakers. Plus, you have the arrogant swagger of those greedy, planet-wrecking, fuel-burning jerks."

"She said I have swagger. Did you hear that?" Lewis nudged Maeve.

"I didn't get the impression she meant it as a compliment," Maeve shot back, holding the young inmate's stare.

"My name's Kor. From the colony formerly known as Ebvar in Dim7. Accused of theft, possession of unsanctioned parcels, and being too charming for my own good." She winked.

Maeve rolled her eyes.

"Listen, I'm not a criminal. I like to consider myself a collector of sorts. A peddler of wares from across the multiverse." Kor held up her bag. "I don't steal. I barter. I trade. People lose things, I find things. It all evens out in the end." She reached into the bag and removed a tall LED lamp, an entire chocolate cake, and a small jade box.

Tessa blinked. How all those items could fit into such a small bag was a mystery. "What are you, like an intergalactic Mary Poppins with that bag?"

"Your Earth references are lost on me," Kor replied flatly, setting the bag carefully on the floor. "Although, I think I may have a few artifacts from your planet in here somewhere. Let me see..." Kor dug around and retrieved a skateboard, a plastic fork, and a yellow-striped harmonica. Isaiah's mouth gaped. He'd gotten a harmonica just like that from Uncle Ming for his sixth birthday, but it had gone missing...

"So, what're you five in for?" Kor leaned back, picking at her teeth with the fork.

Maeve took a deep breath. "Breach of this, violation of that, cracked the space-time continuum, accidentally activated a Transfer portal..."

"Which we broke," Tessa added.

"By accident," Lewis retorted.

Kor let out a long whistle. She scrubbed a hand against the back of her neck. "The MAC decide your sentence yet?"

"No. Soon, I hope." Maeve flashed her most optimistic smile, but it felt fake. "We just want to go home."

Kor's white eyes dulled, her voice grew quieter. "At least you have a home to return to..."

"Maybe not for long. According to Duna, our home planet isn't in the best shape. We want to help, but we're not sure how."

"How noble." Kor eyed them skeptically. "Good luck with that." She eyed their instruments. "What do those do?" she asked nonchalantly.

"They help us play music," Maeve said, holding on to her oboe a little tighter.

"Ahh, I remember the first time I heard some Earthling tunes." Kor's shoulders rolled, her head bobbed. "Chuck

Berry's 'Johnny B. Goode' was my mom's favorite song. She would listen to it when she cooked dinner for my brothers and me. She'd dance around the kitchenette. She said the rhythm was too powerful to resist. We used to laugh so hard at her, at how silly she looked, until we realized our own feet were tapping and our hips were swaying." Kor closed her eyes, savoring the memory. But then a shadow of sadness fell over her face. She opened her eyes, blinking away the image of happier times.

"How did you hear that song?" Dev asked, surprised something from Earth had made it across the Threshold and into homes across the multiverse. "Johnny B. Goode" also happened to be one of his mom's favorite songs. How crazy that he and this girl from a completely different dimension could have that in common.

"You guys blasted that tune into space, remember? The Voyager Golden Record? It topped the MV's charts for at least a decade. Mostly because no other dimensions know how to replicate Earthling music. Which means it was pretty much the only thing on the charts ... except for that weird dotty, pulsy thing that you guys broadcasted from Arecibo."

"You heard that, too?" Dev asked. "Oh man! If my dad were here now, he'd have a billion questions for you!"

"Well, I'd tell him that that Arecibo song sounded more like a broken video game than music. No one understood what you crazy Earthlings were trying to say. It was awful." Kor rubbed her ears, remembering the sound.

Suddenly a grating shriek blared. The Station's AI system

announced, "Earthlings, your sentence has been decided. You will be Released in T-minus nine hours. A sentinel will be sent to retrieve you, at which time you will board a Release pod. End message."

"We're going to be released! Hooray!" Maeve cheered. The others tried to jump up for hugs and high fives, but the electromagnetic shackles zapped them, restricting their movement.

Kor shook her head. "That is *not* what you think it is. It means they are Releasing you into the outer reaches of the cosmos. Think of it like walking the plank off a pirate ship . . . directly into darkspace."

Tessa sucked in a breath. Her hands trembled.

Kor continued, "They'll stuff you in a tiny pod with no nav panel, then launch you into pure nothingness."

"Will there at least be snacks?" Lewis asked. "My suit was fresh out of space biscuits and juice tabs when we got here."

"Not likely," Kor said, giving him a weird look. "You'll perish as soon as your oxygen supply runs out."

"You're joking," Isaiah said. "This isn't happening." His head began to throb.

"Release is less expensive than housing inmates in the penitentiary on Praxalis. And it's considered more humane than tossing criminals into the bile pits, or feeding them to the long-toothed cranks on Jelingor, but I'm not so sure."

"There's no way they'd do that to us . . . would they?" Dev asked. "That Finto guy wouldn't let them."

"But he's nowhere to be found. And we messed up all communication with Earth. What makes you think Finto even knows we're here, let alone cares about us?" Isaiah replied.

"Then my dad will do something. I know it. He's probably already looking for us," Dev said, fighting back the sting of tears. "He'll find us."

Maeve's heart thrummed. She hoped Dev was right, but still, they needed a plan. She was supposed to be a leader, yet she'd never felt more unprepared.

"My advice? Whatever you do, do *not* get into that Release pod," Kor said, re-packing all the items into her bag.

"How do we know you're telling the truth? Maybe you just want to hijack our pod so *you* can escape!" Tessa snapped, her nerves fraying.

Kor's face shifted. "My parents were Released when I was small. I would never willingly switch places with you."

Isaiah looked at the others. "I hate to say it, but I told you so. Ninety-nine point nine percent chance we're D-O-O-M-E-D."

"Stop being so dramatic," Maeve said. "Everything will be fine."

"Seriously?!" Tessa said, astronomically annoyed. "Don't you remember what happened the last time someone said that?"

32

EARTH

ZOEY SAT ON HER BED, FLIPPING THROUGH THE PAGES OF ISA-
iah's Journal of Strange Occurrences and chewing her nails
anxiously. As soon as she came home from school, she had
changed back into her normal clothes and eaten an entire
bag of gummy bears (minus the pineapple ones), but she
still felt off.

Her mother was working late as usual, her father was in
his painting studio in the garage, and her sister was off gal-
livanting somewhere. She hadn't mentioned anything to her
parents about Tessa yet, hoping her sister would show up
before anyone else noticed she was missing. At this point,
she was more irritated than worried.

Tessa had flaked and hadn't appeared at band practice.
Neither had Isaiah, Dev, Maeve, or Lewis, which was completely out of character. They weren't the types to ditch a
rehearsal. Especially Maeve, who never missed a chance
to boss everyone else around. Even Coach Diaz, the

punctuality police himself, was late. When he finally arrived at the field, he was unusually frazzled, canceling practice with little explanation. This was especially odd, given that regionals were only weeks away and their formations were a hot mess.

Unfortunately, Coach left the field before Zoey could grill him for answers about the whereabouts of her sister and friends. She hadn't even been able to find Nolan to return his tuba, so she'd lugged the massive case all the way home with her. The whole afternoon had dissolved into total . . . hmmm, Zoey couldn't even think of a good vocabulary word to describe it other than . . . weirdness.

She returned her attention to Isaiah's journal, emptying the envelope pasted onto the back cover, which contained most of the letters Isaiah had received from his late uncle Ming. She and Isaiah had read through the notes and postcards countless times before, but something about Benni's cryptic message made her reconsider them with fresh eyes.

33

STATION LIMINUS

AS TESSA AND MAEVE ARGUED, DEV LIFTED HIS SAXOPHONE TO his lips and began to play. The first few notes were quiet, soft.

Everyone stopped, stared, and listened. Through the music, they felt Dev's emotions—the shared sadness, the confusion, the fear—all the things words couldn't properly express. Maeve closed her eyes and let the melancholy notes pour over her. She picked up her oboe and joined in, followed by Isaiah, and finally Lewis, whose typically frenetic drumming calmed, becoming a rhythm that felt like a heartbeat. Tessa knew that if Zoey were here, she would play and add to the melody, but Tessa wasn't her sister. The clarinet would be useless in her inexperienced hands.

But there was one instrument she could use: her voice. Normally she was way too self-conscious to sing anywhere but the shower. At this point, what did she have to lose? Dying by embarrassment might even be an improvement over perishing in some space pod.

Tessa began to sing, matching the tones and notes of the bandmates. She felt the scar on her left wrist prickle. Deep beneath the marred skin, the metal plate that the surgeons had implanted grew hot and itchy. In spite of the growing discomfort, she sang louder.

Music filled the holding cell, blossoming in every corner, making them forget—for a brief moment—the reality of their situation. Tessa's wrist grew more and more painful, but she carried on, singing and improvising, accompanied by the instruments.

From somewhere deep inside Kor's bag of questionably acquired goods, a small, shelled creature emerged, slowly, hesitantly. Curled within the pearlescent shell was a child with shimmering gray skin and huge, ice-blue eyes. She turned to look at Tessa, riveted by the vibrations of Tessa's voice. She moved liquidly onto the bench and inched her three-fingered hand closer to Tessa's.

Surprisingly, Tessa didn't flinch. She felt some unspoken thing pass between herself and the child, an understanding. The child placed her palm atop Tessa's. Beneath her silver bracelet, the prickling sensation of Tessa's skin cooled. She took a breath and when she sang again, her voice changed in her throat, words melting from English into an unknown language.

The bandmates paused, faltering for a moment, then kept on playing. The music swelled. It wasn't a piece they had ever rehearsed at band practice, but they played it flawlessly, perfectly in sync. Even Kor was transfixed.

She fumbled inside her sack and retrieved a recording device.

As their improvisation was about to reach a crescendo, the cell doors flew open. The music screeched to a halt. The child withdrew her hand and curled defensively into a tight spiral, rolling quickly back inside Kor's open sack, safely out of sight.

Ignatia stood in the doorway, flanked by Shro and an assortment of guards.

"Explain yourselves, at once!" the secretary demanded.

"We were just having a little jam session to help cope with the fact that we're about to die in darkspace. No thanks to you!" Lewis blurted.

"Precisely what sort of session?" the secretary asked, her horns flaring a bright cerise.

"Music," Isaiah replied matter-of-factly.

The secretary's eyes darted around the cell, searching for something. "How did you generate it? What code sequence did you initiate? What apparatus did you engage to transmit such powerful sound waves?"

"Uhhh...We just played our instruments." Lewis shrugged. "Isaiah on the trumpet, Maeve on oboe. Dev on sax. Me on bench drum. And then Zoey started singing. Which I've never heard before, but dang girl, you've got some pipes!"

Tessa blushed. She couldn't fight the proud smile tugging at her lips.

The secretary eyed them suspiciously. "At the precise moment you began to generate your...*music*...we received a flood of transmissions on this." She held up a thirteen-sided stone the size of an apple. "This triskaidecagon has been dormant since the silvox plague struck."

"Sorry. I'm not following...?" Maeve said.

"Triskaidecagons are highly complex translation devices that allow the council to communicate with sentient beings in all dimensions, regardless of language or dialect, via a cross-universe platform. They are like larger, more sophisticated versions of the pendants we wear." She touched the small, blue stone around her neck. "Thirteen of them are installed in the Station's primary communication hub, one for each dimension."

Shro nodded, explaining further: "The planet of Klapproth exists in Dim2, but a few years ago, a terrible plague struck. To protect the rest of the multiverse, a decision was made by the MAC to place the entire dimension under quarantine to prevent further spread of the virus. A strict interdiction was issued, preventing all travel to and from Klapproth. As head of Defense, it is my duty to make sure the interdiction is enforced."

"Right, but what does all this have to do with that triskadecka-whatsit?" Lewis asked, scratching his head.

"We were led to believe that the virus was capable of infecting both biologic and technologic hosts," Shro explained.

"Meaning it could jump from people to gadgets?" Lewis asked, fascinated, imagining what might happen if his favorite Maxcroft gaming console could get sick with the flu or somehow infect him with a bad cold.

"Indeed," Shro said, nodding solemnly, as though the information was greatly disheartening. "As such, it was deemed necessary to cut all standard communication lines with Klapproth until the virus was under control. Ever since, there have been no incoming or outgoing transmissions with Dim2."

"Until today," Ignatia said. "Something activated Dim2's designated triskaidecagon, and we followed the signal to this room."

"Could the virus spread through that?" Maeve wondered, pointing to the faceted turquoise-blue stone, hoping they hadn't accidentally infected themselves with a nasty bug.

"No. Triskaidecagons work differently from normal communication channels. They are highly secure, encrypted with metaphysical firewalls and sonic barriers, to be utilized only in extreme circumstances. The sudden flood of transmissions could mean Klapproth is finally cured, or it could be a distress call."

"It could also be a ruse, or a trap," Shro added, giving Ignatia a pointed look.

The secretary frowned at the implication. "I have only ever known Klapproth to be a peaceful planet."

"Of course, Your Eminence, but one can never be too

careful with these things. Especially when the safety of the entire multiverse is at stake . . ."

Ignatia lifted her chin regally. "Yes, well, I've summoned our top analysts to review the data. We will not proceed recklessly, but it seems as though the Earthlings' music may provide the key to reconnecting with an important and powerful ally," Ignatia declared. She directed her gaze at the cadets. "You will replicate the sound waves in the auditory lab at once. Please follow me. Time is of the essence."

"So we're not being Released?" Tessa asked, clinging to hope.

"None of you are going anywhere until we figure out exactly what occurred in here."

The secretary swiveled on her heels. "It appears these musically inclined Earthlings may be more valuable than we initially believed."

General Shro nodded. "Indeed."

As Ignatia led the group toward the auditory lab, Shro put his hand on Dev's shoulder. "May I speak with you for a moment?" he said.

"Me?" Dev gulped, pausing as the others moved on.

Shro smiled. "Of course. You are the leader of this group, are you not?"

"Uhhh . . ."

"The secretary is putting great stock in you and your fellow Earthlings' abilities. Do not take this opportunity lightly. You may have arrived here in error, and made a terrible first impression . . ."

"Gee, thanks." Dev wondered where this little chat was heading.

"But this is your chance at redemption," Shro said. "That is no small task. But I have faith you can handle it. I can see it in your eyes, Dev."

"See what?" Dev asked, blinking.

"Leadership. Potential. Ambition."

"Oh." Dev was pretty sure he lacked all of those qualities. He usually just wanted to disappear and blend in. His rules for surviving middle school involved not speaking up, not acting out, and avoiding getting his butt kicked.

But Shro's words felt warm as sunshine, especially inside the cold, sterile Station. Dev leaned into the idea, the possibility of making his mother and father proud. Of securing a better future for his baby sister. Of helping his friends. Of saving the world.

"We'll perform like our lives depend on it," Dev replied.

"That's the spirit," Shro said.

Just then, Quirg scuttled down the hall, racing toward Ignatia as fast as his legs could carry him. "Your Eminence!" he called out.

Ignatia stopped, her face wrought with irritation. "What is it? We are in the middle of something rather important."

"I'm sorry to interrupt. So very sorry! But your counsel is required. Our security team needs to speak with you immediately."

"Shro, could you please go with Quirg? Resolve this issue," she said, waving her hand.

"No, Your Eminence." Quirg shook his head. "They will not proceed without your personal authorization. The Ebvarienne adolescent known as Kor has escaped."

"Again?" Ignatia huffed.

"She's a slippery one," Shro muttered, scowling.

"I'm afraid so." Quirg nodded, his chins wobbling. "Perhaps the door wasn't properly secured after the Earthlings' exit?"

Ignatia looked from the kids to Quirg and back.

Shro cleared his throat and stepped forward. "If it would be helpful, I would gladly take on the lowly task of escorting the Earthlings to the auditory lab while you apprehend this miscreant and lay down justice."

"But I would like to witness this so-called music," Ignatia said, torn. "If they can . . ."

"I know. I know," Shro replied, his voice smooth as glass. "And you will, Your Eminence. In due course. I'm sure the Earthlings would appreciate a little more time to . . . warm up." Shro glanced at the instruments in their hands.

Maeve clutched her oboe tightly. "A little more practice would be a good idea," she agreed.

Shro turned back to Ignatia. "Presently, there is a fugitive on the loose within the Station. Only you can provide guidance for this most pressing issue, Your Eminence."

"Yes." Quirg nodded. "Only you."

"Fine," Ignatia relented. "But I expect to witness this *music* as soon as my duties are complete."

"Not to worry, Your Eminence." Shro bowed. As he rose, he locked eyes with Dev, who nodded gravely. "I'm sure the Earthlings will blow us all away."

34

EARTH

ON THE FAR SIDE OF TOWN, COACH DIAZ KNOCKED ON A TRAILER door. The mint-green siding was sagging and mildewed. He knocked again.

No one had picked up when he had called on the phone, so he figured he would stop by in person on his way home.

A thin woman with bloodshot eyes and a baggy beige sweater came to the door. "What do you want? I already told the last one, we don't need no stinkin' magazine subscriptions."

Coach Diaz held out his hand. "Are you Mrs. Greene?

"It's Ms. Greene. And who's asking? You with the services?"

"What service?" Coach Diaz asked.

"Social services," she spat.

"No, ma'am."

She chewed her lip, which was cracked and bleeding. "What're you selling, then?"

"Nothing, ma'am. I am Raul Diaz, Maeve's marching band coach. She's a tremendous asset to our group, by the way."

"Maaaaaeeve!" The woman turned her head and shouted into the dark trailer. "Get your asset out here! Now! You're in some sorta trouble." She looked the coach up and down.

"No, no. She's not in any trouble, I assure you," Coach Diaz said, wiping a hand across his bald head. He'd begun to perspire despite the chilly, early November air.

"Maaaaaeve!" the woman called again, her eyes glassy. "Where are you, you little—"

"Ms. Greene, please. I just came by to inform you that your daughter's not home. She's at the Gwen Research Center, a NASA field station nearby. We had a school field trip there today. Maeve volunteered for a special sleep study. She's spending the night at the Center with her peers."

"My dad go, too?" Maeve's mother squinted at the whistle around Coach Diaz's neck.

"Who?" he asked.

"Gil Greene. Maeve's grandpa."

Coach Diaz stared at her, confused. "No, I don't believe so. Why?"

"This time of day, he's usually glued to that recliner,

watching his game shows. Today he's gone." She swayed a little, then gripped the doorframe to steady herself. "How much does that sleep study pay, by the way?"

"Oh. There's no compensation. Just, um, experience. Perhaps some complementary space ice cream, or something of the sort." Coach Diaz forced a smile.

The microwave beeped from somewhere inside the trailer.

"I gotta go. Supper's ready," Ms. Greene said.

"Of course. Here's my personal number, as well as Mrs. Minuzzi's. If you have any other questions, please reach out. We'll make sure your daughter is returned safe and sound."

A dark look passed over her eyes. "You sayin' I can't take care of my own kid, Coach?"

"No, not at all." He stepped back, alarmed by the change in her mood.

She glared at him, her nostrils flaring. The microwave beeped again. "Good. Now get lost!" She slammed the door with such force it shuddered on its hinges and nearly knocked Coach Diaz off his feet.

He stood on the stoop, frozen for a minute, trying to figure out what had just happened. Maeve was responsible, kind, organized, and upbeat. She didn't fit into the narrative he'd just witnessed. Then again, she was a star performer. Maybe she put on a game face each day at school to hide her own reality.

Coach Diaz walked to his car, casting one last look at the trailer. Was this run-down, loveless place really where Maeve came home to each night after band practice? His heart ached for her. Her own mother hadn't even realized she was missing.

STATION LIMINUS

SHRO USHERED THE CADETS THROUGH THE EXPLORATORY SCI-
ences wing of Station Liminus. They hadn't visited this
area on their tour with Duna, and the construction dazzled
them. The kids had thought the Gwen Research Center was
cool, but it paled in comparison to where they were now.

There were labs full of robots pipetting glowing liquids
into hovering petri dishes. Alien-looking scientists gazed
through highly advanced microscopes, while others printed
three-dimensional tools with smartwands. Other rooms
offered glimpses of holographic cell dissections, complex
biomimicry, and gravity-defying engineering.

"Whoa," Tessa breathed. She wished Zoey were here to
see this. Despite the fact that they'd had a doozy of an argument earlier that day, Tessa missed her sister. She wondered
what Zoey was doing back home. She'd lost all sense of
Earth time. Was it still afternoon? The middle of the night?

The Station and its inhabitants seemed to use a similar

time system, but she wasn't sure whether the minutes and hours matched up to what they were used to on Earth. Tessa glanced down at her eChron watch, wishing she could send her sister a message. But its face was blank and unresponsive, the batteries likely fried during their Transfer.

"The auditory lab is down this hall, but our team will need a few more minutes to prepare the recording equipment. In the meantime, you can practice in here." Shro gestured to a featureless white wall. A door materialized and swung open.

The practice room was completely purple, floor to ceiling. Even the tables and chairs were a rich lilac color. Isaiah entered and rubbed his eyes. Flashes of alternate realities bombarded his vision, making it hard to focus. Behind the purple walls, Isaiah saw a roaring reactor, firing pistons, flames. He clenched his eyes shut, swaying. Lewis caught him by the elbow.

"Hey, buddy. You okay?"

"Yeah, just dizzy." Isaiah kept the hallucination to himself. He'd already lost his lunch; he didn't want his bandmates thinking he'd completely lost his mind, too.

"Performers typically prep in something called a greenroom. But a purple room will do just fine, too," Maeve declared, perching on an aubergine velvet couch. Now that they were no longer going to be jettisoned into space, she was rather enjoying the oddities and luxuries that Station Liminus had to offer.

"A *green*room?" Shro asked. "That could be arranged."

With a snap, the walls, ceiling, floor, and furniture turned vibrant emerald. "Better?"

"How did you do that?" Isaiah asked, wondering if he had imagined the change.

Shro twirled his fingers. "Simple trick, really. Realigned the prismatic lumi-ratios."

"Right. Obviously," Lewis said.

Shro buttoned up his leather jacket. "I'll return shortly. Make yourselves comfortable. In the meantime, enjoy a little snack. I've heard Earthlings can be rather insatiable." He snapped his fingers and a bowl full of chartreuse starfish and plump sea slugs appeared on the table. They writhed and wriggled.

"Are we supposed to eat those?" Isaiah asked, feeling like he might throw up again.

Shro looked baffled. "They are a delicacy in our dimension. But perhaps you'd prefer something less—"

"Mobile?" Tessa eyed a starfish that had crawled out of the bowl and was making a squelchy escape across the table.

"Of course." Shro snapped his fingers again. The starfish and slugs were replaced by a platter of juicy grapes and tart green apples.

"Much better. Thank you." Maeve smiled, popping a grape into her mouth, savoring the sweet taste.

"Is there anything else I can assist with?" Shro asked.

"Actually, yes. It's sort of freezing in here," Tessa said, rubbing her arms.

"Seriously," Dev agreed, his teeth chattering. Even the

NASA suit's built-in thermodynamic management system wasn't cutting it.

Shro nodded. "My apologies. Station Liminus accommodates such a vast array of species, you never know if your next guest will be warm-blooded, cold-blooded, feriumblooded . . ." Shro pointed to a small dial on the wall. "Feel free to adjust the temperature to a comfortable level."

"This isn't in Fahrenheit or Celsius. How high should I turn it?" Lewis asked, but Shro was already gone, the door closing behind him. "Hmm." He looked at the dial. "How about somewhere in the middle?"

"Sounds good to me," Tessa said, shivering. Behind the wall, gears began grinding. Metal squealed, air popped. A gust of warmth filled the room. "Ah, that's better already," she said, stretching out on the couch beside Maeve.

Isaiah's eyesight blurred. The green walls flared to a jarring orange. The entire room shifted. He squeezed his eyes shut.

"What's wrong?" Maeve asked.

"Nothing," Isaiah said. "Just a headache." He tried to blink away the vision. The glimmers of strangeness he had felt back on Earth were becoming stronger, as though the Transfer process had amplified something within him. Duna had warned them that cellular mutation could happen. The thought was unsettling, but he didn't want to worry his bandmates. Everyone was already dealing with a lot.

"Okay, then let's get started," Maeve said.

They picked up their instruments and began to play,

with Tessa singing along. The room grew warmer. After they'd been rehearsing their music for a few minutes, a metal grate overhead trembled. The bolts holding it in place twisted, popping off one by one, clinking onto the green floor below.

"Look!" Isaiah said, fearing his vision had predicted the arrival of some duct-dwelling spacebeast. But within the ceiling's opening appeared the shimmering face of the shell child.

"Huh?" Tessa stopped singing. "How did you get up there?" she asked.

"Remember the holomap Duna showed us?" Dev said. "The entire Station is laced with ducts running behind walls, above ceilings, and beneath the floors. She must have escaped with Kor, inside that strange bag of hers, and traveled through the ducts."

"But how did she find us?" Tessa asked. "The Station is massive!"

"Maybe she followed the music?" Dev said, giving a friendly wave.

The child's huge eyes darted back and forth, as if trying to assess whether it was safe to enter the room.

"We won't hurt you," Tessa said gently.

"She can't understand you," Maeve said.

"Maybe not, but hopefully she can detect some kindness in our voices and gestures," Tessa replied, smiling warmly. "It's okay. You can come down."

Sure enough, the child descended into the room,

climbing dexterously along the wall like a gecko. She landed nimbly on the ground, her shell shrinking and retracting as she moved, until it was the size of a backpack.

Behind the walls, heaters rumbled. A whoosh of hot air filled the room. Lewis began to sweat.

The child's eyes moved rapidly. She reached for Tessa's hand, squeezing it.

"She's scared," Tessa said. "She's trying to tell us something."

"What is it?" Maeve said, a little impatiently. "Because we really need to keep practicing. There's a lot on the line here. As drum major, it's my job to make sure—"

Before Maeve could finish, the child began pulling Tessa toward the door. Tessa tried to protest, but a shiver zinged through her body, starting at her wrist and moving into her arm and down her spine. Her eyes rolled back in her head.

Out of Tessa's mouth came words in a strange, warbling voice. "You're in grave danger! Leave this place!"

Tessa shook her head, and yanked her hand away from the child. "What just happened?" she said in her regular voice.

The others stared. "You told us, or that shell kid told us *through* you, to get out of here."

Tessa's eyes widened. "Then why are we still in here?"

They scrambled toward the door, but the handle was jammed. The room was becoming warmer and more stifling by the minute.

"Hurry!" Isaiah said.

"Watch out," Lewis instructed. "I learned this move from Ninja Masters. Here it goes! Hi-ya!" He high kicked the door's lockset but it didn't budge. "Youch!!" he hollered, jumping up and down on one foot.

"Hand me your drumstick!" Maeve shouted, wiping sweat from her brow as the temperature soared. Lewis stopped hopping and passed it to her.

She jammed it into the keyhole and wrenched it downward. It snapped in half, splintering like a broken twig.

"Aw, man! Why'd you have to do that?" Lewis groaned. "Now I have nothing to play with!"

"Not a priority at the moment," Maeve said through gritted teeth. "Plus, anything can be used as a drumstick. We'll find you another."

Meanwhile, Dev frantically fiddled with the thermostat on the wall, trying to reprogram the heat. The dial was stuck. A message flashed on its small, circular screen, but it was in an alien language he couldn't read.

Isaiah's head pounded. He pressed his thumbs to his temples, trying to dull the sensation and the doomy premonition that accompanied it. He knew the shell child was right; they needed to get out of this room as quickly as possible.

"Stand back!" Lewis picked up a chair from the seating area and slammed it against the door. The chair cracked to pieces. "That was actually kinda fun," he said, wiping sweat from his brow and reaching for another chair.

"Enough destruction, Lewis!" Maeve yelled.

Tessa wasn't sure what she should do to help. She tugged at the neck of her suit, which suddenly felt way too tight. Then she remembered Shro leading them into the room. The entry door had sort of materialized from a blank wall. Perhaps there was another exit somewhere? Maybe the whole lumi-ratio reconfiguration thing had obscured it . . .

Tessa pressed her hands along one wall and then another, running them up and down, feeling for something, anything, that might indicate a hidden doorframe or handle. The shell child watched, then joined her, mimicking the movement.

The walls were all smooth. Nothing to grab hold of. Nothing . . . wait. Tessa backtracked. There! She couldn't *see* anything unusual on the plain, green-hued wall, but she *felt* a square-shaped knob. It was metallic, cold to the touch. She twisted it to the side. It clicked. Clicked again. She pushed, but the wall held fast. She twisted the knob another half rotation, leaned all her weight forward, and fell through the opening, landing in the hallway face-first.

"You did it!" Lewis shouted.

"Are you okay?" Dev asked, lending her a hand.

She rose to her feet and brushed herself off. Her nose was bleeding, but other than that she was okay. "I'm fine," she said, wiping the blood away, staining the sleeve of her green-and-silver mesh suit. "But let's get outta here. That room gives me the creeps."

The bandmates fled into the hall, clutching their instruments, all except Lewis, whose drumstick was unsalvageable. "This way!" Maeve directed.

"Wait!" Tessa shouted, stopping in her tracks. "The shell kid. Where is she?" They looked up and down the hall. "We can't leave her in there!"

"She's the one who warned us. I'm sure she got out safely and is hiding somewhere," Dev said, hoping it was true.

"Don't go back in there," Isaiah warned. His head throbbed. He couldn't help but feel like the headache was somehow related to whatever was happening, or about to happen, in that room.

"I'm going back," Tessa said stubbornly. She and the child shared something, some sort of bond built through sound and song. Despite the cadets' protests, she turned and ran.

As she neared the greenroom, a deep boom reverberated through the hall. The floor shook. A fiery blast burst from the open door. The force of the explosion knocked Tessa backward, throwing her off her feet and onto the ground. She lay there, stunned and barely conscious, her nose continuing to bleed.

A siren wailed. The cadets scrambled toward Tessa, dragging her to safety, far away from the intense, searing heat. A few seconds later, a deluge of water gushed like a waterfall from a massive overhead sprinkler. The roaring fire hissed and smoked, eventually dying out.

Maeve knelt down and gently wiped water and blood from Tessa's face. "What were you thinking, Zoey?"

"I'm not Zoey," Tessa murmured, drifting in and out of consciousness. "I'm Tessa."

"Uh-oh. This is bad. She hit her head really hard," Maeve said. "She thinks she's Tessa."

"Actually . . . She's telling the truth," Dev said, coming to her side.

Tessa slowly sat up, her ears ringing and her muscles aching a little. "It's true. I should have told you all sooner." She dabbed her sleeve to her nose, which had thankfully stopped bleeding. "I'm not Zoey. I'm Tessa. We switched places for the day."

Maeve gawked, feeling all kinds of confused.

"Say whaat? A clothes-swap prank? That's epic!" Lewis laughed. "A maneuver only identical twins could pull off. Nicely done." He offered a fist bump, which she returned weakly.

"Zoey and I got into a fight this morning and I dared her to trade places with me. I didn't think she could last an hour in my shoes."

"Well, you do wear ridiculous shoes," Maeve pointed out, thinking about the spiky-toed booties and platform wedges Tessa typically wore.

Normally, Tessa would take offense to a comment about her wardrobe, but instead she just laughed. "Let me tell you, I've never been as grateful for practical footwear as I was today, especially while running from imploding greenrooms and self-destructing walkways."

"I can't believe you lied to us all day," Maeve said, still processing the information.

"I shouldn't have. I'm really sorry. I wanted to say something, but everything happened so fast." Tessa studied the floor tiles. "And I wasn't sure you'd like the real me."

Maeve looked Tessa up and down with new eyes. She was irked by the deception but even more irked that she hadn't picked up on it. Zoey used to be her best friend: how could she have missed something like this? "I did think it was odd you didn't play your clarinet once."

"I *can't* play. I was terrified the council was going to make me perform on the spot and find out I was an imposter. You saw what they did to that Oolg! You heard Ira say that they take honesty super seriously. I was afraid." She bit her lip. "I hope you can forgive me."

Maeve reached out and squeezed her hand. "It's okay. Just don't lie to us again."

"I won't. I promise. And I apologize if I acted weirdly to any of you. I wasn't always sure how the real Zoey would react in some of the situations we've been through today."

"For the record," Isaiah said, chiming in. "I knew all along."

The others swiveled around. "You did?"

He shrugged. "The makeup and bracelet gave you away. The real Zoey never wears jewelry. Or mascara."

"You're right." Tessa lifted up the silver cuff bracelet on her left wrist, the one that hid her scars. "I fell off a tractor when I was little. The scar from my surgery is so ugly. I hide it with this."

"It doesn't look that bad to me," Lewis said. "It's actually sort of badass."

She laughed.

"And the real Zoey despises anything pineapple flavored. When you ate those gummies, I knew something was up," Dev said, glad to finally get the information off his chest.

Tessa nodded. It was true. She had slipped up with the candy, too. She supposed this meant Zoey won the bet.

"Wait, you both knew about this?" Maeve balled up her hands into fists. She hated being the last to know things.

Tessa gave Maeve a friendly smile. "Listen, I'm sorry. I really am. If it's any consolation, in spite of the near-death parts of the day, I've really enjoyed hanging out with you all. I can totally see why my sister loves her fellow band geeks."

Dev's face flushed bright red. "She said she *loves* us?"

Tessa laughed. "You know what I mean!"

"Speaking of near death . . ." Isaiah got up and stepped hesitantly toward the charred doorway. All that remained of the emerald couches and tables was soot.

The cadets gathered around and assessed the damage. Tessa felt as though a weight had been lifted after revealing her true identity, but her stomach twisted with worry. She hoped the shell child had escaped safely.

"Oops. We did it again," Lewis said with a resigned shrug.

"Seriously, what the heck happened in there?" Maeve said, eyeing the blackened room from a safe distance.

"Zoey, er, I mean Tessa and that shell kid saved us from becoming toast," Lewis replied.

Isaiah nodded solemnly. "Burnt toast."

Ignatia's horns pulsed with color, vermillion and furious. Slamming her fist on the onyx table, she rose from her seat. It was an elegant wingback chair, iridescent black and violet, tipped with emerald feathers and hooked claws. "Why were you in that room?" Ignatia demanded. "You were supposed to be in the sound lab!"

The cadets were assembled in Ignatia's private office now, which should have been less intimidating than appearing in front of the entire council, but the kids were uneasy, standing together in a clump in the center of the room with Shro and Quirg beside them.

Ignatia's voice was sharp. Behind her loomed an entire wall of books in a variety of sizes—some minuscule, some as big as refrigerators. A few were positively ancient looking with tattered leather spines; others new and shiny, clad in glinting metal dustjackets. A single, snaking vine studded with tongue-shaped purple leaves grew from a black ceramic pot on the floor. The plant wound its way up the walls toward the square of simulated sunlight on the ceiling that illuminated the otherwise dark chamber.

"Shro led us there to practice," Maeve said, pointing to the general.

"It is true. And for that I am deeply, deeply sorry," Shro said with a remorseful bow.

Ignatia glowered. "Station Liminus is a state-of-the-art facility. You claim this was a heating malfunction? How is that possible?"

"They did destroy an expertly engineered Transfer portal. I wouldn't put this past them," Quirg grumped.

"Your Eminence, the biobots assessed the damage. It appears someone activated the incinerate feature on the room's control panel," Shro explained.

Lewis smiled apologetically. "My bad."

"Never underestimate an Earthling's capacity for destruction," Quirg huffed.

"Are any of you injured?" Ignatia asked, looking at the dried blood smeared beneath Tessa's nose. She hadn't had a chance to get cleaned up before Quirg whisked them away to Ignatia's chambers.

Maeve shook her head. "No, thankfully. Just shaken up."

"And hungry," Lewis added. Maeve glared at him. "What?" He shrugged. "I have a very active metabolism, okay?"

None of them mentioned the shell child, though they were still concerned for her well-being and grateful for her warning.

"Then how did you get that?" Ignatia asked, pointing to Maeve's arm.

She hadn't realized that the sleeve of her suit had torn when they scrambled from the greenroom. Now her entire forearm was exposed, the bruises impossible to hide. Maeve's face flushed dark red. "It's nothing," she mumbled.

Ignatia pressed a button on her wristlet. "Duna!" she said, summoning the young delegate. They entered a moment later, as though they had been waiting right outside the door.

"Yes, Your Eminence?" they said politely.

"Please escort the Earthlings to a suite within the diplomatic quarters. And make sure they receive a proper meal."

Shro's expression hardened. "What about the sound studies? The lab is ready now. I prepared all the equipment."

Ignatia shook her head, her swirling silver braids softening the stern angles of her face. Isaiah studied her, sensing a glimmer of remorse in her eyes. She had overseen the vote to release them a few hours earlier; he hoped she did feel sorry.

"These Earthlings have endured enough for one day," Ignatia said. "Keep in mind, they are delicate creatures, not as hardy or robust as Vermaskians or Izoxis. Therefore, I think they deserve some time to rest and recuperate. We will reconvene the musical explorations tomorrow morning."

36

EARTH

ZOEY FIDDLED WITH HER WATCH AND SENT A TEXT MESSAGE.

Hey, Nolan. It's Zoey.
Just wanted to let you know that I have your tuba.
I can bring it to school on Monday.
Unless you need it over the weekend.

My tuba?

Yeah, that big ol' horn you play in marching
band.
Remember?

I know what a tuba is, Zo.
But you don't have mine.
I brought my tuba back from
practice.
It's in my living room.
I'm looking at it right now.
In fact, my mom is bugging me to
practice.

Zoey eyed the case on her bedroom floor suspiciously. Gage had said he'd stolen Nolan's tuba. And Nolan was the only tuba player who went on today's field trip. So what was inside that case?

Yo? Zo? You still there?

Yeah, sorry. Never mind.
I was just joking around.

You feeling okay?

Yeah, why?

Idk. You seemed . . . off today.
During the field trip.

I did?

Just quieter than usual, I guess.

I'm fine, Nolan.
But thanks for checking in.
See you Monday.

Okay, see ya.
Have fun playing that mystery
tuba . . .

STATION LIMINUS

DUNA LED THE CADETS THROUGH STATION LIMINUS TO THEIR accommodations.

"One minute we're total rejects, and the next minute we're like celebrities," Lewis mused, giving a goofy Mr. America wave to the crowd of onlookers who peeked out from labs and offices as they passed. "Man, fame is a wild ride."

"I wouldn't exactly call it fame, but today has been quite a roller-coaster," Maeve said, rubbing her hands absent-mindedly over her bruised forearm. She was grateful none of her bandmates had asked her about it yet.

As they passed Gate Hall, Dev spotted a team of biobots and humanoid supervisors in bright yellow jumpsuits trying to repair the portal they'd damaged on arrival. Sparks flew as the welders attempted to fuse the broken doorway.

"Yikes, we really did a number on that portal," Lewis muttered guiltily, following Dev's gaze.

Duna paused. "Do not feel so bad. You're not the only ones who have encountered challenges with entry and exit procedures."

"We're not? Because that Quirg guy seemed pretty mad at us."

Duna sighed. "Quirg can be a curmudgeon. He and his staff do their best to secure and monitor each doorway, but occasionally they break or glitch out on their own. Dimensional membranes are dynamic and unpredictable. Sometimes creatures wander through with little warning."

"When you say creatures, what do you mean exactly?" Tessa asked.

"We once had a rare permadon, a flock of downy piffells, and even carnivorous rakoomas. Those caused quite a scene. Just last week, a large black-and-white mammalian quadruped entered the Station. Apparently, it had a sack full of venom and made a very frightening call."

"Yikes," Tessa said, inching away from the entrance to Gate Hall.

"If you're interested in wildlife, we can take a slight detour and stop by the Menagerie on our way to your suite. It houses some of the multiverse's most fascinating animal life, rehabilitating and protecting many endangered species. It's a fairly new initiative here at the Station, but one I hope will continue to expand. And directly across from that is our Arboretum, which supports an astounding plethora of flora, fungi, and more. Plants are cultivated, hybridized, and studied for agricultural and biomedical uses, as well as to stock the MV seed bank. I'd be glad to show you."

"That would be awesome. Thanks, Duna," Tessa said, drawn to Duna's warmth and inquisitive spirit. She liked that they didn't hide their genuine interest and enthusiasm for the world. Until recently, Tessa had always regulated her reactions to things, worried she might come off as too nerdy or weird. She dreaded being judged or ridiculed by Blake, Gage, and the other popular kids. All she wanted was to be liked by them, to be one of them. But she was starting to feel like she was drifting from those feelings and those friendships.

"Duna," she said, "there's something I need to tell you."

"Yes, Zoey?" They smiled, their russet eyes bright.

She sighed. "That's just it. I'm not Zoey, like I told you earlier. My name is actually Tessa. Zoey and I look identical."

"She is your dimensional doppelgänger, then?" Duna asked, not quite following.

"Sort of. She's my twin sister. We switched places for the day and swapped clothes. She's stuck back on Earth."

Duna looked perplexed. "Is this a common Earthling game? The clothes-swap?"

"No." Tessa shrugged, still feeling embarrassed about the whole thing. "It was definitely a one-time switch. I'm a lot happier just being me."

"As you should be," they said. "The multiverse is full of

parallels, mirrors, and doppelgängers, but there is only one true you."

Tessa nodded gratefully. "My sister and I, we drive each other crazy, but I love her. And right now, I really miss her." Tessa looked down at her smartwatch, wishing she could get in touch with Zoey. Even just to send a goofy meme or string of ridiculous emojis. "She should be here instead of me. She would handle all of this so much better."

Duna shook their head. "Remember what I said earlier? About fate, about *th'ahnai*? Keep that in mind, Tessa. Perhaps there is a reason you are both where you are." They paused. "I, for one, am glad *you* are here."

"Thanks," Tessa replied softly, surprised that she was starting to feel the same.

STATION LIMINUS

AS THE CADETS EXPLORED THE ARBORETUM AND MENAGERIE with Duna, Dev thought of his family with a pang of sadness. As a botanist in search of the latest drought-resistant crops, his mother would love to see all the incredible plants on display in here. His father would go crazy for the innovative technology throughout the Station.

And Sejal would giggle and clap for the Menagerie's cuddly bear-monkey-marsupials called poleers and the tiny pink unicorn lizards called kikews. The massive megaphantes looked uncannily like the woolly mammoths that had gone extinct on Earth long ago, but these had three golden tusks. He couldn't wait to tell his family all about the things he was seeing as soon as he returned home. *If* he returned home, that was. His chest tightened with worry.

After their tour, the cadets arrived at their suite and were delighted to find that it was a whole lot nicer than the holding cell they'd been stuck in before. It was spacious with a cozy lounge, five private bedrooms, and a spa-like bathroom. The main room was illuminated by stalactite chandeliers coated in glowing lichens. The floor was made of swirling, deep green malachite tiles. Abstract digital art adorned the walls.

"Wow. Aside from the whole nearly-getting-blown-up thing, this is the life!" Maeve said, flopping onto an asymmetrically shaped sofa, sinking into the delicious softness of the overstuffed cushions.

"I'm glad you find it agreeable," Duna said. "There is an entertainment system with several streaming holovid channels, as well as our top gaming platforms. I highly recommend AstroBlastersVII, but good luck passing level eight. The big boss is unstoppable." Duna grinned. Even though they were a high-powered dimensional delegate, they were still a kid at heart.

"Alien video games? Whaaat?" Lewis could hardly believe his eyes. He picked up a controller and clutched it lovingly to his chest.

"Each room has a cumulo-bunk." Duna opened one of the doors, revealing a bed that was actually made from a cloud. It floated like a huge, puffy cotton ball in the center of the room. A neatly folded set of pajamas was stacked inside a dresser made entirely of clear glass, and assorted day clothes hung in the mirrored closet.

"Is this for real?" Tessa asked, incredulous. She kicked off her shoes and climbed into the cumulo-bunk. The plush, white mist was softer than kitten fur and moved to fit every contour of her body. "I could get used to this."

A bell dinged. "Ah, your food has arrived! The secretary has ordered a special meal for you, featuring signature dishes from several of our delegate dimensions."

"Room service!" Lewis said, doing a happy dance. "Fancy!"

Duna crossed the suite and opened the main doors. Tessa hopped down and followed the others, her mouth watering.

Servers entered, wearing shiny uniforms and funny tufted hats. They wheeled in large catering carts loaded with cloche-covered platters. The servers arranged the feast on a round table in the suite's dining room while Duna described the dishes and the unusual ingredients used in each one.

As they lifted the bronze cloches, aromas both familiar and strange filled the air. One platter was piled high with dumplings, each filled with brightly colored vegetables and fragrant spices. Another revealed a crock of burbling fuchsia soup with crackled soy cubes for dipping. There was a roasted suckling firduck with a honeybalm glaze, sticky buns sprinkled with black salt crystals, and a platter of writhing blue tentacles.

"Ack! Those are still alive!" Tessa replaced the cloche quickly before the meal made a run for it.

The kids gathered round and dug in, gorging on sweets and savories. The flavors and textures of the multiverse delighted (and occasionally disgusted) their palates. Duna was pleased to see them enjoying themselves.

"Thank you for all this," said Tessa, dabbing her lips with a napkin. "After a rough day, this is such a treat."

"My pleasure." Duna smiled. "Oh! And I almost forgot to show you the spa." They crossed the room and opened a frosted glass door. "Here are the rain showers, a soaking tub, and a geothermal sauna."

"I think we'll skip the sauna," Maeve said, still slightly traumatized by the exploding greenroom incident.

"How insensitive of me." Duna placed their hand on their chest and lowered their head. "On behalf of the MAC, I want to express my utmost sympathy for the near-miss accident you endured today."

"You mean the fiery chamber of doom?" Isaiah asked, looking up from nibbling an ear of rainbow-kernel corn. "You don't actually think that was an accident, do you?"

Duna's hand dropped to their side. "What are you implying? That a member of the Multiverse Allied Council tried to kill you?"

"Incinerate us, technically." Isaiah took another bite. "The doom-o-meter was off the charts."

Duna's expression shifted, their youthful eyes growing weary. "That is a weighty accusation."

"Well, they'd been discussing Releasing us. Why not just save a fancy pod and toast us to a crisp?" Isaiah popped a crunchy tofu cube into his mouth.

"I doubt there is anything nefarious at play here, but I will look into it, quietly," Duna said, their brow furrowed.

"If it weren't for that shell child..." Tessa said, her

mind wandering as she twirled some spicy red pasta with her fork.

Duna stopped short. "That *what?*"

Tessa dropped her fork on her plate and clasped a hand over her mouth. Maeve shot her a piercing glare.

"Nothing. No one. Never mind."

"You must tell me, I implore you."

Tess bit her lip. Crap! Crap! Crap! How could she have been so stupid?

Duna walked over to a wall vent, unscrewed the grate, and tapped some sort of signal. The vibrations echoed down the ducts. A minute later, a ceiling panel moved aside and the small child climbed down.

"There you are! I've been looking for you everywhere!" Duna scooped her into a warm embrace.

"You know her, too?" Tessa asked.

"Yes, though she is a bit of an enigma. From what I can tell, she cannot speak. She senses vibrations, though. I think she is a citizen of Klapproth, a beautiful planet in Dim2."

"I thought Dim2 was quarantined? Shro said there was a plague," Dev said, backing away in case the child was contagious.

"It was. Or, still is, technically. But I do not believe her to be infected or a threat in any way. I think Queen Eryna sent the child here to help reestablish communication with the alliance, but I can't figure out what information she wishes to convey. If she has chosen to trust you, you must promise to keep her safe. I am working to learn more. But until then, it is best if she remains hidden. I am not sure how the rest of the council will react to her appearance on the Station."

"Of course," Tessa replied.

The shell child moved closer, her ice-blue eyes eager, her sensory ports twitching, detecting sound waves and signals the others couldn't hear. She reached for Tessa's hand, as though she wanted to tell her something.

"What is your name?" Tessa asked intuitively.

The child's eyes closed, as did Tessa's. Then out of Tessa's mouth came the word, *Virrrrrrrriiii*. The *R* trilled, rolling and tumbling off Tessa's tongue.

Tessa's eyes flicked back open. "Your name is Virri?" she asked.

The child beamed.

"That's amazing," Dev said, coming closer. "Ask her something else."

"I think she wants to send a message. I'm not sure how, but I can feel it."

Virri held Tessa's hand tightly, then looked at the instruments on the nearby table. "She wants you all to play your instruments, like you did in the holding cell," Tessa said.

Without hesitation, the cadets grabbed their instruments.

They waited for Tessa's cue. When she closed her eyes and began to sing, the others followed along, letting the music lead them somewhere new. They did not perform a rehearsed marching band piece; there was no strict structure to their music, but it flowed freely from all of them, with Virri's hand gently resting on Tessa's.

As Tessa sang, what came from her lungs, throat, and lips was not hers; she was a conduit. As the music ebbed and flowed, Tessa's voice took on ethereal, ephemeral shapes and sounds. Bells chiming, waves lapping, wind through trees. At the end, the ensemble's music had transformed into the gentle, melodic hum of a conch shell pressed to an ear.

Virri's pale gray skin shimmered. She removed her hand from Tessa's and the music faded. Duna and the cadets sat in serene silence for several minutes.

"You've given Virri a voice, and in turn, found your own," Isaiah said to Tessa. "Just like Benni predicted. It's all very poetic, don't you think?"

"Poetic, or just plain freaky?" Lewis said, wide-eyed. "You're basically an opera-singing alien translator."

Duna's lynk suddenly pinged. They pulled it from their pocket. "The council summons me. Before I depart, is there anything else you need?"

Dev set down his trumpet. "Like Virri, we need to send a message home. We've been gone for a while and I'm sure our families are worried about us."

The others nodded, struck by a sudden bout of homesickness.

"Unfortunately, our comms with Dim14 are temporarily disabled. It appears your misguided Transfer caused more damage than initially thought. I will see what can be done and report back as soon as communication is restored."

"What about the triskaidecagon? Ignatia said each dimension has a designated one that operates on a separate communication channel. Maybe we could send a signal home using that?"

Duna considered this. "I will see what I can do. Only Ignatia has access to the trisks. I will approach her and see if your dimension's unit is operable at this time." They smiled gently. "I know how hard it is to feel disconnected from those you love."

"Thanks, Duna."

"You are very welcome. I will see you in the morning." They walked to the door. "Until then, please look after Virri. Enjoy your meal and rest well. Tomorrow is a new day with infinite possibilities."

As soon as Duna shut the door, Isaiah turned to the others. His skin prickled. The only way he could describe it was . . . an inkling. Not quite a premonition, but something similar. "We need to send a message home now. Not later."

"I agree," Dev said. "If we can reach my dad, he might be able to help."

"How?" Tessa asked. She wanted to get in touch with her parents just as badly, but Duna had just said comms were down.

Lewis was sitting at the table using a pair of serrated chopstick-like utensils to stuff his face with crispy orange noodles. In between bites, he absentmindedly drummed the utensils on the table in a subtle *tap-taptap-tap* rhythm.

Across the table Virri watched and listened. She tapped a rhythm back.

"That's it!" Dev cried, practically jumping from his seat and spilling a bowl of thornmelon soufflé.

Virri tucked inside her shell and rolled under the table.

"Sorry," Dev said, crouching down to comfort Virri. "I didn't mean to startle you. Lewis, your drumming... it reminded me of something." Dev knocked his knuckles on the table. "Morse code! My dad and I use it all the time, more as a joke than anything."

"Okay, cool father-son bonding tidbit, but how does that help us now?" Maeve asked.

"If we transmit a message in Morse code and convert it to electrical pulses, we should be able to send it over long distances." He looked around the suite at the holovid screen and gaming device. "I bet we can use what we have in here to build a radio."

"I love your enthusiasm, Dev, but we're on a state-of-the-art space station." Maeve planted her hands on her hips. "Do you really think we can build a better homemade device than whatever they're running on board?"

Dev's eyes sparked with new energy. "We can try."

39

EARTH

DR. KHATRI EYED THE BROKEN COLLIDER WARILY. "WE CAN FIX it. We can repair the portal," he said, willing it to be true.

Dr. Scopes stood at his side. "I'm not so certain. The damage looks irreparable. Without the Syntropitron, that is." Her makeup had begun to smudge, her eyeliner forming dark circles beneath her tired eyes. "We'll need to build a new portal. Start from scratch."

"We don't have that sort of time! My son and his friends could be suspended somewhere—anywhere—within the multiverse, lost in another dimension! Facing inhospitable conditions, gruesome beasts, or worse." Dr. Khatri slumped down, sitting on the floor. He threw his hands up. "And I thought sending him to sleepaway summer camp was nerve-racking!"

"Don't worry, Dr. Khatri. The NASA sound lab is fully staffed, listening and scanning the radio waves and satellites nonstop. If the kids send a transmission, our team will pick it up and alert us immediately." She pursed her lips. "In the meantime, I'll search Professor McGillum's computer, see if I can hack his encrypted files. Maybe there are mechanical plans or diagrams that we can use to construct a new collider. If we move quickly, perhaps we can have a new portal up and running in a week or so."

"A day, Dr. Scopes! We have twenty-four hours. Tops."

She took a step back. "Yes, sir."

He touched the charred wall beside him, rubbing the oily residue between his fingertips. "What if we located a natural portal? You and I have both heard murmurings at conferences."

"You're not referring to Bermuda, are you? Because rising seas swallowed the Triangle. Even if we wanted to approach the vicinity, we'd need a seaplane, or a ship," Dr. Scopes replied.

"I know. Perhaps there are other dimensional tears closer to us? If we could find one and adapt it..." He rose to his feet. "I'm going to contact our colleagues at other institutions. I'll scan the dark web, see if there's any chatter on the catastrophysics boards. Search missing persons logs and UFO sightings in the police database. The Area 51 folks are pretty tuned into this stuff. I'll call them as well."

She exhaled. "You know that's all conspiracy theory mumbo jumbo."

Dr. Khatri turned, looking her in the eyes. "Maybe so, but these are desperate times, Dr. Scopes. We can leave no stone unturned. There are children in jeopardy and I will explore all options, no matter how crazy they may seem."

KLAPPROTH

FAR ACROSS THE MULTIVERSE ON A BEAUTIFUL BUT ISOLATED planet, Queen Eyrna's crystal glyph began to spin, slowly at first, then faster. The sound pattern was soft, low in frequency, losing some of its edges as it traveled across spacetime. She clutched the stone to the sensory port in her chest, letting the song reverberate through her many-chambered heart. Finally, she sensed a voice. A channel opened within the fabric of the cosmos, like a single pinprick of light in a pitch-black sky.

She listened, absorbing the message into her heart. She sang, her powerful voice rising above the froth and spray of the sea, louder than the crashing waves, sending a response in return, making a wish for its safe passage.

41

EARTH

ZOEY STILL HADN'T HEARD BACK FROM TESSA, AND SHE HADN'T made much progress with Ming's letters. She was flipping through the Journal of Strange Occurrences when she heard the front door open.

"Tessa?" her mom called.

"Up here!" she yelled, realizing she was still technically playing the role of her sister. "Just...uh...doing some homework." Her mom never bugged her when homework was involved.

"Could you please come downstairs for a minute, honey? Dad and I need to talk to you."

She could hear something in her mother's voice. Tiredness, yes. But something else, too. Something she wasn't used to hearing. Zoey's stomach flip-flopped. Had they found out about the swap? That she'd taken Tessa's math quiz for her? That she'd stomped on Gage's already injured foot? That she'd basically lied her way through an entire school day?

"Tessa?"

"Yeah! One minute," she said, stalling. She did not want to go downstairs to face her parents and fess up about the swap.

Her mom hollered up the stairs, "We brought home takeout. Supino's Pizza. Mushroom and pepperoni."

Zoey's stomach rumbled. She supposed the letters and journal could wait a little while longer . . .

STATION LIMINUS

"YOU WANT ME TO DO WHAT TO THE WHAT-WHAT?" LEWIS ASKED, horrified.

"Take the gaming console apart so we can use the wires and circuits to build a radio and send a signal home," Dev explained, handing Lewis a tiny cocktail fork. It wasn't exactly a screwdriver, but the utensils from the catering carts were the closest things to tools they had at the moment.

"But I haven't even reached level two of AstroBlasters-VII!" Lewis whined, thumbing the controller, shooting orbs of yellow light at a rogue asteroid.

"Priorities, Lewiston. Ever heard of 'em?" Maeve said. While she didn't personally feel the need to send a message home, she could appreciate why the others wanted to contact their families. Especially Dev, since it was his father who was hopefully going to get them all out of this dilemma and arrange for the actual Earthling envoys to take their place on the Station.

"I just started playing! One more minute. Pleeeease?" Lewis begged, firing a discombobulator at a pack of slobbering, six-headed space wolves.

Tessa's foot pattered impatiently. "You act like we're on vacation here."

"It's sort of like a mini-vacation," Lewis replied, not looking up from the screen, his fingers flying across the controller. "Watch this. Blam! Boom!" He detonated a hydrogrenade and sent a fleet of warships to their demise.

"Okay, I'm cutting him off." Tessa walked across the room and disconnected the console's power supply.

"Hey!" Lewis pouted. "You're all mean. And boring. And super mean."

Tessa said, "Do you want to get home and save the planet, or not?"

"I was about to do exactly that, until you unplugged me!"

"This is real life, Lewis. Not some silly video game."

"If only we didn't have to give up our cell phones during the field trip. Then we could just call home!" Lewis lamented.

"You think we'd get service out here?" Dev asked, peering out the suite's triangular windows at the inky, vertiginous darkspace beyond.

Tessa touched her smartwatch. Its face was blank. The battery completely zonked.

"Listen," said Isaiah softly. "My mom had to deal with my dad passing away when I was a baby. Then my uncle disappeared into thin air. My mom is strong, but I don't think she could handle losing me, too. She's probably a wreck right now. I need to let her know I'm okay."

"Isaiah's right. Come on. Let's focus. We need to work together." Maeve gave Lewis a pleading smile.

"Fine. I'll help." Lewis reluctantly unscrewed the game controller, pulling out wires and springs. He handed the parts to Dev. "But Dr. Scopes denied the existence of the multiverse during our visit. There's no way she's going to come looking for us here," Lewis said.

Dev wedged a butter knife into a remote control and opened its power pack, removing small, pill-shaped batteries. "She might not. But my father will. We just need to access the universal beta channel and broadcast an SOS signal. With some luck, NASA's radio telescope will pick it up and send help. Or at least inform our families that we're all alive."

"For now," Lewis mumbled, stripping parts from the game console.

EARTH

"MOHAN, TELL ME PRECISELY WHAT IS GOING ON." MINA KHATRI looked at her husband pointedly.

He pulled a heavy atlas from the bookshelf, flipping frantically through the pages, running his index finger across the maps, searching for something.

"It's confidential," he said. "I'm not authorized to say a word to anyone." He didn't like keeping things from his family, but Mayor Hawthorne had made him promise to keep a wrap on the situation.

"I am not anyone, Mohan. I am your wife. Dev was due home from band practice two hours ago." She frowned.

He continued shuffling his papers, upending his home office files, seeking any clues that might lead him to the missing kids.

"Where is our son?" Mina asked, interrupting his search.

He took a deep breath and straightened his shoulders. "Dev and a few of his friends volunteered for a sleep study at the Center."

"They what?"

"It was an honor to be asked, frankly." His chin twitched. He was a terrible liar.

"And you just let him do it? Without consulting with me first?" Her face was a mix of fury, outrage, and confusion, with a sprinkling of hurt.

"I'm so sorry, dear." Mohan reached out and took her hand in his. "I should have asked you. But the research team needed to fill the spots quickly, and Dev really wanted to do it. I didn't want to get in his way. He hates when I embarrass him. I wanted to be a cool dad." He hung his head in shame. He *had* wanted to be a cool dad, to impress Dev's friends, to connect with his son. And now, impossibly, he'd lost them all.

He took a ragged breath. He needed to keep it together, keep his mind clear. "Besides, I work at NASA. Dev is in capable hands with my colleagues. I trust them."

Unfortunately, this wasn't entirely true anymore, and Mohan felt a deep stab of guilt.

"Dev was anxious at first. You know how he hates the dark. But he thought about what you told him this morning. Remember? About facing his fears?"

Mina Khatri studied her husband's face. "Yes, I remember."

"It's just one night. Tomorrow is Saturday, so he's not missing any school. His teachers agreed it was a valuable learning experience. He may even get extra credit."

"I just worry about him, all alone."

"He's not alone. He's with his friends from marching band. I met them today. A nice group. Kind, smart, resourceful kids. A little goofy, but that's good for him. He needs to loosen up a little."

Mina sighed. "Well, I am happy to hear he's making some connections. I know this move has been difficult for him." She looked up, her eyes sharp and clear. "But I want him home tomorrow."

"Absolutely, dear." Mohan gave her a peck on the cheek.

He shut the door to his office and exhaled a heavy breath. Then he began sorting through his files again, madly searching for evidence of a natural portal. One that he and Dr. Scopes could reach quickly, before it was too late.

STATION LIMINUS

"WE'VE BEEN AT THIS FOR OVER AN HOUR, AND ALL WE'VE made is a gigantic mess," said Tessa miserably.

Virri peered over Dev's shoulder, watching intently as he worked to rebuild the disassembled electronics. "You have to make a mess before you make a masterpiece," Dev said, undeterred.

"More like a messterpiece," said Maeve, holding up a frayed wire.

"Lucky for us, I won first place in the Junior Electrical Engineering Challenge back in San Francisco." Dev wasn't normally one to brag, but his nerd skills were coming in pretty handy. "I think we're getting close. We just need to connect these last two circuits," he said. He looked around. "But we don't have the right tools. I need a soldering iron and some alligator clips, or something similar. See if you can find anything that might work."

Isaiah searched under the sofa, and Lewis rummaged through the catering cart. Virri's face lit up. She moved swiftly across the room, unscrewed a floor grate, and disappeared. A second later, her head popped back up. She waved.

"I think she wants us to follow her," Dev said, hoping Virri might lead them to the tools they needed.

"Down there?" Tessa was not a fan of small, dark spaces. Especially ones that led into the deepest recesses of an unfamiliar space station.

"Um, guys, maybe Tessa and I should hang back?" Maeve suggested. "In case Duna comes to check on us, or give an update about the trisk."

Tessa felt a surge of gratitude.

"Okay," Dev said. "That makes sense. Hopefully we won't be too long. We'll just grab some supplies and dash back here."

"Good luck," Tessa said. "And be careful, okay?"

"What is there to be afraid of?" Lewis asked with a nervous laugh.

As soon as Virri and the boys were gone, Tessa turned to Maeve.

"So." She rocked back on her heels.

"So," replied Maeve. "What now?"

"We wait, I guess."

There was a tension in the air, an awkwardness that Tessa needed to address. "Listen, I don't know what happened between my sister and you, but I know she still cares about you. A lot."

Maeve tried to keep her face stony and unreadable, but it was hard to put on a mask all the time. "She has a funny way of showing it."

"What did happen? I mean, if you don't want to talk about it, I get it..."

Maeve blinked. "She really didn't tell you?"

Tessa shook her head. "Nope. She and I used to talk about everything, but we've sort of drifted since middle school started. Plus, she's good at keeping secrets. She's like a vault that way. Sometimes it makes me so frustrated, especially when I want her to spill juicy gossip." Tessa walked over and sat on the sofa, sinking into its cushions. Maeve joined her, sitting a few feet away. "Twelve hours ago, I wanted to rip her head off. I guess that's just how sisters are sometimes. Now, I'd do anything to see her. To hug her." Tessa shrugged, refusing to let herself cry.

Maeve had never seen Tessa Hawthorne-Scott so vulnerable. She felt like maybe it was safe to open up to her. "Zoey ran into my mom and me at the pharmacy one day after school. My mom was making a scene, demanding more pills. The pharmacist said she'd maxed out her refills. My mom got...a little out of control. She's usually not that bad in public. But she's had a tough time since we lost the farm, and my stepdad left, and my bratty half sister moved in with us..."

"That sounds hard."

"It was." She paused, then corrected herself. "It is."

"I'm sorry you're dealing with all that."

"Well, it's not like I really have a choice, do I?" she said, feeling an ache in her chest. "Zoey's the only one who really knew what was going on. I told her some stuff, but not everything. When we left the pharmacy that day, Mom lost it in the parking lot. She was screaming at me, like the whole thing was my fault. Zoey saw and she was really upset. I was so embarrassed.

"She said she was worried my mom might hurt me, or someone else. I told her I could handle it. Calling the cops just brings more attention to the problem, and makes Mom angrier. But Zoey wouldn't listen to me. Since then, life at home has been even rougher than usual.

"I know Zoey was just trying to help, but I couldn't help blame her a little. And when we both went out for drum major, and I got it over her, I figured it was the end of our friendship for good." She sighed. "I'm not sure how to get back to a good place with her, to be honest."

Tessa nodded. "She can be stubborn."

"You got that right."

"And she's so righteous about everything," Tessa said. "She gets that from our mom. It's not necessarily a bad thing. It comes from a good place, it's just..."

They fell quiet, thinking.

"You should try talking to her," they both said at the same time, then laughed.

"Seriously though," Tessa said. "You shouldn't be afraid or ashamed to ask for help. If you need it."

"Thanks," Maeve said softly.

"If my watch worked, I'd send Zo a message right now. She'd lose her mind if she knew you and I were, like, bonding," Tessa said, smiling.

"Is that what we're doing here?" Maeve asked, arching an eyebrow.

"Yeah." Tessa nodded. "I think it is. And you know what? It's nice."

Maeve smiled, hugging her arms around herself, rubbing the fading bruises. Maybe Tessa was right. It was okay to ask for help now and then. Maybe she didn't need to carry everything on her shoulders all the time.

STATION LIMINUS

ISAIAH, DEV, AND LEWIS NAVIGATED THE BOWELS OF STATION Liminus, following Virri through the dark passages until they arrived at the repairworks. From their view under a large floor grate, they could see that the room above them was filled with equipment, spare parts, and machinery. It was empty except for a lone watchman, who was eating a green sandwich and scrolling through his lynk instead of watching the surveillance camera footage projected on one wall.

"See that?" Dev whispered, pointing at a rack lined with tools and dense clusters of colored wire. "Everything we need is up there."

"We'll have to create a diversion, distract the watchman so that we can pop up and grab the supplies," Isaiah said.

"Oh my gosh," Lewis breathed. "Easiest prank ever."

"Really?" Isaiah and Dev asked skeptically.

"Yeah. I'll crawl through a little farther and pop up in the hallway. Then . . . ding, dong, dash!"

"What if someone sees you?"

"It's quiet now, seems like everyone in the Station is sleeping. I'll knock on the door. Big guy will get up to answer it. In that time, you two grab everything we need and slip back under the floor. I'll meet you back at the suite."

"You really think you can dash that quick?"

Lewis looked insulted. "I'm a Wynner. And I'm on the track team, duh."

"I thought you quit."

"I did. But whatever. I'm still pretty fast. I got this. No worries, okay? This is a basic prank. Amateur hour."

"Let's hope so," Isaiah said, not exactly sharing Lewis's confidence.

Lewis climbed deeper into the underfloor duct until he found a grate leading up to the hallway. Virri carefully unscrewed the bolts holding it in place, then returned to the others.

In the chamber beneath the repairworks, Dev and Isaiah waited for the sound of Lewis's knock. The room above them was filled with the faint ambient hum of motors buzzing and machines grinding away within the Station's nearby core. Thankfully, these noises drowned out the sounds of Virri gently unscrewing the grate overhead.

"Where is he?" Isaiah hissed, listening for Lewis's signal. "It shouldn't be taking this long . . ."

"Any minute now," Dev said, watching the door.

Then, right on cue, *knock knock knock!* The night

watchman put down his sandwich and went to the door. He opened it.

"Wait a minute," Isaiah whispered, grabbing Dev's sleeve before he popped up like a gopher. "That's not Lewis."

Dev slunk back down, his heart beating wildly. "What? Who else could it be?"

"Look. It's Shro."

They stayed as still and silent as possible, their breath coming fast and shallow. They had a hunch that the general would not be pleased to find them "borrowing" tools and sneaking around in the middle of the night.

"What's he doing?" Isaiah said quietly.

"I don't know. He's speaking in another language. I can't understand."

The watchman clomped across the room and adjusted one of the projections on the wall. He flicked through a reel of footage. Shro waved his hand. Barked some sort of order. The watchman paused the frame.

"That's Kor," Dev said. "That video was recorded in the holding cell earlier today. Look. We're there, too."

Shro leaned over and tapped the screen. He enlarged the image, zooming in on a blurry figure beside Tessa. The resolution wasn't great, but Dev and Isaiah knew it was Virri. Shro's face reddened to an even deeper shade. Beside them, Virri trembled. Dev turned to comfort her. Her eyes were wide and fearful. She slipped noiselessly away, disappearing into the dark labyrinthine ducts.

Dev wanted to call out for her, but they couldn't risk

getting caught. On a separate screen, they caught a glimpse of Lewis ducking down a hallway, heading away from the repair room. Luckily, Shro and the watchman were too busy inspecting the holding cell footage to notice the live feed.

"Where is he going?" Dev frowned. The whole plan was unraveling. In his frustration, Dev bumped his knee on the side of the narrow duct.

Shro bristled and cocked his head, his ears pricking. Dev and Isaiah froze, barely daring to breathe. Finally, Shro turned and strode back toward the door. The watchman followed. The two of them conversed in that unfamiliar language before Shro departed. In the split second they turned their backs, Dev reached up and grabbed whatever supplies were within arm's reach, then ducked back down beneath the floor as fast as possible.

He pulled the grate back over his head and secured it just as the watchman returned to his seat. The man looked around the room, his eyes roving the walls and floors, then he shrugged and went back to eating his green sandwich and scrolling through his lynk.

Isaiah exhaled. "That was a close one."

"Tell me about it. I don't even know if I got the right stuff," Dev said, shocked by his own bravery. He wasn't one to act so impulsively, but something had compelled him to move. His fingers were still tingling with the thrill of it.

"You have got to be kidding me! Look," Isaiah whispered, pointing to one of the surveillance monitors. On its screen they spotted Lewis rummaging around in a refreshment cart and stuffing something into his pockets. He jogged out of view.

"If he seriously ditched us for snacks, I'm gonna kill him," Dev said, fuming.

They retraced their path and reemerged in the suite.

"You made it back alive!" Tessa cheered.

"Was there some doubt that that was going to occur?" Dev asked.

Tessa bit her lip. "No, but Virri came racing back here with panic in her eyes, so we worried something bad happened."

"Virri? She's here?"

Virri peeked out from her pearlescent shell and gave a small, frightened nod.

"Something really spooked her," Tessa said.

"Shro, that's what," Isaiah said.

Maeve rushed over to them. "What? You ran into him? Did he catch you?"

"No, but we saw him. He was reviewing security camera footage from the holding cell. He seemed really curious and kind of upset about Virri. We couldn't understand what he was saying, but maybe it has something to do with her breaking quarantine."

"Um, guys, where's Lewis?" Dev asked, placing the tools on the floor beside the partially constructed radio.

Tessa frowned. "What do you mean? He's not with you?"

"He was supposed to create a diversion, but he disappeared. And then we caught him on camera nabbing a midnight bite from a refreshment cat," Dev said, tinkering with the new tools and parts.

"Go figure!"

Maeve looked worried. "We've gotta go look for him. The Station is huge. He could be lost."

Just then, there was a knock at the door. "I'll get it," Maeve said. She opened it, but no one was there. "What the—?" She craned her neck around the corner.

Then Lewis jumped out from behind the door. Maeve screamed.

"Got ya, suckers!" He wiggled obnoxiously. "Ding, dong, dash!"

"Grrr, where have you been?" Maeve snapped. "We were getting worried!"

Lewis clutched a hand to his chest. "Wait, was Maeve Greene worried about *moi*?"

"We're a team, Wynner. Of course I was worried. Especially when you nearly jeopardize our plans to save the whole frickin' world. Now get in here." She pulled him inside.

He flopped onto the sofa. "Sorry, dudes. I had to abort the mission."

"Yeah, we noticed," Dev said, irritated that they hadn't been able to get all the supplies they needed.

"I saw Shro coming down the hall and had to hide. But I did take a little pit stop on my way back to the room," Lewis said, grinning mischievously. "I figured there had to be a kitchen on the Station since they cooked up that feast for us. I broke in and grabbed us some potatoes."

"You did what? You heard what they did to that Oolg who stole seeds!" Dev and Lewis had never fought before, but Dev was furious. "You want to get us thrown in jail over potato chips, just because you have the munchies?" he yelled.

Lewis made a face. "Listen, I was in full stealth mode. No one saw me."

"We saw you," Dev said. "On camera actually."

"Huh? Oh, well, whatever. I didn't get caught, okay? And you won't be mad for long, once you see these. Check 'em out." He pulled two potatoes from his pockets. "Ta-da!"

Tessa stuck out her tongue. "You want us to eat raw potatoes?"

"No. Gross." He shook his head. "A potato contains sugar, water, and acid. Certain types of metals—particularly zinc and copper—react with the potato, effectively becoming electrodes, one positive and the other negative. Electrons flow between the metals inside the potato, making a small electric current. Don't you remember that experiment we did in science class last year?"

The cadets stared at Lewis in disbelief.

"What?" he said, expecting a slightly more excited reaction. "Contrary to popular belief, I actually pay attention in class from time to time."

"Dude, you are a genius." Dev instantly forgave his friend, delivering a palm-smacking high five.

Maeve snorted. "Okay, let's not get too carried away. But

yes, Lewis, you did good. Now let's see if those spuds actually work."

Dev took the electrical wires they had stripped from the gaming system and attached them to the rudimentary transmission panel and oscillator board he'd built with the other materials. He flicked a metal tab, practicing the series of dits and dahs, testing out the Morse code message they had agreed to transmit back to Earth. He ran the wires through the potatoes and twisted the ends together to close the circuit. He tuned the makeshift capacitators.

"Okay. Ready to go," Dev said, preparing the main switch. "Tessa, on my signal, flip the brass lever."

"Got it," she said.

"Three ... two ... one ... Go."

Nothing happened.

"It's not working," Dev grumbled. "Even with the potatoes."

"Let's try again," Tessa said.

Dev reconnected the circuit and adjusted the oscillator, watching as bright green light flickered along the copper path, then died out. "The circuit's messed up. The wiring must be wrong. I need to fuse the joint, I think, but I don't have a soldering iron."

Lewis leaned over. "We can't give up that easily. We just need a little extra oomph."

"Ah yes," Maeve laughed. "That highly technical unit of measurement ... the oomph."

Virri came closer, intrigued by what they were doing. Dev rewired the radio again, realigning the knobs. He switched it on.

"Three . . . two . . . one . . ."

Virri closed her eyes, as if sensing the electrical current. Just as Tessa pulled the lever, Virri tapped a finger to the problematic wire. A spark shot out, crackling and flaring with fluorescence. The wires sizzled. The panel cleaved. A puff of smoke rose into the air. Dev coughed and waved a hand in front of his face. He looked down. The whole contraption was singed, cracked right down the middle.

"It's destroyed! Our invention is ruined. Virri!" he yelled, losing his temper again. "Why did you do that?"

Virri shrunk away, retreating into her shell and rolling behind Tessa's chair.

"Don't yell at her. She was just trying to help." Tessa gave Virri's pearly shell a gentle pat. Virri poked her head back out tentatively.

"Hey, look on the bright side. Baked potatoes!" Lewis held up a smoking potato covered with a blackened rind of char. He bit into it. "Yikes! Hot!"

Tessa also felt a strange burning sensation creeping from her wrist down to her fingers. "Hot is right. Ouch!" she cried, running to the bathroom and dabbing her skin with a damp towel. Her entire hand was tingling.

"Are you okay?" Maeve asked.

"Yeah, mostly. The electricity from the circuit must have zapped me a little. I have a metal plate under my skin from that old injury. I think it reacted in a weird way." She rubbed her wrist. "I'm fine, it just feels weird. Like it's buzzing."

"Uh, Tessa?" Isaiah said. "That's because it is. Look."

The face of Tessa's eChron watch lit up. Its screen glowed, crowded with new messages. Each time a new one loaded, the watch vibrated.

"Holy cow! I guess Virri's oomph jump-started the battery or something! It hasn't worked since we got here."

The cadets gathered around and Tessa showed them the messages.

"Wait a minute," Isaiah said, always picking up on small but important details. "Look at the time stamp on this one. Your sister just sent it a half an hour ago."

"So?"

"So, that means your smartwatch is somehow receiving data from across the Threshold," Isaiah said incredulously.

"Which means maybe, just maybe, it can also *send* data." Dev nearly jumped for joy.

The cadets cheered.

Virri shrank away sheepishly.

"Oh, it's okay," Tessa said when she noticed Virri's worried eyes. "We're not upset with you. The radio broke, but this may work even better. You helped us. Thank you."

Virri looked up. She reached for Tessa's hands and squeezed them. Tessa squeezed back. Then Virri crawled up the nearest wall, opened a ceiling grate, and disappeared back into Station Liminus's ducts.

46

EARTH

DR. KHATRI HAD ALREADY HAD SEVERAL CUPS OF STRONG, caffeinated tea, but he needed another. His eyelids drooped and his energy waned, but he refused to rest until he found evidence of a natural portal.

He shuffled to the kitchen and placed the kettle on the stove. While he waited for the water to boil, he flipped the television on and surfed the channels aimlessly.

The local newscaster announced, "Rolling blackouts are on the rise throughout the city of Conroy and surrounding counties."

Mayor Hawthorne's photo flashed on screen.

"The mayor promises to work with the energy council to ameliorate the situation, but business owners and individuals are growing increasingly frustrated by the situation."

The video cut to a reporter interviewing two old men, one of them holding a pitchfork, the other holding a shotgun. A dilapidated silo appeared in the background.

"When the power goes out, my cows can get past the electrical fencing. At first, I thought coyotes were picking them off. Then I suspected the MegaAg folks. But now I think it's something else!"

The reporter spoke into her microphone. "The owner of Miss Mary's Dairy claims that a total of six animals have gone missing in a matter of weeks. Police are investigating."

The farmer spoke again. "My buddy and I, we staked out the perimeter this time, sure we'd catch them MegaAg folks kidnapping our cattle. We spotted the cows, just beyond the fence, trotting toward the old Greene silo."

"It was sort of hard to see, because mist and fog always settle around that place. It's in a natural gulley," Gil Greene added.

Ray Harkis's face lit up. "We had our eyes on one cow, a sweet little Holstein who lost her way. Then, all of a sudden—poof! The poor gal disappeared into thin air. Spookiest thing I ever saw." He blinked. "My buddy Gil saw it too, didn't ya?"

"Sure did. With all them quivers wiggling the ground around these parts, we think maybe a sink hole opened up."

The kettle whistled. Dr. Khatri turned off the stove, but he didn't bother to pour himself a cup of tea. Instead, he picked up the phone and dialed a number with shaking fingers.

"Dr. Scopes," he said. "I'm sorry to call so late."

"It's fine. I'm up," she said, sounding tired. "Is this about the kids?"

"Yes." He tried to calm his breathing. "I think I've located the nearest dimensional tear."

She perked up. "Where? New Guinea? Panama? West Virginia?"

"Right here in Conroy." He shut off the television. "Meet me at the eastern border of the MegaAg seed fields, near the old Greene silo."

"That's private property. How do you expect to get access at this hour?"

Dr. Khatri glanced at his wife's MegaAg credentials and ID badge on the kitchen island. She had conflicted feelings about working for a big agricultural conglomerate, but they paid well and supported her research into drought- and blight-resistant strains of rice and soy.

"Leave that to me," he said, picking up the badge and slipping it in his pocket.

STATION LIMINUS

"YOU HAVE 74 NEW MESSAGES."

Tessa scrolled through the texts from Zoey on her smartwatch.

if I break my ankle in these
shoes, I'm blaming you.
wow, how do you stand hanging
out with Blake? She is insufferable.
I just saw the Hart McAubrey
poster in your locker. LOL
I knew you had the hots for him!
You are so cheesy

. . .

how's the field trip?
be nice to my friends, okay?
don't embarrass me, okay?
take some notes if you see
anything cool, okay?
ugh. I wish I was there . . .
if Isaiah seems gloomy, try to
cheer him up

if Maeve is moody, give her
space.
. . .
you didn't tell me you had a math
quiz today? Argghhhhh!
you are literally the worst
I'm going to intentionally flunk it
for you.
JK. I'd never do that.
Aced it! booya!
you can thank me later.
wow. ungrateful much?
. . .
Are you ignoring me?
Really? Really?
. . .
Whoa. Did you feel that quiver?
It was sort of scary. We had to
hide under the desks.
The lights are still out.
Hope everything is okay at
NASA.
text me back, pls?
. . .
WHERE ARE U??????
I'm at band practice waiting
outside the locker room to change into our normal
clothes like we planned and you're not here.
. . .
Are you and Lewis pranking me
right now?
I feel like this is a prank . . .
. . .
Fine. You WIN!
I said it: YOU WIN.
It was actually really hard to be
you today.

I give you a lot of credit.
You can style me for a whole
month. Happy now?
Hello . . . ?
Seriously, T. What is up with you
today?

. . .

WTH?!?
MOM IS FREAKING OUT. DAD
TOO. WHAT IS HAPPENING?

. . .

YOU VOLUNTEERED FOR A SLEEP
STUDY AT NASA?
YEAH, RIGHT *eye roll*
WHERE ARE YOU AND WHAT ARE
YOU *REALLY* DOING?
YOU BETTER NOT BE HOOKING
UP WITH GAGE BEHIND THE BLEACHERS.
I AM SO NOT COVERING FOR YOU
AGAIN.
PS—He is a terrible human.
If you heard the way he talks to
me and my friends, you'd get it.
You deserve better.
Much better.

. . .

Tessa, I'm scared.
Mom is acting extra weird. Dad
is eerily quiet.
I'm sorry about our fight. I said
awful things.
Please don't stay mad.
If this is about the swap, it's
over. You win.

. . .

HELLO? EARTH TO TESSA?
ANSWER ME. PLEASE.

Tessa finished reading the last message. She wasn't sure what time it was on Earth, but she typed a message and hit send.

She waited. And waited. Nothing. Tessa tried once more. This time, the watch made a *swoosh!* sound indicating the message had been sent.

A small icon popped up. She showed it to the other kids.

"It says delivered, but unread. Zoey usually takes her watch off at night. We can try again in the morning. She's probably sleeping now."

"Speaking of which, we should do the same. We're never going to play well tomorrow if we're sleep deprived." Maeve yawned.

Dev caught the yawn next, then Lewis. They were exhausted. A few hours of shut-eye sounded more delicious than the twelve-course feast they had eaten earlier (minus the wriggling tentacled things).

They said good night and retired to their cloud beds.

Isaiah tossed and turned. His mind was racing, his nerves raw and jumpy. He thought about the changes in vision and the inklings he'd had—the need to leave the greenroom, the importance of connecting with their families back on Earth.

Duna had said Transfer could have some unexpected effects. Isaiah had been sick when he arrived, but when the nausea faded, something else replaced it. Something Isaiah didn't have a name for and didn't know what to do with. There was a sensation thrumming through him, some unidentifiable energy that needed an outlet, like the radio's electrical current. Something that had become amplified since he crossed the Threshold.

He walked to the dining table and spotted a lonely, charred potato. Lewis had actually eaten the other one, which was pretty gross, but that kid seemed to eat just about anything. Except for live starfish. He drew the line there.

Isaiah studied the potato, thinking back to Nolan's tuba during the field trip. He focused his eyes on it. He wondered if he could make it move without touching it. He squinted. He willed the potato to move. He blinked. Wait? Had it just wiggled? He leaned closer to check. Nope. It was in the exact same spot. He tried again. The potato refused to budge. Maybe he hadn't acquired some new superpower after all. Still, he was too restless to return to bed.

While the others slept soundly, he slipped out the door and wandered through the quiet Station until he arrived at Gate Hall. The looping structure rotated slowly, doorways shifting and changing as they passed.

He looked through a porthole, then leaped back as an enormous sea creature swam by. Another window revealed a fiery sunscape, flaring with bursts of white-hot gas and light. Through the keyhole in a red wooden door, he spied an idyllic hillside dotted with . . . wait, were those cows? He stepped back and rubbed his eyes. Then, far in the distance, he spotted a slim, shadowy figure wandering Gate Hall.

Isaiah ducked behind the frame of a heavy stone door, pressing his body flat to the wall, hoping he hadn't been seen.

He peered around the stones. The figure opened a door, looked in, closed it again. Over and over, the shadowy figure opened and closed doors, as though he was searching for something, someone, someplace. Isaiah squinted, trying to make out the figure's face, but he was too far away. Technically, there was no day or night in the liminal spaces between dimensions, but the Station's lights were dimmed for the designated eight-hour sleeping interval required by most species for essential energy restoration.

"Hey! You!" a guard shouted, and ran toward the figure with a club raised. The man opened a wooden door and jumped across the Threshold. The door closed behind him and the wall instantly shifted from wood to concrete. The guard slammed an angry fist against the wall.

"Almost got him this time," he muttered to himself.

Isaiah's heart stopped as the guard swiveled and made eye contact with him.

"Earthling?" The guard strode in Isaiah's direction. "You shouldn't be out here unaccompanied, especially at this hour," he said gruffly, grabbing Isaiah by the arm. "I will escort you back to your chambers."

"I was just looking. I wasn't planning to open any of them," Isaiah stammered.

"I should hope not. You never know what might come crawling, creeping, or screaming out of these doors."

"Who was that person you were chasing?" Isaiah asked.

The guard turned, his four pale eyes scanning Isaiah. "You saw him, too?"

"Of course I did."

The guard loosened his grip on Isaiah's arm. "Some call him the Traveler. Some call him a ghost. Those of us who work the late shifts see him from time to time, but he's a tricky one. No one's ever gotten a good look at his face. Some say he's traveled so much, he no longer has one."

"He's faceless?"

"Perhaps. Some species experience cellular degradation after too many Transfers—similar to the way digital images lose their resolution when compressed and sent back and forth. Some individuals are more susceptible than others."

Isaiah thought of Dr. Scopes, the way she had looked airbrushed, her face missing contrast and edges. Maybe she had hopped between dimensions too many times? Then again, Dr. Scopes had vehemently refuted the possibility that other dimensions even existed. Isaiah shook his head, his thoughts jumbled.

"Why do you chase him?" Isaiah asked.

"We have orders to catch the Traveler. He's trespassing. Visitors to the Station must be authorized by the council."

They turned the corridor and took a shortcut past the Menagerie. The nocturnal animals prowled through simulated night. Some glowed, flaunting their bioluminescence in the darkness. The colossadon bellowed, a mournful call that echoed through the halls. Even though Duna had said during their tour that the creature was vicious, Isaiah felt sorry for it. How lonely to be the last of its kind.

"Don't go sneaking around again," the guard advised when they arrived at Isaiah's suite.

Isaiah nodded, the image of the Traveler seared into his brain.

"Next time I find out you're out after curfew, I won't be so kind."

"I understand," Isaiah said, entering the room and locking the door behind him.

He tumbled into his cloud bed and fell into a deep, dreamless sleep for the first time in months.

48

EARTH

DR. KHATRI SWEPT A FLASHLIGHT ALONG THE GROUND. "WATCH out for cow pies and black holes."

"Ah yes, my idea of Friday night fun." Dr. Scopes high-stepped over clods of dirt and clumps of grass.

"There!" Dr. Khatri whispered excitedly. "I knew it!"

The portal was hard to miss. At the base of the old silo, the ground eroded into a gaping hole, with bursts of quantum lightning glinting along its jagged edges.

"Stay back or I'll shoot!" someone yelled through the darkness.

Dr. Khatri and Dr. Scopes froze, then slowly raised their hands over their heads. A flashlight shined in their eyes.

"You cow-nappers?" the voice asked.

"No." Dr. Khatri squinted into the blinding lights. "We're scientists. We work at NASA. And we need access to that . . . sinkhole." He couldn't possibly tell them that he suspected the hole was actually a portal to another dimension.

"NASA, huh?" The man turned off his blinding flash-light and switched on a camping lantern.

"My granddaughter went there today for a field trip. Red-head. Sweet girl," said a second man, stepping into the light.

Dr. Khatri squinted, trying to get a better view of the men he was addressing.

"Yes, I remember her. Very bright. Loads of potential. A flair for the dramatic. Maeve was it?"

"Uh-huh. That's her." Gil Greene lowered his shot-gun slightly.

Ray Harkis jutted his chin out. "You think my cows stumbled into that?" He pointed.

Dr. Scopes looked into the portal. It was black with swirling iridescence, as though a slick of oil had pooled on top. "It's quite likely," she said. She stepped closer and felt the energy pull her, like a magnet. Dr. Khatri grabbed her coat and yanked her back.

"Don't get too close," he warned. "It's acting like a black hole. It has a strong gravitational field."

"Where does it lead?" Gil asked.

"That's what we intend to find out," Dr. Scopes said.

"I can tie a rope round your waist and lower you in, like we used to do with the old water well," Ray offered.

"No, thank you," said Dr. Scopes. "It's too unstable right now."

"She's right. We need to run some tests and see if we can stabilize the, err, sinkhole before venturing in or getting the kids to exit."

"Kids? We didn't lose any kids. We lost cows!"

"Right, of course. My mistake," Dr. Khatri said, quickly fixing his error. "And it is our goal to bring them all back, safe and sound. As quickly as possible."

"I like the sound of that," Ray said with a satisfied nod. "How can we help?"

"Dr. Scopes, secure this area with the assistance of these fearless dairy vigilantes. Make sure no one goes near the portal. I will return to the Gwen Research Center and gather supplies."

"Good idea," said Dr. Scopes. The two farmers nodded as well.

"I'll be back soon." Dr. Khatri set off across the fields, just as dawn was beginning to peek over the horizon.

49

STATION LIMINUS

THE KLAPPROTHI CHILD APPEARED IN DUNA'S SLEEPING chambers unannounced.

Duna bolted upright in their cumulo-bunk. "Virri?" they said groggily. They reached for their lynk and checked the time. "It's so early. What's going on? Is everything okay?" They sat up and rubbed their tired eyes. They had been up late, worrying over the possibility that a member of the MAC might have tried to incinerate the Earthlings. Why would a council member, or members, want the cadets dead?

Virri crossed the room and placed a small, round pearl in Duna's palm. She curled their fingers around it tightly, hoping to convey the importance of it, the need for it to be kept safe.

"What is it?" Duna asked, inspecting the pearl carefully, holding it up to the light. It was warm to the touch. Its surface swirled as it hummed with energy.

Virri touched a finger to her heart, then her lips, then she touched the sensory port on the side of her head.

Duna had never seen a Klapprothi pearl in real life, but they remembered from their history books that they were known to contain great multitudes of information. Entire epics could be compressed and layered within the lustrous spheres. For centuries, the people of Klapproth used pearls as storytelling devices, as a way to pass on information from one generation to the next, to communicate across space and time, to capture memories in the form of gems and preserve them. In the days before her dimension's interdiction, Queen Eryna had often attended MAC meetings with an impressive strand looped around her neck. She had said wearing the necklace was like carrying the history of her people with her at all times.

Duna looked down at the object in their palm. Pearl-making was believed to be a lost art form, replaced by newer, sleeker technology like lynks, hyperdrives, and gamma-radios. But here was a real pearl, right in the palm of their hand.

"Is this . . . a message of some sort?" Duna asked. "Something I need to listen to?" They tapped their ear to show what they meant.

Virri nodded excitedly. The Earthling's music had successfully activated Dim14's triskaidecagon, allowing Virri to send a sonic message back to Klapproth. In return, Queen Eryna had transmitted a single granular note, which crystallized deep within Virri's chest. She had spent the past several hours crafting the pearl, unraveling the message encoded within the grain of sand, and building upon it, wrapping it in layers of mucus, which hardened into a durable, beautiful shell. Virri looked at Duna earnestly. She did not have Tessa to help make her understood, but she tried to convey to them the seriousness of her request.

Duna nodded solemnly. They clutched the pearl. The humming grew more intense, but whatever story was contained within it wasn't audible to their frilled Mertanyan ears. They would need to find something to amplify or decode the message.

Duna looked at Virri. "Thank you for trusting me with this. I will see what can be done."

50

EARTH

JUST AS DR. KHATRI PULLED INTO THE GWEN RESEARCH CEN-
ter parking lot, his phone rang.

"Mayor Hawthorne! I'm so glad you called. There's been
an encouraging development..."

"Yes," she said breathlessly. "I have something exciting
to tell you as well. We received a message from Tessa."

Dr. Khatri stopped in his tracks. "Tessa? I thought it
was Zoey?"

"Long story. They're identical twins and they switched
places for the day. The important thing is that we've established a line of communication."

"Really? How?" Dr. Khatri's voice hitched in his throat.

"After an unfortunate hacking incident during my
last campaign, I gave my girls eChron watches that oper-
ate over a secure network. Somehow, Zoey is able to send
and receive texts between Earth and this other dimension.
There seems to be a delay between messages, but at least

we're getting through. And you'll be glad to know that the kids are all safe."

"Oh, thank goodness." He blinked away tears. "Tell Dev I love him. Tell him this . . ." Dr. Khatri proceeded to dictate an entire text message, and then quickly explained his discovery of the portal at the dairy farm. "Valerie, why don't you and your daughter meet me at the MegaAg field? I am gathering some materials from NASA now, but then I'm heading right back to the field. We can work on a new plan together and keep in touch with the kids through Zoey's watch."

"Absolutely," she said. "We'll be there soon."

STATION LIMINUS

THE CADETS AWOKE AS SIMULATED SUNLIGHT BROKE THROUGH the clouds in their rooms. Someone knocked insistently on the door to their suite. Tessa stumbled out of bed and opened the door, expecting to see Duna. Instead, Shro loomed large, his sinewy jaw pulled into a grin.

"Good morning," he said, swooping past Tessa and entering the suite uninvited. He held a black box tied with a delicate white ribbon. "I brought breakfast. Pastries fresh from the commissary." He placed the box on the dining table and looked around. He spotted the broken radio. "What do we have here? An arts and crafts project?"

"Oh, it's nothing. Just a tuner for our instruments," Maeve lied, shifting into performance mode, brushing aside the charred electronics.

The other cadets slowly shuffled out of their cloud bunks, sleepy-eyed, still wearing their matching pajamas.

Shro eyed them warily. "You'd better hurry and get dressed. The entire council is assembling as we speak."

"I thought we'd only be performing for you and Ignatia, and maybe a few lab technicians?" Dev said.

Shro snorted. "On the contrary. Every delegate in the Multiverse Allied Council is keen to witness your musical abilities." His gray eyes grew cool. "They want to see what all the fuss is about."

"Good. We can't wait. We love a challenge," said Lewis, puffing up his chest. He felt confident after their practice session last night and their teamwork building the radio. Which hadn't actually worked, but still, it was the effort and collaboration that counted, right? Plus, it eventually led to something good.

Shro nodded. "Very well. A Station guide will arrive in forty-five minutes to escort you to the auditory lab. Make haste. The council's time is precious and its members do not like to be kept waiting."

"We'll be ready," said Maeve, opening the door, eager for Shro to leave.

He strode across the room, his curved back rippling beneath his leather jacket. He glanced back at the box of pastries. "Do be sure to eat something. You'll need energy for your big performance. It would be such a shame if it didn't go well."

As soon as he left, the kids showered and dressed as fast as they could. Tessa pulled on a copper-and-ivory tunic and a pair of matching leggings that she found hanging in her room's closet. She laced up stylish yet sensible boots, happy to see that they fit perfectly. She did a little twirl in front of her mirror and caught a glimpse of her watch on the bedside table. She slipped it on and tightened the strap. A moment later, it vibrated.

"A message came through the eChron!" she shouted.

The others gathered around, wearing variations of the Station-issued copper-and-ivory attire. They peered at the watch's glassy face, eager for news from home.

"There's definitely a delay between sending and receiving info," Dev said, looking at the time stamps. "But that's better than nothing." He was elated and relieved that they could communicate with Earth using the watch.

A chain of texts flooded the smartwatch's screen:

Geez. It's about time you texted me back!
I thought you were totally ghosting me. Jerk.
Anyway, I'm glad you're okay.
Say hi to my friends. I'm glad they're okay, too.
I showed Mom and Dad your message.
Mom burst into tears.
Then she finally confessed that you're not doing a sleep study after all.
Surprise, surprise—NOT!

. . .

Uh-oh.
Bad news: Mom has lost her dang mind!

Seriously.
She said you were stuck in some
other dimension!
Yeah, okaaaaay, Mayor Cray-Cray.
LOLOLOL
. . .
Um, wait, what?
Your other messages are just
downloading now . . .
. . .
Hold up—
YOU'RE ACTUALLY IN ANOTHER
DIMENSION?!?!?!?
WITHOUT ME?!?!?!
OMG. The FOMO struggle is real
crying face emoji
If you're not already dead, I'm
going to kill you.
JK. Sort of.
. . .
So, YAY. No one is actually crazy
and no one is actually dead (yet).
Big news: Mom talked to Dev's dad.
He's all excited that you guys are
alive and able to send messages to me.
He said, and I quote:
"Tell Dev-i-doodle that his father
loves him to infinity, but not beyond
because infinity goes on forever-
ever-ever-ever-ever . . ."
You get the idea.

Tessa looked at Dev. His face was bright red, but for once
he wasn't embarrassed, just grateful. They kept reading.

Anyway, Mom's all excited
because Dev's dad found a portal.
Not the thing you guys broke
(you're in BIG trouble for that, btw)
There's another one, out in some
field.
Yo? Are you getting my
messages, or not?

. . .

I repeat: Dr. Khatri found a
portal!
happy dance
He and his coworker think they
can use it to bring you home.
But it's dangerous,
They need to run some tests.
Mom's taking me with her to
check it out.
She says we need to stay in
constant contact.
So, text me back!
Hellooooo?

. . .

FYI Mom called me a "critical link"
(in case you were starting to feel
like the more special twin)

. . .

Oh! And tell Isaiah I have his
Journal of Strange Occurrences.
Benni gave it to me. Isaiah left it
on the bus.

. . .

I'll message you as soon as I
know more.
Stay tuned . . .

52

STATION LIMINUS

"WELL, THAT'S ENCOURAGING," SAID LEWIS, ONCE THEY'D FIN-
ished reading the messages. "Now all we need to do is play
some sweet tunes, get those councilors boogying, and convince them not to blast us into space."

"Right. We just have to buy enough time for my dad to
stabilize the portal," Dev said.

"Then we can go home and tell everyone that
planet Earth is about to self-destruct. Yippee," Lewis
deadpanned.

"Yeah, I'm not looking forward to *that* conversation."
Isaiah grimaced. "It's so...doomy."

"It'll be okay. The grown-ups will know what to do,"
Dev said. "All we need to worry about now is our music."

"That should be easy enough," Maeve said. She turned
around. "Wait. Where are our instruments?"

They looked in each room of the suite. "I could have
sworn we left them right here before going to sleep..."

They searched high and low, but the instruments were nowhere to be found.

"Aw, man." Lewis flopped on the couch. "Without our instruments, we are so dead. Like super dead. The deadest."

"Stop it. We'll improvise if we have to." Maeve took a deep breath and put on her best game face.

"Improvise with what?" Dev asked. "We can't all sing like Zoey, er, I mean Tessa."

Tessa was busy rummaging through her closet. She was looking for the instruments, and also some accessories to jazz up her outfit.

"Do you think someone stole the instruments?" Dev said.

"Impossible. I made sure to lock the door before we went to bed," Maeve said, pointing to the deadbolt on the suite's main entry.

Isaiah's face flushed. "Uh-oh."

"What?" Maeve asked, glaring at him.

He swallowed the lump in his throat. "I sort of left the suite last night."

"You what?"

"I couldn't sleep. I went for a walk, just to clear my head."

"Did you lock the door behind you?"

Isaiah shook his head guiltily. "No."

Maeve's hands balled into fists, but she kept her voice calm. "Were the instruments here when you got back?"

Isaiah blinked. "I don't know. I was so tired by then. I fell right asleep."

"Great. Just great!" She planted her hands on her hips and shook her head.

The wall beside them rattled. Lewis jumped back. The ventilation grate opened and Virri appeared.

"Did you take the instruments?" Tessa asked, running to the child.

Virri grabbed Tessa's hand and tugged her toward the vent. "I think she wants us to follow her. Maybe she knows where they are!"

"She wants us to crawl in there again?" Isaiah asked, eyeing the narrow metal shaft. He hadn't exactly enjoyed their underfloor expedition the night before.

"Do you have a better plan?" Maeve asked.

They all looked at one another blankly.

"Didn't think so. Let's go."

The cadets wove through the winding ductwork on their hands and knees, following Virri in the darkness.

"For the record, I am very claustrophobic. I hope you all recognize the sacrifice I am making for you right now," Tessa said.

"Much appreciated," Maeve replied, rolling her eyes.

Up ahead, Virri slowed, pausing to feel for sound vibrations that would hopefully lead them in the right direction. She turned left, then doubled back.

"We're supposed to perform for the council in half an hour, and we're wandering around aimlessly," Isaiah said.

"I'm sure Virri knows where she's going," Tessa said, hoping it was true.

A strange smell wafted through the ducts.

"Come on, Wynner!" Maeve groaned, pinching her nose. "Rude, rude, rude!"

"Seriously, dude," Dev said, waving his hand in front of his face. "We are in close quarters here!"

"What? It wasn't me!"

"Sure it wasn't." Maeve coughed. The stench was becoming more pungent by the minute.

"Hey, whoever smelt it dealt it," Lewis rebuked.

"Um, actually . . . I think *she* dealt it." Tessa stopped and gazed down through a large ceiling grate.

Below, the mighty colossadon roared, standing atop a gigantic pile of dung.

Virri trembled, her glacial blue eyes wide. She tucked herself into her shell.

"Why did Virri lead us directly above the Menagerie?" Dev whispered, peering through the open louvers at the beast below.

According to Duna, the colossadon was one of the Menagerie's most impressive specimens. Weighing several thousand pounds, it looked like a mix between a T. rex, a saber-tooth tiger, and a great white landshark. Its jaw flashed with thousands of razor-sharp teeth; its yellow eyes glowed. Its claws—prized by big-game hunters and traders—slashed through the enclosure's leafy underbrush like machetes. Duna had told them that colossadons were the ultimate apex predators. This particular one had allegedly *eaten* all the other colossadons in its home range on Jelingor, making it exceedingly rare and undeniably terrifying. Ignatia had convinced the council to keep this specimen in captivity at the Station to study it and protect it from poachers who would otherwise kill it for its valuable claws.

"Let's keep moving. Fluffy here doesn't seem to like our company," Lewis said, inching forward.

The colossadon's nostrils flared and its pupils dilated. It circled and charged the triple-thick transparent plastene wall of its enclosure. The kids flattened themselves on the bottom of the metal duct to keep from tumbling around and falling through the grate.

"Why does she keep ramming that wall?" Dev asked, watching the creature's strange behavior.

"Maybe she's trying to shake us out from the ceiling so she can eat us?"

"Not helpful, Isaiah," Maeve hissed.

The colossadon rammed the wall again, howling a mournful, bone-chattering call.

Virri crept toward another enclosure, with Tessa and the others following behind. Maeve looked down. "Wait a minute. Is that ... a cow?"

"Looks like it," Dev said, leaning over to get a better view. "Duna said a black-and-white quadruped stumbled through a Gate recently. Maybe this is the same creature?"

Maeve squinted. "Wait. Do you see that? Look!" She pointed to a tag attached to the cow's ear. It was hard to see from up so high, but she could make out the letters *MM*. "Oh. My. Gosh."

"What?" the others asked.

"That cow is from Miss Mary's Dairy. The farm next to our old place." Maeve's chest tightened. She shut her eyes, holding back tears. The fact that a single cow could potentially reduce her to a blubbering mess was disconcerting. Especially when there were more important things on the line.

"You okay?" Tessa asked, touching Maeve on the arm.

"Yeah, it's just . . . that cow brings back memories, that's all. I haven't really been missing home that much since we got here, but I miss *that* version of home."

The cow mooed.

"I miss our farm. I miss that life." Maeve sighed. "You know, Gramps and I used to help Ray and Mary during calving season at the dairy. I might have even helped bring that ol' gal into the world. Isn't that wild?" she said, looking at her fellow cadets, then down at the cow again. She moved across the duct.

"Maeve? What are you doing?" Dev asked.

"I just want to get a better look." Truthfully, she wanted to pet the cow, to nuzzle her, to smell her grassy sweetness. But that was crazy.

"Maeve, seriously," Isaiah said uneasily. "Don't get too close. The ducts up here are full of vents. They might not be able to support our weight."

Just then, the colossadon rammed its plastene partition,

shaking the entire structure. Maeve was knocked off her hands and knees. She rolled onto her side. The grate beneath her creaked.

"Get off of that!" Dev shouted.

But it was too late; the hinges gave way and Maeve tumbled down into the pen below.

"Maeve!" Lewis screamed.

She gripped the edge of the opening. Her fingertips were white and straining. "Help me!" she cried. The colassadon sniffed and turned its attention to the girl dangling like a snack inside its enclosure.

Lewis grasped her wrists and pulled. Tessa wrapped her hands around Lewis's waist and held tight.

Maeve's face flashed with terror. The colossadon reared up on its hind legs. It snapped its massive jaws, its teeth glinting. Maeve could feel its hot breath on her shins. She pulled her knees up to her chest, just out of reach of the creature's open mouth.

"I won't let you go, Maeve," Lewis said. "I promise."

"You'd better not!"

The colossadon thumped down on all fours and turned away, snorting angrily.

"It's leaving. Thank goodness. Quick. Pull us up," Lewis shouted. The others yanked with all their might.

All of a sudden, the colossadon tossed its head and rammed the partition again, sending both Maeve and Lewis tumbling downward, clinging to each other like a chain. Tessa held on to Lewis for dear life. Dev, Isaiah, and Virri grabbed Tessa's legs and tried to pull her backward. Dev had never considered himself particularly buff, but his friends' lives were at stake and he felt a burst of untapped strength.

The colossadon eyed the cadets. Now it could surely reach Maeve. It reared its head, clawing the ground and preparing to pounce.

Isaiah's ears rang. Heat built up behind his eyes. His racing heart stilled. A sort of calm fell over him. Time slowed. He blinked and found his vision crisper and clearer than ever before. He focused all his energy on the tree beside the colossadon, a thick-trunked palm studded with leafy fronds. He stared at it, thinking about how it had felt to drop that tuba on Gage's foot back at NASA. How he had harnessed his anger, his fear. He felt those same things now, more intensely than ever. Energy surged through him; pressure gathered until it was almost unbearable.

Maeve screamed. The colossadon roared. Isaiah's vision flared, white and hot. A pulse of light arced, striking the tree. The huge palm cracked as though it had been struck by lighting and toppled onto the beast, stunning the animal just long enough for the cadets to wrench Lewis and Maeve up to safety. Virri quickly bolted the grate back in place and scrambled away from it.

The cadets lay on their backs in the duct, heaving deep, ragged breaths.

"No one hurt or eaten?" Lewis asked, checking to make sure everyone was okay. Maeve could barely speak, but she was unharmed.

"Wh-what was that?" Tessa asked, dazed. "Where did that blast come from?"

Isaiah's head was pounding. He looked down into the enclosure. Below, the colossadon bucked the tree off of its back as though it were no more than a twig. Still, in the moment, it had been enough. Enough to save his friends. He rubbed his eyes. They stung and were tender to the touch. He studied the splintered tree. Could he really have done that? With his mind alone?

He hadn't been able to move a dinky potato the night before, but now he could suddenly fell an entire tree? The thought sent a shiver down his spine. Something stirred in his chest. For once, Isaiah wasn't afraid. He didn't feel doomy or full of dread. He felt powerful, alive. He didn't share any of this with his fellow cadets, though. Not yet. He needed to figure it out himself before telling anyone else.

53

EARTH

DR. KHATRI HURRIED INTO THE GWEN RESEARCH CENTER AS the Conroy sky blushed apricot-pink. On weekday mornings, the building would be buzzing with activity at this hour, but it was Saturday and Dr. Khatri was grateful to be alone. He couldn't afford any distractions. He needed to gather the necessary equipment and return to the portal as expediently as possible.

As he hurried toward the quantum studies supply room, he heard muffled sounds coming from Dr. Scopes's office. He stopped. He crept closer, listening, pressing his ear to the door.

Thump! Bump!

He pulled a master set of keys from his pocket and unlocked the door. He pushed it open.

"Hello?" he called, stepping inside. Something rustled behind Dr. Scopes's desk. He rushed over, hoping it might be one of the missing children.

On the floor, bound and gagged, was Professor McGillum.

"You!" Dr. Khatri yanked the gag from his mouth roughly. Professor McGillum cried out, cowering behind the nearest chair.

"How dare you construct a collider without consulting with the department!" Dr. Khatri shouted. "Do you have any idea—"

"Mohan! Stop! Please!" the professor croaked, his throat dry, his eyes struck with terror. "It wasn't me! Genevieve is behind this. She's a fraud!" He coughed and wheezed. "She received some sort of urgent message during the field trip. The kids were having lunch in the café, so she asked me to look after them for a moment. I agreed." He scrunched up his forehead, trying to remember each detail.

"A few minutes later, the building shook. I assumed it was just a quiver, but then a second jolt hit. I thought we'd been hit by a bomb, the impact was so powerful. I helped the teachers evacuate the students and then I ran down here, only to find Genevieve clutching her crystal paperweight and speaking some alien language into the pendant necklace she always wears."

The shock of gray hair on his head stood on end. "I told her we needed to get out of the building, but she refused. When I asked her what was going on, she turned and looked at me with eyes made of ice. Then she blasted me with some sort of stun gun. It knocked me out cold. When I finally came to, she was gone and I was tied up."

Dr. Khatri let the information sink in. "How do I know you're telling the truth?"

"She cannot be trusted, Mohan. I've suspected for some time that she was receiving private research funds from some very shady investors. I can't help but think there is a connection to whatever happened yesterday." He pulled himself to his feet and shuffled through the files on Dr. Scopes's desk. "Here. See for yourself."

Dr. Khatri inspected a glossy pamphlet advertising some sort of paradise for the elite. A thirteen-pointed logo was embossed in gold foil on the front.

"She was recruiting billionaires, promising them passage to a utopian world—on another planet in another dimension."

"But why?" Dr. Khatri asked, confused.

"I don't know. But here are the highest bidders. Not exactly the cream of the crop, if you know what I mean." Dr. Khatri read the list of names. Oligarchs. Warloads. Billionaire bad boys.

"Is she trying to profit off her access to NASA equipment and research?"

Professor McGillum shook his head. "I wish I knew. I don't understand her intentions. All I know is that she is not the person we thought she was."

"Clearly," Dr. Khatri agreed. He opened an envelope on her desk and unfolded a letter from someone named Salvido Finto, an executive with EnerCor, the world's leading energy producer. According the letterhead, Mr. Finto was based out of Italy and was in charge of the corporation's global drilling and mining efforts. The letter was addressed to Ms. Genevieve Scopes, Ambassadorial Advisor for the World Intelligence Organization. He paused. "Have you ever heard of the WIO?"

Professor McGillum shook his head. "Never."

"I suppose it could be related to the UN? Or NATO?"

"She must have been working for them undercover." Professor McGillum logged on to her computer and pulled up an email from her private server. "Look! On September first, Genevieve contacted Finto and offered him a position, a diplomatic post of some kind with the WIO, in exchange for continued access to his drilling sites."

"Drilling sites? I'm having a hard time following," Dr. Khatri said. It had been a long twenty-four hours and his head was spinning.

Professor McGillum unrolled a map on the desk. It was marked with at least a dozen *X*s scattered on nearly every continent, indicating various EnerCor bases and headquarters. Two blue stars also appeared on the map—one outside of Milan, Italy, in a small town called Luciana. The other was smack dab in the middle of Conroy, Ohio, at the Gwen Research Center itself.

"So, Dr. Scopes built the collider," Dr. Khatri said. "Which means she knows more about the children's whereabouts than she's letting on."

He was devastated. Emotions surged through him: relief that the kids were alive, fear that they might still be in danger, anger that Dr. Scopes put them in this position. He squeezed his eyes shut as frustration welled up. He felt like a fool. "Ian, I am so sorry I suspected you."

Professor McGillum waved his hand. "No need to apologize. She is cunning. She deceived us all, but we can still make this right."

"Yes, I intend to." He picked up the phone and dialed Mayor Hawthorne's number. "Dr. Scopes's deception ends now."

STATION LIMINUS

"HEY PUNKS," A VOICE ECHOED THROUGH THE DUCT.

The kids stared as Kor crawled toward them.

"What's the matter? Colossadon got your tongue?" she snickered. Her white hair was disheveled, her capsule bag slung across her back. The beast below roared. "Yikes. You guys pissed that thing off, too?"

Lewis nodded silently, still in shock.

"Wow. You have quite the track record."

"You would know all about records. How many times have you escaped from jail?" Maeve replied. "You're a wanted criminal, after all."

"Look who's talking." Kor shot Maeve a feisty look.

Maeve glared back. "We are highly valuable assets on a mission to restore interdimensional diplomacy and stave off planetary collapse. Thank you very much."

"Ohh, fancy. How'd you score that gig?" Kor pretended to be impressed.

"We just played our music and this little glowy rock started doing something special," Lewis explained.

"Wow. So technical. Your brain's capacity for highly advanced concepts is astounding. It's shocking you humans only barely learned to cross the Threshold," she said sarcastically.

"Get lost, Kor," Tessa snapped. She did not have a good feeling about this girl.

"Okay. Good luck with your little concert." She paused. "Though I would have thought you'd need these." She pulled a brand-new drumstick out of her bag.

"Whaaat?" Lewis gawked.

"Oh, you like this, huh? I got another just like it." She reached her hand deeper into the bag and retrieved a second drumstick. "I got one of these, too." She pulled out Maeve's long, skinny oboe.

"Where did you get that?"

Kor shrugged. "Where do you think? I acquired it from your sleeping quarters last night."

"You acquired it? Really?" Maeve seethed, moving closer to Kor so she could snatch it from her hands. "You mean you stole it."

"Stole. Acquired. Potato, potahto, I say."

"Hey! Did you take our baked potato, too?" Lewis asked angrily. "'Cause I was saving that for breakfast."

"Give us back our instruments," Dev said, getting madder by the minute.

"Okay, okay" Kor sat back and perused the contents of her bag. "I'm willing to make a trade."

"A trade? That's ridiculous," Maeve said. "They belong to us. Give them back."

"I mean, I could always 'accidentally' drop them down there...with that thing." Kor gestured to the colossadon. "Bet she plays a nice allegro on the flute."

"It's an oboe, okay?" Maeve hissed. "Why is that so hard for everyone to understand? They don't even look or sound alike!"

Kor scooted back. "Whoa. Attitude much?"

"Calm down everyone," Isaiah said. "Kor, what do you want in exchange for the instruments?"

She leaned forward and met his eyes. "What I want is your word."

"Our word?"

"Yes. That when you get off this Station you'll take something with you. I promised someone I would deliver some items personally, but I have some...important business that I need to deal with first." She pulled a glowing magenta stone the size of a Rubik's cube from her bag. It illuminated the dark duct with pulsing pinkish light. Virri watched carefully.

"What is that?" Isaiah asked, mesmerized.

"It's a rare ore from Virri's dimension."

"Wait a minute, you're not giving us that nasty bug, are you?" Lewis said, making a face.

Kor frowned. "What are you talking about?"

"The virus that's ravaging their planet. The reason Shro ordered an interdiction."

Kor shook her head. "The silvox virus is not as bad as Shro wants everyone to believe. The interdiction is a cover."

"For what? Does the council know that?"

"Not sure exactly. But the Queen of Klapproth paid me these to transport some very precious cargo to the Station." She held up the cube.

Maeve looked at Kor suspiciously. "What sort of cargo?"

"You Earthlings sure do ask a lot of questions. In this case, you don't need to know. Better if you don't." She pulled out four more cubes, each glowing the same shade. "I promised someone special I would bring these to him."

"Ooh, someone has a boyfriend," Lewis teased.

"It's my grandfather, you wingnut. Promise me you'll transport the cubes to Earth in Dim14 and I'll hand over the instruments."

"Are these illegal? What if we get caught with them?" Maeve asked.

"Yeah, I don't think this is a good idea," Dev agreed.

"They're not illegal, but they are valuable. They're made from regenerex."

Dev looked at the others. "Isn't that the ore the council wanted us to help them mine?"

"Probably," Kor said, giving a nod. "This stuff is mad valuable. It's the most concentrated fuel source in the multiverse, plus it's environmentally friendly and can naturally self-renew, so it never runs out. But there's a super limited quantity and every dimension wants to get their hands on it. Apparently there are some deposits of it running beneath

Klapproth's ocean floor, and there are deposits in a few other dimensions, but it's almost impossible to extract."

"Which is why the council wanted us to help find more of it," Maeve said. "Though I don't know the first thing about mining."

"So, why does your grandfather need these cubes so badly?" Tessa asked, still distrustful of Kor and her motives.

"His omniabus broke down and he can't get back home," she replied.

"His what?"

She huffed. "His time-traveling, dimension-hopping vehicle. Duh."

"Excuse me, what?" Isaiah said, wanting to make sure he'd heard her correctly.

"He was passing through Dim14 a while ago, and since you Earthlings only managed to build a few functioning portals, my grandfather's been trapped on your dumb planet ever since. He needs the regenerex to fix his bus, okay?"

"But . . . how will we find him when we get back to Ohio?" Dev asked.

Kor shrugged coolly. "Don't worry about that. He'll find you."

Tessa looked down at her watch. They were wasting time. "Fine," she said. "We promise to bring the cubes home with us. Happy now?"

"Good choice," Kor said, her lips curling into a smile. She took the cubes and pressed them between her palms, one at a time, flattening them into paper-thin squares. She handed one to each cadet. Isaiah was surprised that it felt as light as air. "Keep them somewhere safe."

"Yeah, yeah," Lewis said, slipping his into his back pocket. "Now hand over those sweet drumsticks."

Kor doled out the instruments. When she was done, she wiped her hands. "Nice doing business with you. I always enjoy a fair trade."

Dev raised an eyebrow. "Not sure that counted as fair, but whatever . . ."

Kor made a trilling sound deep in her throat and opened her capsule bag wide. Virri rolled across the duct and slipped inside, giving a friendly wave before disappearing within the mysterious expanse of Kor's Mary Poppins bag. "See ya," Kor said, before crawling away in the opposite direction.

"I don't trust her as far as I can throw her," Dev said as soon as Kor was gone. "Who knows what these cubes really are? What if they get us in more trouble?"

"We didn't really have a choice. Let's get a move on." The cadets shuffled through the ducts, hunched and crawling on their hands and knees. "Hustle up," Maeve instructed, getting back into her role as drum major. She looked over at Tessa's watch. "We have a concert to play in five minutes. Aten—"

"Ahhh!" Isaiah screamed as the grate beneath him and Tessa buckled under their shared weight and gave way.

STATION LIMINUS

DUNA WAS SEARCHING FOR A WAY TO UNLOCK THE MESSAGE contained within the Klapprothi pearl. They had a hunch that the Station's translation equipment might be helpful, so they had slipped across the Station before the cadet's musical performance to try and find a solution. Their attempts hadn't worked yet, but they planned to stop by the Station's encyclomedia desk later that day to request additional information about the unusual gem.

Before leaving, Duna decided to surf the various radio channels, listening for a frequency that might activate the pearl. They twisted the dial to the left, then the right, picking up mostly static and the Voyager Golden Record, which played on repeat in the low frequency channels.

Duna was about to disconnect their headphones when a voice caught their attention. The channel's translator filter made it impossible to tell who was speaking, but Duna's ears perked up. They raised the volume, listening carefully.

Only one voice was audible, coming through in broken, patchy fragments.

"I am sorry to bother you at such an early hour, but I have an important update. It appears a stowaway has found her way onto the Station. Yes, I'm sure. Thanks to that slippery little Ebvarienne wretch, no less. We should have offed her long ago, when we got rid of her parents. Yes, I know I cannot change the past . . .

"What's that? The stowaway? Ah. I suspected something when the trisk was activated. It was. Yesterday. Quite concerning indeed. When I reviewed the video footage, my suspicions were confirmed. I know. We cannot allow Eryna to reestablish contact with Ignatia. I understand. It would compromise everything. We are finally so close to achieving our goals. I agree.

"Yes, I do believe the council will reverse their vote. Oh, please. The Earthlings are no threat whatsoever. A nuisance, yes. But a threat? Not at all. I thought to exterminate them early on, just to simplify matters, but that didn't work out as I planned. These so-called cadets are likely to doom themselves. Oh, yes. They are positively predisposed to disaster. It comes quite naturally to them, in fact. They're not cut out for life in the multiverse. Hahaha. I know. It's hilarious. They don't stand a chance.

"No, Finto has not made contact with us. No, he never returned. What a coward. But I am sure our associate is dealing with him.

"What's that? Ah, I see. Mhmm. The triskaidecagon? I

have already swapped out Dim2's with a fake and destroyed the original. I did indeed. Last night. As soon as I identified the Klapprothi stowaway. Thank you for saying that. I appreciate your praise.

"This morning when the Earthlings play their little music, nothing will happen. The fake trisk will not activate. Ignatia will see that the initial transmission was merely a glitch. Nothing to concern the council over.

"Then, of course, the council will see how terribly useless the humans are. Yes, I will enjoy that part very much. Following a rousing and eloquent speech made by me, the council will surely proceed with an expedited vote to compactify Earth. Oh, yes. Not to worry. I will make sure everything goes according to plan."

56

STATION LIMINUS

ISAIAH AND TESSA FELL NEARLY TWENTY FEET. THANKFULLY,
a huge pile of hay, and not dung, broke their fall. And thankfully, they had fallen into the cow's enclosure this time, and not some voracious spacebeast's pen.

"Are you guys okay?" Dev asked, sticking his head out of the opening.

"Yeah, I'm fine," Isaiah said, rubbing his elbow. "Just bruised I think. How about you, Tessa?"

"I'm okay," she said, standing up and dusting off her copper tunic.

It was still early, so the Menagerie was unstaffed. But any minute, the techs and vets would be coming in for morning feedings and health checks.

"We have to get out of here," Isaiah said. The friendly cow sauntered over and licked his face.

"I know," Tessa agreed, scratching the cow gently behind the ears. Sure enough, the tag on its ear was from Miss

Mary's Dairy. The coincidence was strange, but Tessa remembered what Duna had said about fate. Maybe all of this was happening for a reason.

She peered around the pen. She lifted a bar on the door and helped Isaiah exit the enclosure without setting the cow loose. "You stay here," she told the animal, rubbing its nose.

"Now what?" Isaiah asked. "There's no way we can climb back into the ceiling ducts now."

Tessa looked up at their friends, whose worried faces were gathered inside the opening. "We'll take the main corridor and meet you at the lab," Tessa said.

"Bring our instruments, okay?" Isaiah added.

"You got it." Lewis flashed a thumbs-up.

"Do you know which way to go?" Tessa asked Isaiah once they were in the Menagerie's main exhibit area.

"Not exactly. But there's one of those interactive holo-maps." He pointed.

They crossed the room and looked at the map, trying to get their bearings. They had just charted a fairly direct route to the sound lab when a loud voice shouted, "Stop! You there!"

They wheeled around to see a khaki-clad creature keeper wielding a gun-shaped contraption. "What do you think you're doing?" he yelled. "Trying to steal the colossadon hatchlings, are you?"

"Hatchlings?" Isaiah said. So that was why she was ramming the wall and howling. Her babies were on the other side.

"They nearly went extinct thanks to smugglers and poachers like you!" the keeper yelled, moving closer.

"We're not smugglers," Tessa said. "Believe me, if we wanted a pet, we wouldn't choose one of those. We weren't—" Before Tessa could explain, the creature keeper fired his tranquilizer.

Blat! Blat!

"Tessa! Run!" Isaiah yelled.

The darts whizzed through the air. The first one missed, but the second pierced the fabric of Tessa's copper leggings and lodged deep into her thigh. The potent stundrug began coursing through her veins almost immediately. She swayed. Her bones turned to jelly, her mind to mush. She stumbled to the left, to the right, to the left again. Isaiah reached out to catch her. They both crashed into the holomap.

"Guards!" The creature keeper called for reinforcements. He lunged for Isaiah and pinned him to the ground.

Tessa's vision was a blur of color and light. She dragged herself to her feet, but the drug was too strong. Her eyelids fluttered. The control console beeped as Tessa's limp hand dragged across the interactive floor plan. Blue walls turned red, orange walls turned white. Clicking sounds echoed through the Menagerie as cages and pens unlocked.

Tessa crumpled to the floor. Everything went dark.

57

EARTH

"I CANNOT APPREHEND OR ARREST DR. SCOPES," MAYOR HAW-
thorne said into the phone as she stepped through tall,
damp grass.

"You must!" Dr. Khatri said, his voice urgent. "She is a
criminal. A fake. Professor McGillum and I found proof in
her office."

The mayor paused beside the old Greene silo. "No, Dr.
Khatri, please. What I mean is I cannot arrest her because
she's . . . gone."

"What? Did you say gone?" Dr. Khatri rubbed a finger in his ear. Surely he had heard the mayor incorrectly.
Sometimes service was patchy out in the agricultural areas
of the city.

"I'm so sorry," Mayor Hawthorne said. "My daughter
and I just arrived at the MegaAg field. Gil Greene and Ray
Harkis are here. They saw her jump into the portal."

Dr. Khatri couldn't believe what he was hearing. "She fell through the portal?"

"She didn't fall. Ray says she jumped, intentionally."

He strode across the office. "Tell me, what condition is the portal in?"

The mayor paused. "The portal is gone, too. It closed up in her wake." She turned on the camera and held up her phone so that Dr. Khatri could see the field and the silo. There was no sign of the gaping hole or flashing quantum lightning.

"That was our only hope," he muttered miserably. "How will we ever reach the children now?"

58

STATION LIMINUS

"WHERE ARE YOUR FELLOW EARTHLINGS?" IGNATIA INQUIRED impatiently. The delegates were gathered inside the auditory lab, ready to experience the power of the cadets' so-called music.

Maeve, Dev, and Lewis fidgeted uncomfortably on the small stage at the front of the room.

"They'll be here any minute," Maeve replied, forcing a smile. Tessa and Isaiah were supposed to come directly to the auditory lab, but time was ticking by with no sign of them.

"Did you enjoy your breakfast?" Shro asked expectantly from his seat in the front row.

Something about his tone made Lewis uneasy. For once, he was glad he hadn't eaten anything. None of them had. There hadn't been enough time.

"Very much," Maeve lied, not missing a beat. She gave her stomach a pat for emphasis.

Ignatia rapped a bony knuckle on the table. "Enough small talk. We don't have infinite time at our disposal. You will begin without the others," she commanded. The delegates took their seats.

"We can't," Maeve said, stalling. "We're an ensemble. A team."

"You'll play fine as a trio, I'm sure. Show my esteemed peers how you activated this." She held the triskaidecagon in the air. It was glowing a fainter shade of turquoise than yesterday, but it was still impressive. The delegates gasped.

"What should we do?" Dev whimpered, his stage fright rearing its ugly head. His breath was shallow, his chest tight, his shirt damp with perspiration.

Maeve bit her lip. "The show must go on . . ." She counted them in.

Dev lifted the saxophone to his quivering lips, and—

BLERRRGGHHH!!!

"What in the multiverse . . . ?" Ignatia covered her ears.

Dev looked down, bewildered. Had that noise really come from his regular old brass sax? He fixed his grip and tried again. Five . . . six . . . seven . . . eight . . .

BLERRRGGHHH!!! GAARROOMFFF!!!

It sounded almost like an elephant trumpeting.

"Let me try again," Dev said, his hands shaking.

"You got this." Lewis nudged his shoulder.

Before Dev could play another note, the floor rumbled.

"This feels like a quiver," Lewis said, steadying himself.

GAARROOMFFF!!! Through the large glass observation window, the kids and delegates watched a three-tusked megaphante plow through the hall, with a stampede of purple oryx galloping at its heels.

An alarm wailed.

"Breach! Breach!" the Station's central AI announced through the speaker system. "Creature breach reported from the Menagerie."

"Yes, I can see that. How many specimen enclosures were compromised?" Ignatia demanded, pressing a small button on her wristlet.

"Seventeen," the AI replied.

"But surely not the—"

The colossadon's mighty roar shook the walls of the sound lab, leaving a spidery crack in the glass observation window.

The color drained from Ignatia's horns. Havoc erupted as delegates scrambled out of their chairs, trying to flee.

"Calm down! Everyone, stay put! You are safer in here than out there. Shro! Lock down the room. Stay calm!"

Blat! Blat! Blat! Tranquilizers fired as creature keepers pursued the runaway animals. The colossadon roared again, whipping her spiked tail. The keepers scattered and ducked. She thundered toward Gate Hall, seeking an escape route, with four small hatchlings clinging to the fur of her underbelly.

A screeching pack of rakoomas darted past the window next.

Ignatia pressed her wristlet again. "Connect me with the Menagerie manager. At once!"

A second later, a gray-skinned man appeared as a holovid, floating in the center of the room.

"Yes, Your Eminence?" he said over the din of squeaking, hissing, and buzzing.

"Precisely what transpired at your post?" Ignatia barked.

"We discovered a pair of humanoids, who we believe to be smugglers, meddling with the Menagerie's enclosure controls. The creature keeper on duty subdued the thieves, but not before they caused significant damage."

"Was anyone injured?" Ignatia asked.

"Affirmative," the holovid said. "Lino, our habitat specialist, was bitten by a hungry crark. A second staffer was stung by a swarm of calypso wasps."

"Where are the smugglers now?" Ignatia asked.

"They're being held in custody," the holovid answered.

"Show them to me!" Ignatia ordered. Her horns flared a furious shade of scarlet.

A second holovid image appeared. Isaiah and Tessa were slumped over, tethered to chairs with electromagnetic shackles, their heads lolling, delirious from the lingering effects of the stundrug.

Maeve was appalled. "They're not smugglers! They're our friends! What did you do to them?"

"Your Eminence, please," Duna said. "I'm sure this is a misunderstanding."

"We didn't mean to cause so much trouble, I promise," Dev pleaded.

"That's becoming a common refrain with you Earthlings," Ignatia snapped. "Disruption and destruction follow you everywhere, it seems."

"What a pity. We had such high hopes for your kind," Shro said, pouting.

"This is all wrong!" Dev shouted. "We were only in the Menagerie because someone stole our instruments and we went looking for them."

"And yet you found them, I see. Where exactly were they hidden?" Shro pressed, unperturbed by the chaos just beyond the lab's walls.

Dev shot Lewis a look. They couldn't rat Kor out. Even though she had caused this mess. Virri was with her now. If the MAC found Kor, they'd find Virri, too.

"We, uh, found them, in, um . . ."

Quirg snarled. "Just as I suspected. They are incapable of being truthful. It was a mistake to bring them here! Look what they've done to our beautiful Station! I can only image the state of the Gates, probably trampled by the megaphantes."

"Please," Maeve said. "Let us explain . . ."

"Silence!" Ignatia narrowed her violet eyes. "You three are complicit in this crime." She hammered her fist on the table. "Guards, seize them!"

59

EARTH

ZOEY COULDN'T BELIEVE HER MOTHER HAD AGREED TO LET HER go to the Gwen Research Center at the crack of dawn and help search for a portal into the multiverse. If her sister wasn't actually trapped somewhere in another dimension, it would have been the coolest mother-daughter outing ever. But Tessa was in trouble, and so were some of Zoey's closest friends. She would do whatever it took to help them. First, though, they needed to make a quick stop at home.

Zoey scaled the stairs two at a time. The morning had turned cold and rainy, and she had gotten soaked in the field near Miss Mary's Dairy. She ran to her room to change into some dry clothes and to grab Isaiah's journal, just in case it might come in handy. As soon as she opened the door, she stubbed her toe. Hard.

"Ouch!" She hopped up and down until the pain subsided. What had she bumped into? That's when she saw it: the tuba case. She had been so distracted by pizza and interdimensional text messages during the night that she had completely forgotten about it. She unlatched the case and it fell open, revealing a long metal tube with dozens of buttons and rings running up and down its length. It looked like a souped-up grenade launcher.

Nolan was right: It definitely wasn't his tuba, or any tuba for that matter. Where had Gage found such a thing? She didn't dare touch the instrument, or machine, or whatever it was, so she carefully closed the case and flipped it over. On the bottom, a small silver-and-blue sticker said: *Property of NASA*. She figured she had better return it. And luckily, she and her mom were heading there now.

60

STATION LIMINUS

"WHERE ARE WE? WHERE ARE OUR FRIENDS?" TESSA MURmured blearily. Her questions echoed off the walls of the cell. She was still dizzy and her muscles felt weak, but her head was finally clearing.

Isaiah's eyelids fluttered. "Uncle Ming?" he mumbled. "Is that you?"

"Isaiah," Tessa said. "It's me, Tessa. Wake up!"

He wiped a dribble of drool from his chin and looked around. "What's going on?"

"They locked us up. We need to get out of here and find the others."

A single light bulb flickered from a wire overhead. Impenetrable concrete walls loomed on four sides, wrapped with sharp strands of barbed wire that not even Virri could scale without tearing her hands and feet to shreds.

Isaiah tried to stand up, but the shackles held firm, zapping his ankles with electric shocks.

"We're stuck," he said. "There's no way out."

There was a faint knock on the door. It creaked open. Tessa looked up, terrified that their moment of reckoning had come. She reached over and grabbed Isaiah's arm. She squeezed tightly, unable to speak.

"Room service!" a voice called.

Tessa and Isaiah exchanged confused glances.

A member of the catering staff appeared, wearing a navy-blue uniform and a funny silver hat. She pushed a refreshment cart into the cell.

Tessa gawked. Her brows knit together. "Dr. Scopes?" she said, incredulous. "Is that you?"

"No way." Isaiah hunched over despondently. "Must be a doppelgänger."

"Shhh! It is me," Dr. Scopes said in a conspiring whisper. "Come. We need to hurry." She crossed the room and used a special tool to unlock the shackles.

"How did you get here?" Tessa asked, stretching out her sore limbs.

"I've been working with Dr. Khatri and your mother, Mayor Hawthorne, to locate another portal. We found one. And just in time, it seems."

"Is Dev's dad here, too?" Isaiah asked.

"No, he stayed back on Earth to help coordinate our return journey. We don't have much time. Where are the others?"

"We don't know," Tessa said.

Dr. Scopes's eye twitched. "Okay. I will figure something

out." She dabbed her eyelid with her finger, fixing her smudgy eye shadow. Isaiah stared at her. Her whole face looked blurry and melty. But he didn't have time to dwell on it; there were more important things to worry about.

Dr. Scopes leaned over and parted the blue velvet curtain that ran around the huge refreshment cart. "Get in. You must stay out of sight. Be silent and still."

"Great. Another small space," Tessa mumbled as she climbed into the cart. At least it smelled like freshly baked cinnamon rolls and thornmelon tarts instead of colossadon dung.

Isaiah followed, tucking his knees under his chin. Dr. Scopes closed the curtain and wheeled the cart out of the cell.

Once safely stashed in the darkness, Tessa messaged Zoey with her smartwatch. Dr. Scopes had come to their rescue!

61

EARTH

ZOEY READ THE MESSAGE IN THE CAR ON THE WAY TO NASA, her eyes darting back and forth. She typed in a frantic reply.

**Tessa—whatever you do,
do NOT go with Dr. Scopes.
Do not trust her.**

There was no response.

**Answer me. Please!
If you're reading this, get away from her.
Run. Hide. Go anywhere, just get away. NOW.**

A minute passed, and then another.
Finally, the watch pinged with a reply.

It's too late, Zoey.
We already did.

62

STATION LIMINUS

AS QUIETLY AS SHE COULD, TESSA SHOWED THE MESSAGE TO Isaiah. Her heart jackhammered her ribs.

"What do we do now?" she whispered in the darkness. "We have to find the others and warn them."

The cart slowed. Dr. Scopes stopped and pulled a ringing device from her pocket.

"Yes?" she said, speaking softly. "I found two of them. Where are the other three?" There was a long pause. "On floor seven? Cell nine-B? I'm on my way now. Yes. I know. Of course I'm in disguise. Do you think I'm some sort of neophyte? Yes, yes. Fine." She hung up and continued pushing the cart.

"Bingo," Tessa whispered to Isaiah. "Floor seven, cell nine-B."

"How are we supposed to beat her there?" Isaiah whispered back.

Their cart slowed to a stop. The kids huddled together, making sure their elbows and feet weren't sticking out.

A robotic voice addressed Dr. Scopes. "Halt! You have reached a mandatory checkpoint."

"Checkpoint?" she asked. "Is that normal protocol?"

The robot beeped with irritation. "Following the Menagerie breach, additional checkpoints have been established to ensure the comfort and safety of Station passengers."

"I see . . ." said Dr. Scopes, clearly irritated.

The robot beeped again. "Cite your destination and task."

"Upper wing. Diplomatic salon replenishing," Dr. Scopes replied.

The robot scanned the cart's digicode. "Affirmative," it answered.

A second cart pulled up to the checkpoint and parked next to theirs.

"I'm returning to the galley for more vellwaffers," its driver told Dr. Scopes. "The Nharlites are insatiable today."

Dr. Scopes chuckled, playing along. "You should see how many pints of moonrye they can toss back after a grueling Transfer!"

"Now is our chance," Tessa said. She slid the curtain aside.

"Are you crazy?" Isaiah hissed.

"Probably, but I'd rather be crazy than dead."

As carefully as possible, they slipped from their cart into the refreshment cart parked beside them, pulling the curtains closed behind them. Dr. Scopes continued to

chat with the catering staffer about voracious Vermaskians and gluttonous Quomions. From a thin gap in the
curtains, they could see Dr. Scopes's foot tapping anxiously on the floor. Finally, the conversation wrapped
up and the two carts parted ways, heading in opposite directions.

A few minutes later, the cart carrying Tessa and Isaiah
rolled into a bustling galley. Pots and pans clanged, grills
sizzled, and helium burners flared.

"How do we get out of this thing without anyone noticing?" Tessa asked. The kitchen was a swirl of activity with
alien-looking chefs, dishwashers, and waitstaff moving in a
frenzied culinary choreography.

Isaiah peeked out between the curtains, careful to
remain hidden. Across the room, he spied a towering pile
of shiny yellow fruits with purple spots. Isaiah eyed one
at the very bottom of the stack. He squinted, focusing his
energy on that single fruit. He channeled the sensation he
had felt earlier, remembering the way he'd willed the tree in
the colossadon's habitat to fall.

His vision started to blur; the space behind his eyes
grew hot and bright. The fruit moved—just a slight wob-
ble. He squinted harder, focused more intensely. The fruit
wiggled again. He imagined reaching out and grabbing the
shiny sphere, yanking it free from the pile.

And then, just like that, the fruit dislodged, bouncing
off the table and across the floor. A second later, the entire
tower collapsed in a terrific yellow-and-purple avalanche.

The kitchen dissolved into chaos as the cooks slipped and tripped over the rolling, runaway fruit.

This was their moment! The two cadets made a mad dash for the exit.

"That was lucky! But we have to get to the others before Scopes does," Tessa said once they were safely out of the kitchen.

Isaiah paused to catch his breath. He looked around. The security guard had taken a special route through the service corridors last night when he escorted Isaiah back to their suite.

"This way," Isaiah said. "I know a shortcut."

63

EARTH

"I AM SO GLAD YOU'RE HERE," DR. KHATRI SAID, GREETING Mayor Hawthorne at the main entrance of the Gwen Research Center. He introduced her to Professor McGillum. "Where is Zoey?" he asked. "I thought she would be accompanying you?"

"She forgot something in the car. She'll be here any minute," Mayor Hawthorne replied, straightening her hunter-green blazer. Even though it was Saturday, and she was technically off duty as mayor, she felt it was important to dress well. Her business suits were like a form of armor in that way.

Dr. Khatri tried to keep his own nerves at bay. "Any word from the kids?" he asked.

Mayor Hawthorne nodded. "Yes, they're on some sort of station, like a space station, perhaps? I'm not sure exactly. But according to Tessa's most recent text, Dr. Scopes just arrived."

Dr. Khatri's eyes grew wide.

"Zoey told them to stay away from her. But Tessa said it was too late."

"Too late? What else did they say?" he asked frantically.

The mayor looked distraught. "Nothing yet. Tessa hasn't responded to the last few messages."

"Oh, dear. This is worse than I thought." Dr. Khatri walked in brisk circles around the foyer. "Professor McGillum, we must work faster to find a solution."

"How can I help?" Mayor Hawthorne asked, eager to assist. Children's lives were on the line. She would mobilize the entire municipal government, if need be.

"We need to either find another portal or repair the quantum collider here at the center. Unfortunately, it was badly damaged when the kids disappeared. I don't think it's salvageable, at least not without my Syntropitron."

"What's that exactly?" asked Mayor Hawthorne. "You mentioned it before, I think?"

"It's a large, tubular invention that rewinds the effects of cellular entropy. We hope one day to scale the technology to restore environmental degradation. But our current prototype should be capable of repairing equipment like the collider." He frowned. "Although right now it's useless. Because it's missing. Dr. Scopes and I thought Professor McGillum had it, but he clearly didn't."

Mayor Hawthorne racked her brains, trying to think of possible leads. "Could the kids have brought it with them? Might Dr. Scopes have taken it?"

"Not likely," Dr. Khatri replied. "Dr. Scopes probably would have used it if she had access to it. Especially if she wanted to travel through a portal all along. It's possible the device got misplaced during the disruption at the Center yesterday. Professor McGillum and I have searched the building high and low but haven't found any sign of it."

Just then the doors flew open. "Hey, guys!" Zoey said brightly. "Sorry to keep you waiting. Had to go back for this." She held up the heavy black case that Gage had mistaken for a tuba.

"Where on Earth did you find that?" Professor McGillum said. "Mohan, look!"

Dr. Khatri turned. "Is that—?"

Zoey gave an apologetic smile. "I'm sorry, I think it belongs to you, or someone here at NASA. I'm not sure what it is. One of my classmates accidentally brought the wrong case home after the field trip, thinking it was a musical instrument."

Dr. Khatri practically leaped with glee. "Zoey! You are brilliant!"

"Uh, thanks?" she said, handing him the heavy case, grateful to be rid of it.

Dr. Khatri laid the case gently on the floor. He opened it gingerly. His eyes twinkled. "Yes," he breathed. "This is exactly what we need. There's no guarantee it will work, but it's our best shot. All of you, come with me. Hurry. There's no time to waste."

64

STATION LIMINUS

DR. SCOPES STEALTHILY WHEELED THE LARGE REFRESHMENT cart inside the interrogation chamber. She looked left, right, up. The room was empty.

Perhaps she had been given the wrong location? She was about to pull her lynk out of her pocket when she noticed the curtains on the refreshment card were askew. She knelt down to fix them. She blinked. She tore the curtains open. Tessa and Isaiah were gone.

A guttural, alien scream escaped from her lips. She rubbed a hand across her face, smearing her peach blush, revealing leathery scales below the mask of makeup. Her eyes glazed over with icy fury.

Across the Station, Shro's lynk buzzed. He answered it, listening carefully. "You lost them? How is that possible!" He growled and stormed around his office. "Find them.

Scan the entire Station if you have to. What? You did that already? And nothing?"

He shook his head. "Do it again. If the Earthlings are still on board, the heat maps will pick up their exact locations. Yes. That's what the Menagerie staff have been using to catch all the runaway creatures."

Shro exhaled, growing angrier by the minute. "The only thing that could scramble the sensors is regenerex, and there is no way the Earthlings could be in possession of *that*.

"No more excuses," he growled. "We must find those pestiferous Earthlings before the rest of the council does. I no longer care about the subterfuge. I have reason to believe the stowaway escaped the Station today with incriminating evidence. I believe she was assisted by the humans. Yes, I'm serious!" he boomed.

"I will not allow the Earthlings to jeopardize our plan, not at this stage. We've come too far. I want them caught. I want them destroyed. If the heat scans fail, you may need to take more extreme measures. In fact..."

The wheels in his mind began to turn. "There are still dozens of animals running wild around the Station. It could be a useful diversion. Adding another creature to the mix won't draw any extra attention. Yes, I know the risks!"

Shro seethed. "I don't care how you do it, just get those cadets, NOW!" He disconnected the lynk and threw it across the room, shattering it into hundreds of fractals.

STATION LIMINUS

65

"STAY OUT OF SIGHT," DEV SAID. "WE'RE FUGITIVES NOW." ISA-
iah and Tessa had busted them out of the interrogation cell
and now all five cadets were on the run.

"Wow, that sounds so cool," Lewis mused. "I've never
been a real fugitive before."

Isaiah made a face. "If we get caught we're dead, so it's
not *that* cool."

"Come on, guys. We need to find Duna," Tessa said.
"They'll know what to do."

The kids ducked behind a waste disposal unit on the
perimeter of the Arboretum. There were clusters of armed
guards at every turn. Since the Menagerie breach, security
was tighter than usual.

"Don't forget that Scopes is still on the loose," Tessa said.

Maeve frowned. "Are you sure about her? I thought she
and Dev's dad were working together to help us."

Tessa showed them the messages on her smartwatch. "Looks like she was a traitor all along."

Dev thought about his dad. He'd always spoken so highly of Dr. Scopes. He was sure her deception cut his father deeply. Dev wished he were home so he could give his dad a hug.

"If only Virri were here," Tessa said, peering around the corner of the disposal container. "She seems to know every inch of this place and all the best hiding spots."

"Quick. Someone's coming." Isaiah pulled them into the Arboretum. Most of its staff had been called in to help locate the missing animals, so the greenhouse was empty. The cadets hid behind a massive leafy succulent, like an agave plant but larger, with unusual geometric markings running along its thick leaves.

The door opened. "That's her!" Tessa hissed. "That's Scopes. Get down."

Dev flattened himself against the wall. "Did she see us?"

"I don't know. But something happened to her," Maeve said. "She looks . . . weird."

"She was wearing a catering uniform last time we saw her," Tessa said.

"No, not her clothes. Her face, it's . . . lizardish."

Tessa peeked between the fronds. Sure enough, Scopes's face was covered in scales. As they watched, her body morphed from human to something more reptilian. "She's a shape-shifter!" Isaiah breathed.

The Arboretum door opened again and the cadets heard someone else approach. A moment later, they spotted Quirg through the dense screen of leaves.

"What are they doing together?" Maeve whispered.

"They must be in cahoots. Shhh." Dev held a finger to his lips.

Tessa strained to listen. "They're speaking in another language. I can't understand what they're saying."

"She doesn't look too pleased with him," Dev noted. Scopes was pointing a finger at Quirg, her reptilian face twisting angrily. She shoved a lynk in his doughy hands and stormed away.

Quirg looked down at the device and shook his head. He exited the Arboretum, shuffling back toward the Station's core.

66

EARTH

DR. KHATRI AIMED THE LONG, CYLINDRICAL TUBE AT DR. Scopes's shattered paperweight, the thirteen-sided one they had found on her desk earlier. Dr. Khatri figured it was an easy enough repair, a good way to run some preliminary tests and warm up the Syntropitron. The machine hummed, then shot an arc of light across the room, instantly repairing the paperweight. Not a scratch or crack could be seen on its faceted crystal surface.

"Remarkable!" Mayor Hawthorne said.

Zoey, who hadn't been at the NASA field trip, was equally impressed. But the destroyed quantum collider was much bigger and more complex than a paperweight. Could Dr. Khatri's invention really fix that and bring her sister home?

"Everyone, protective visors up! Safety measures engaged. Cross your fingers and your toes," Dr. Khatri said, walking over to the damaged collider. Wishful thinking was by no means scientifically effective, but it couldn't hurt. Especially in dire circumstances such as these.

Mayor Hawthorne reached for her daughter's hand.

"Ready? Aim. Repair!" Dr. Khatri pulled the trigger.

The room exploded with light.

STATION LIMINUS

QUIRG RELUCTANTLY WALKED DOWN GATE HALL, STOPPING IN front of a heavily barricaded door. He checked the message on the lynk once more, then slid the titanium bolt aside. He unlocked the steel bars and entered a passcode, disarming the shock field.

He opened the door. He inhaled, then whistled. A pack of hideous, six-headed wolves approached, sniffing and snarling. Their matted gray-green fur was flecked with dried blood, and their fangs were sharply pointed. Their forked tongues flicked, their eyes a glowing amber.

Quirg held out the Earthlings' musical instruments, letting the beasts find the scent. Their noses twitched, their ears pricked. Then Quirg whistled once more—the hunting call—and set the beasts loose. They set off at a brisk trot, their claws clicking on the polished moonstone floor.

"This way!" Tessa insisted. Ever since Dr. Scopes and Quirg had left the Arboretum, the cadets had been searching the expansive greenhouse and grow rooms for a back door where they could escape and sneak off in search of Duna.

"No, this way!" Maeve shook her head, her red hair falling into her eyes. She brushed it aside and pointed to a room full of lush tropical orchids in every imaginable color. "We're going in circles."

"We are not!" Tessa marched toward a metal stairway that twisted like a curling grapevine and ascended to an upper level.

"Ugh. You are just as stubborn as your sister," Maeve huffed, ducking behind a large jade plant.

Tessa scowled. "I'm sure I saw a doorway up here. Are you coming, or not?" She continued to climb.

"We already looked there!" Maeve threw up her hands. "You have absolutely no sense of direction!" She stomped up the metal staircase behind Tessa, with the other cadets trailing behind.

Isaiah stepped onto the landing, glancing down at the riot of colorful wildflowers below. "If you two keep arguing, we're all going to get caught," he said anxiously.

"She always wants to be the boss, but I'm sick of it!" Tessa rolled her sleeves up, feeling hot from climbing the steep steps and agitated from arguing with Maeve. "I remember seeing an exit up here. I'm sure of it." She spun around, nearly bumping into a blue-and-white porcelain vase with a creeping vine spilling from its mouth.

Maeve gritted her teeth. "Why should we believe you? You lied to us before."

Tessa scoffed. "You said you forgave me! And why would I lie about something like this?" she said. "Don't you think I want to get out of here alive, too?"

"Enough!" Lewis said. "I know this is stressful, but we have to work together."

Maeve turned, surprised that Lewis was the voice of reason for once. Then, out of the corner of her vision, she spotted a pack of hideous, wolf-like creatures weaving between some prickly cacti.

"Uhhh, guys?" She slowly raised her hand and pointed, slack-jawed. The kids swiveled around.

The animals froze, tails rigid, noses high. They locked eyes with the kids.

"I don't remember seeing *those* in the Menagerie," Dev whispered.

"Me neither. But I battled some terrifyingly similar monsters in AstroBlastersVII last night. These look even scarier," Lewis said, taking a slow step backward, nearly toppling a potted sapling.

"Do you think they can smell fear?" Tessa whimpered.

"Oops." Lewis shrugged. "That's not fear. That was me. Sorry."

The wolves hunched down into predatorial position, getting ready to pounce.

Maeve's voice was quiet but firm. "On my count... three... two..."

Before she could finish, Tessa screamed, "Run!"

The kids flew through the Arboretum and back into the main lobby, sprinting as fast as their legs would take them. The wolves drew nearer and nearer. The kids no longer worried about staying hidden; their only concern was staying alive.

They bolted through a crowd of bewildered constituents, toppled a cluster of biobots. They shoved a yellow hoverdisc aside, scattering a pallet of joule springs and spools of data cables. The beasts yipped and howled, savoring the thrill of the chase.

"I'll distract them. You find Duna!" Isaiah shouted as he peeled off from the group, running toward Gate Hall.

"Isaiah! No!" Maeve called. "We have to stick together!"

The kids zigzagged and ran to catch up with Isaiah.

"For once I'm grateful for all those track practices," Lewis said, his long legs propelling him forward.

"There he is!" Tessa shouted, catching a glimpse of Isaiah around the corner.

"Run faster!" Maeve screamed. "They're gaining on us!" She could hear the beasts' awful snarls. She could smell their rancid breath.

Lewis sped down the hall, skidding and knocking into a refreshment cart. Cups and saucers smashed to pieces. Scalding licorice tartea sloshed across the floor. The beasts slipped on the sticky liquid, their paws burning, their legs splaying.

The kids finally caught up with Isaiah. Together, they

tore through Gate Hall, putting distance between themselves and the wolves. They rounded the bend, then suddenly came to a halt, their path blocked by a formidable wall. A sign across the front read: *Restricted Access. This portion of Gate Hall closed for repairs. (PS—It was the Earthlings' fault.)*

"Fantastic," Dev panted, catching his breath.

The kids backed into the corner. They pushed on the wall. It wouldn't budge.

"We're trapped!" Tessa cried.

The pack of beasts advanced, their gait slowing. One of them limped, licking its wounds. The others barked, revealing fangs dripping with saliva. The kids had no weapons, nothing to throw or fight with other than their bare hands.

Isaiah reached out and grabbed the handle of the nearest door, looking for an escape route.

"You don't know where that leads!" Maeve said.

"Pretty sure anything is better than being eaten, which is what's gonna happen if we don't do something!" He twisted the handle but it was locked. He pounded his fist on the door, yelling for help.

The beasts lowered their heads, stepping closer, stalking their prey. The kids stumbled. Lewis tripped and fell to the floor, pulling the others down with him. They crawled backward on their hands and knees until their bodies were pressed against the locked door.

The beasts' amber eyes glowed, their forked tongues

flicking the air hungrily. They bayed, howling their hunting call.

Lewis reached out and grabbed Maeve's hand. She looked at him, her face stricken with a mess of emotion. She squeezed his hand back, then reached out and grabbed Tessa's hand. Tessa reached for Dev. Dev reached for Isaiah. One by one, they all linked hands. The beasts howled again. The kids flinched, feeling the beasts' hot breath on their faces.

A shrill whistle pierced the air. The slobbering wolves stilled, their ears pressed to the sides of their skulls, their tails dropping between their legs.

Shro appeared down the hall. He shouted a command and whistled again. He marched forward, his heavy boots clacking loudly on the floor. He stopped a few feet from the children and snapped his fingers. The beasts whimpered and retreated behind his powerful legs.

"Oh, thank goodness." Tessa slumped back, a wave of relief washing over her.

"Are we happy to see you!" Lewis said with a wide, grateful smile.

Shro chuckled. "I wish I could say the same." His expression shifted, hardening into a bitter scowl. His eyes revealed a darkness that sent shivers down their spines.

STATION LIMINUS

SHRO STRODE FROM SIDE TO SIDE, LOOKING THE COWERING cadets up and down. "I can't decide what would be more satisfying: to see you humiliated in front of the entire council, released into darkspace, or devoured by my trusty companions here." He stopped and tapped a finger to his sinewy chin. "Hmm, decisions, decisions."

Tessa, Dev, Lewis, Isaiah, and Maeve huddled together on the floor. "You agreed that our musical abilities might be helpful. Why are you so angry? What did we do wrong now?" Dev asked, trembling.

Shro stepped closer, his shadow falling over them like a death sentence. "Aside from the distractions, the disruptions, and the destruction?"

"The Menagerie incident was a misunderstanding. We told the council already, we didn't mean to cause any harm," Maeve said firmly.

"Oh, I'm sure you didn't." Shro sneered. "And yet, by traveling here, you interfered with something much larger than you could possibly imagine."

"Like what? Some plot to take over the entire multiverse?" Lewis said sarcastically.

Shro blinked, his carmine skin turning a deeper shade of red.

"Hold up—you're not actually planning to do that, are you? What are you, from Dim8 or something? Duna told us all about that drama." Lewis almost laughed, but Shro's frigid expression stopped him.

Shro clenched his jaw. "The Empyrean One will rule the multiverse one day. Planet Earth's degradation was the perfect cover for our experiments."

Dev stared. "Your what?

"Under the direction of the Empyrean One herself, my associates and I have been using your planet as a large-scale laboratory to nurture a very unique strain of Cataclysmosis, a highly contagious, destructive virus. It's been incubating on Earth for quite some time now." He arched an eyebrow. "Perhaps you've noticed some anomalous planetary behaviors? Quivers? Shivers? Flickers, per chance?"

"Seriously? You caused those?"

"Well, I can't take all the credit. You humans helped expedite the process, of course, with your reckless use of resources." Shro smirked. "The quivers and flickers are side effects of the virus as it matures, deep beneath your planet's crust."

The kids stared back, openmouthed.

"How did you manage to do that?" Dev asked.

Shro flashed a self-satisfied smile. "It was quite easy. We infiltrated one of your larger energy corporations and subverted their mining and drilling operations." Shro stepped closer, the wolves whining behind him.

"Once the virus is ready, we will release pathogens into the atmosphere, where they'll get sucked through dimensional tears and spread throughout the multiverse, infecting planet after planet. An unstoppable ripple effect will ensue."

"Wait, what tears are you talking about?" Dev asked.

"Our team has been hard at work, strategically puncturing your dimensional membrane for the past several years. That hole in the ozone layer? The one that exacerbated the warming effect and melted the majority of your ice caps? That was us." He beamed with pride.

"Why would anyone want to rule a bunch of sick planets?" Lewis asked.

"The Empyrean One will not only be ruler but savior of the multiverse. She will be revered. Celebrated. Worshipped. Altars will be constructed in her honor."

"How do you figure?" Maeve frowned. "Everyone will despise her."

"Very much the opposite. You see, Cataclysmosis is nearly impossible to cure. Only the Empyrean One possesses the antidote. Therefore, she possesses immeasurable power. The multiverse will be in the palm of her hands, at her mercy. And those of us who help her will rise at her side."

"How do you plan to release the virus?" Tessa asked, horrified.

"That is our biggest challenge." Shro clamped his hands together. "In order to activate and release the pathogens, we must exert a compressive force on the entire planetary body." He cracked his knuckles.

Dev cringed. "Like compactification?"

"Precisely. My, you Earthlings are a quick study." Shro winked wickedly. "The virus must appear to originate wholly from Dim14. Your insipid Earthling civilization will be our scapegoat." He looked down at the pin on his lapel, the symbol of the MAC. "But a compactification cannot occur without the council's support."

"They'll never agree to that," Maeve said defiantly.

"I beg to differ. Thanks to the destruction you caused during your short stay on Station Liminus, I'm confident I can now easily convince the council to reverse their earlier aid package and compactify your planet in a more expedient time frame." He laughed again, enjoying himself far too much. He clapped. "Congratulations. You've successfully doomed yourselves and all the people you love."

Dev fought back tears. "What if the real Earthling envoys had traveled here? The smart, special ones. Could they have stopped this?" he asked, riddled with guilt and despair.

"Ah." Shro pursed his lips. "You five miscreants clearly weren't our first choice, but in some ways, you made things easier for the Empyrean One. You see, the so-called elite Earthlings weren't actually skilled or special. One of my associates, working as a mole, simply auctioned off once-in-a-lifetime trips to the highest bidders. We contacted rich, morally corrupt individuals—oligarchs, oil barons, warlords—who agreed to persuade the council in favor of compactification, in exchange for safe passage to an exclusive paradise in Dim8."

"Dim8 doesn't even exist anymore," Tessa said, fidgeting with her shirt sleeve. "What about Mr. Finto? Does he know about this?"

Shro snorted. "Finto was merely a pawn. And according to my associate, he is no longer with us. It seems he couldn't handle the rigors of dimensional diplomacy or Transfer."

Tessa took a deep breath. "So, it was all a scam? You lied to Ignatia and the whole Multiverse Allied Council?"

"Yes, indeed. So many delicious lies. So much delectable deceit." Shro rubbed his palms together. Heeling behind his muscular legs, the six-headed wolves whined. "You're hungry, aren't you?" He scratched one under the chin. Its tail wagged. "Waiting so patiently for your supper, eh?" He watched the kids squirm, an evil glint in his eye.

"Please, don't do this!" Maeve begged.

Isaiah turned around and banged his fist on the nearest door. He wrenched the handle and cried for help once more, to no avail.

"Keeping you alive is far too risky." Shro snapped his fingers. "Especially now that I've told you so very much." The beasts fanned out around the kids. They pawed at the ground, growling.

The cadets held tightly to one another, no escape in sight.

Shro put his fingers in his mouth, ready to whistle the attack signal, when the door behind the kids flew open.

An arm reached out, gripped Isaiah around the waist and yanked him backward, sending him tumbling out of Gate Hall. Linked together, hand in hand, the other kids were dragged through the open door. They free-fell into black nothingness, out of reach.

Shro bellowed; the wolves howled. Before they could follow across the Threshold, the door slammed shut. A burst of fluorescent quantum lightning crackled. The door morphed, disappeared.

The cadets screamed, falling down, down, down.

They dissolved into pixels and atoms and stardust.

And then they were gone.

69

L'ORESS

A GULL SCREECHED, DIVING INTO THE SURF WITH A SPLASH.

Isaiah blinked up at a cerulean sky. His bones ached, his stomach twisted with nausea. His ears felt like they'd been stuffed with cotton. Somewhere in the distance, he heard the gentle lap of waves, the soft rustle of palm fronds.

"My nephew," a gentle voice said. "We are together again."

"Uncle Ming?" Isaiah said, his head spinning.

"Yes, it's me."

"Am I asleep? Am I dreaming?" Isaiah licked his lips, tasting salt and blood.

"No, you are very much awake." Ming placed a gentle hand on Isaiah's elbow, helping him sit up.

Isaiah rubbed his eyes. His uncle's face came into focus. The man's skin was tanned and weathered, his features muddled and hazy. His clothing was tattered, his hair grayer than Isaiah remembered. But it *was* him. They hugged. Isaiah couldn't believe it. His heart felt like it might explode.

"Uncle Ming!" He hugged his uncle tighter, then pulled away. "I'm so happy to see you, but I'm so confused. Where are we?"

"We're on L'oress, a peaceful, idyllic planet in Dim1."

"Okay, but what are *you* doing here? Where are my—?" Panicked, Isaiah looked around. He heaved a sigh of relief when he spotted Tessa, Lewis, Maeve, and Dev walking across the beach, shaking sand from their clothes, shoes, and hair.

"Uncle Ming, these are my friends," Isaiah said, standing up to introduce the others.

Lewis squinted in the bright sunlight. "Is this, like, heaven or something? Are we dead?"

"No. Thanks to my uncle, we're alive." Isaiah turned to Uncle Ming. "You saved us."

Ming smiled. "I heard rumors that young Earthlings had arrived on the Station. I hoped it might be you, Isaiah. But I could not be sure. So I ventured across the Threshold one more time, even though the trip takes quite a toll on me." He sighed, his smile fading. "I slipped into Gate Hall one evening to look for you, but I was chased away by those bothersome guards."

"That was you?" Isaiah said, his heart thrumming. "You're the Traveler?"

Ming chuckled softly. "Is that what they call me?" He shrugged bashfully. "I have become a bit of an interdimensional nomad, a restless wanderer." He sat down in the sand, clearly exhausted. He let the waves wet his feet. "But not by choice."

"What do you mean?" Isaiah asked, sitting beside him. The others gathered round.

"For whatever reason, I am stuck here in the multiverse." Ming looked around at the beautiful beach. "It's not a bad place to be, I suppose. But it's not home." He turned to Isaiah. "It is so good to see you. I have missed you and your mother every single day."

Isaiah swallowed. "Everyone back home thought you died." His throat felt raw. "Except me."

Ming pulled him close. "I would have come back if I could. I tried. Countless times. Which is why I look like this." He touched his wizened face; he looked as though he had aged a decade in the year or so that he'd been gone. "No matter how many doors I opened in Gate Hall, none of them led me home."

Ming reached over and plucked a stone from the sand. He skipped it across the surface of the water. "It pained me tremendously to be apart from you. I can't imagine how much your mother worried. But after I stumbled through that dimensional Rip in the Philippines, I was never able to find a way back."

Isaiah wiped his eyes. He knew his uncle would never have abandoned them.

"How did you piece together the clues I left in my letters?" Ming asked.

"I didn't," Isaiah said, thinking of his journal. "I couldn't figure the letters out. Zoey and I read them a million times, but we never made any big breakthroughs. Everyone told me they were nonsense."

"Well, they were," Ming laughed. "Somewhat. I encrypted them. I only trusted you and your mother with the information. I created a cipher, a way to crack the encoded messages, but I got lost before I could send it to you." He paused. "Wait . . . if my letters didn't lead you to a portal, how did all of you get here?"

Lewis grimaced. "Long story. Mostly my fault."

"One of my dad's colleagues went rogue and constructed a quantum collider," Dev said, not wanting Lewis to feel bad. "We activated it and ended up at Station Liminus."

"Interesting," said Ming thoughtfully.

"It was an accident . . . a series of coincidences . . . I don't know . . ." Isaiah looked around. They were on a beach more beautiful than any postcard. Every color was saturated, the intensity amplified. The water was crystal clear, the sky cloudless.

Ming nodded. "The multiverse contains just as many mysteries as dimensions." He pulled something from his pocket. It was the size and shape of an index card but made of plastic, printed with a complex table of symbols, letters, and numbers. "You may not have needed my letters to cross the Threshold, but they may come in handy in the future. Here." He gave Isaiah the cipher.

"I was on assignment two years ago, photographing a fishing village in Vietnam when I stumbled upon a suspicious-looking off-shore drilling operation," Ming explained. "I did some investigating and discovered it was an EnerCor rig. The fishermen told me that when the rig arrived—seemingly overnight—nearly all the fish disappeared, and the underwater currents became erratic.

"When word got out, a self-proclaimed global watchdog group called the World Intelligence Agency intervened. I hoped they would dismantle the rig and restore the fishing shoals, but instead they paid the fisherman to keep quiet. It was concerning, but I was so busy with work that I didn't have time to think about it too much.

"Then, on my next assignment, all the way across the globe in Peru, I discovered a similar story. This time, the locals reported even stranger incidences, like WIO agents materializing out of thin air, and unexplained energy surges. The whole thing felt . . . off. I started tracking and mapping EnerCor sites, which I began to suspect linked Earth to some sort of parallel or alternate dimension. I worried that if EnerCor or WIO agents caught on to my investigation, they might try to silence me. So I wrote everything down and sent it to you."

Isaiah thanked his uncle and carefully slipped the cipher into his back pocket with the compressed regenerex cube. His pulse raced as he considered everything his uncle had just told them. He quickly filled his uncle in on Shro's plans, connecting the two parts of the story.

Ming listened carefully. "I knew there was something bigger afoot, but I never imagined it was so sinister."

"Our families need us now more than ever." Tessa longed to see Zoey and her parents. To make sure they were safe. "Our world is on the brink of collapse."

"At the hands of some extra evil dudes," Lewis added.

"And it's up to us to save it," Isaiah said.

Ming shook his head forlornly. "I wish I could do more to help, but I've never successfully crossed back into Dim14."

"That's okay," Isaiah said, resting a hand on his uncle's shoulder. "One step at a time. Right now, we just need to get back to Station Liminus."

"The place you just escaped from? You want to go back there? So soon?" Ming scratched his head.

Isaiah nodded. "We have to get back to the Station and stop Shro before he convinces the council to compactify Earth."

"And simultaneously unleashes a super virus intended to wipe out half the multiverse and enslave the rest." Maeve stood up, feeling energized. "We can't just sit around on this beach. We have to do something!"

Ming looked at the kids, marveling at their bravery, determination, and leadership. "Even if you stop the vote, how do you plan to return to Earth?" he asked.

"My dad's at NASA now with Tessa's mom and sister, working to repair the collider," Dev said. "Hopefully it will be ready soon. But first, we need to interrupt the council's meeting."

Ming rose to his feet. "In that case, I may be able to help."

"Really, Uncle Ming?" Isaiah said hopefully.

Ming smiled, squinting into the sun. "I know my way around the Station pretty well. Most portals connect through Gate Hall, but not all of them. We'll need to sneak you in through a back door of sorts."

Lewis hopped up. "Okay, we're listening . . ."

"We must move quickly. This way." Ming walked to the water's edge and dove into the ocean.

"Where are you going?" Isaiah called over the crashing waves. "We need to go to the Station, not go for a swim!"

"There is a portal at the edge of the reef," Ming said, treading water and waving them toward the horizon. "It materializes briefly at sunset."

Lewis looked up at the sky, turning from blue to bright orange and pink. "Which is basically now. Let's move, people!"

"There better not be sharks or stinging jellyfish on this planet," Tessa mumbled, dipping a toe into the salty surf.

One by one, they swam out to the reef. It was teeming with fish and sea turtles. If they weren't in such a rush to save the multiverse, Maeve would have enjoyed snorkeling around for a while.

"There! Do you see those rays of dancing light coming up from a crack in the coral?" Ming said as they got closer to the portal. "That's where you need to go. There's a large rock blocking the entry; I'll dive down and push it aside, holding the portal open as long as I can. Once you're right above the opening, take a deep breath of air and dive straight down. Don't stop until you cross the Threshold. You'll feel a magnetic pull and crushing pressure, but that's normal."

"Oh, goody," Lewis said. Maeve splashed him playfully. He splashed her back.

"What about you?" Isaiah asked his uncle, worry creasing his brow.

Ming shook his head dismissively. "Don't worry about me. I'll make sure everyone finds their way through the portal, then I'll follow." In reality, Ming knew he couldn't handle another Transfer. His last trip to the Station had drained him more than he'd let on. He wagered he had just enough strength left in him to hold the portal open for the kids, though not a whole lot more. But he knew if he told his nephew this, Isaiah would insist on staying behind with him on L'oress. There was too much at stake; Ming couldn't let that happen. The Conroy Cadets were Earth's only hope.

"One thing to keep in mind," Ming said as they gathered together above the reef. "You'll enter the Station through the plumbing valves on the nineteenth floor. You may be a little soggy upon arrival, but it's better than coming through Gate Hall with a pack of hungry space wolves ready to devour you."

"Very true," Dev agreed.

"What do you say? Ready?" Ming asked.

"Ready as we'll ever be," Tessa replied.

Ming paused, exhaling a long breath. "You kids are going to change the world, I know it," he said. "Don't let anyone tell you otherwise. And remember, there's always more to the story." He turned to Isaiah and smiled warmly. "See you on the other side, kid." He took a deep breath and disappeared beneath the waves.

Isaiah watched him go. "See you on the other side, Uncle Ming."

One by one, the cadets dove down, kicking and swimming toward the light.

70

EARTH

THE ROOM SMELLED OF BURNING RUBBER AND BARBEQUED steak.

"Did it work?" Zoey asked, fanning the fumes away. Her safety goggles had flown straight off her face, landing several feet behind.

"It's too soon to say," Dr. Khatri said, popping his head up, looking around the quantum collider lab. The Syntropitron was heavy in his hands, the tip of its barrel sparking with flecks of bright light. He set it down carefully and stepped around the overturned storage unit he'd used as a makeshift barricade.

"Look!" Professor McGillum said, touching the wall. The previously charred and melted panels were restored to a smooth, pristine white.

Mayor Hawthorne moved beside her daughter protectively. "Are you okay?" she asked.

"Yeah, I'm fine, Mom. You?"

"I'm all right." She kissed the top of Zoey's head.

An orange laser beam cut through the smoke and steam.

Beep! Beep!

They all jumped back.

There was a fizzle, a pop. A long hiss.

The air cleared, revealing a glittering cylindrical structure in the center of the room. An array of glowing buttons adorned a curved console. A screen blinked to life.

A soothing AI voice announced, "System: Activated."

STATION LIMINUS

"ORDER! ORDER!" IGNATIA RAPPED THE RUBY GAVEL ON THE onyx table.

The council was in a state of turmoil. An emergency session had been called and delegates and constituents yelled between the aisles. Accusations flew back and forth; tempers flared.

"I said ORDER!" Ignatia's powerful voice reverberated off the faceted walls. She swept her arms wide, her indigo robes undulating dramatically.

Hidden behind a row of seats in the very back of the meeting chamber, the children crouched down lower, waiting for the right moment. Isaiah tried to focus, but he was distraught. His uncle hadn't arrived as planned and Isaiah's heart felt heavy. He worried something had gone wrong with the portal. He held on to hope that his uncle would come soon, but there was no time to waste.

"We will now hear General Shro's case in favor of compactification," Ignatia declared.

Shro moved to the central podium, his broad back straining against his jacket. He regarded the delegates and bowed graciously before them. "My esteemed peers, as you know, the Earthlings caused unprecedented damage and upheaval during their short stay on Station Liminus. Despite our warm hospitality and our best efforts to work with them, they were resistant, defiant, and disrespectful of our culture and policies. Their own delegate, Mr. Salvido Finto, never even returned to the Station on his planet's behalf. He chose instead to leave the fate of his dimension in the hands of a bunch of raucous children."

Several constituents heckled and hollered insults from the crowd.

"I know," Shro cooed, stoking the embers of hate glowing in the eyes of the audience. "Earth did not send their best and brightest. They sent frauds. Thieves! Liars! Criminals whose very presence threatens the sanctity of our great multiverse!"

A wave of discontent rolled through the meeting chamber.

"Order!" Ignatia hollered. "Order!"

Shro's wiry muscles rippled beneath his leather jacket. He waited for the crowd to settle.

"Instead of embracing our generous offers of collaboration, the lowly Earthlings destroyed Station property, unleashing mayhem, and"—he paused for effect—"caused serious injury to one of our top staff members."

The audience gasped. Some shook their fists and claws with fury. Beaks clacked, snouts grunted crossly.

"Excuse me? If I may interject?" Duna approached the podium. Shro shot them an icy glare, but Ignatia nodded acquiescently.

Duna produced a sheet of pixel paper. They held it up for all to see. "To follow up on General Shro's last statement, I received word that Lino, the creature keeper whose arm was bitten by a crark during this morning's unfortunate animal breach, has successfully regrown his maimed limb."

Shro scowled.

Duna continued. "As a reminder, Lino is a member of the Echinus race, capable of sophisticated appendage regeneration, much like starfish and harp lizards."

Noisy chatter erupted down the aisle. The kids, still hidden, breathed a sigh of relief, grateful not to have dismemberment weighing on their consciences.

"Very good. Thank you for sharing that important update," Ignatia said. "General Shro, please proceed with your closing statements."

"It would be my pleasure," he replied. "As you may know, our sentries apprehended the Earthlings, but alas, they escaped." The crowd gasped. "Yes, unfortunately it's true. They are currently on the run, somewhere beyond Station Liminus." He shrugged. "Who knows? They may be hiding out in one of *your* dimensions, plotting terrible acts of violence . . . or worse."

The audience pulsed with ire, discord, and fear.

Shro shouted, "Mark my words: I will not rest until I find the Earthling fugitives, even if it means traveling to the ends of the multiverse." Shro raised a fist in the air. The audience roared. "Justice must be served. Dim14 will pay for its misdeeds!"

"Yes, well, that will require a vote, General Shro," Ignatia said, trying to regain control of the meeting.

"A vote, then," Shro said, riding the surge in support from angry council members and constituents. "I move to halt all aid and compactify Earth at once!"

"Compactify Earth! Compactify Earth!" Quirg chanted on cue.

Dev's skin felt hot, his insides roiling with anger as the chant grew louder. Maeve closed her eyes briefly and tried to get into character, envisioning herself as a warrior about to venture into battle. Tessa bit her lip and sent a text message to Zoey, telling her how much she missed her. Isaiah glanced over his shoulder, hoping Ming would appear. Lewis peeked under the seat and picked up a pack of vellwaffers that must have fallen off a catering cart. He unpeeled the wrapper and took a bite. Maeve heard the rustling sound and opened her eyes. She shot him a look.

What? he mouthed. *Some people stress eat, okay? Don't judge.* Maeve rolled her eyes before turning her attention back to the council.

"Compactify Earth!" Xol shouted.

Ignatia put her hands up to silence the chant, which was catching on like wildfire.

Duna returned to the podium, pushing back against the swell of ill will. "Stop! All of you. We cannot act so brashly. Shro, you misrepresent and diminish the Earthlings. We were never able to explore the potential of their abilities. We must give them another chance."

"How can we give them another chance? They fled!" Shro cackled. "They are fugitives, cowards, wanted criminals! They are—"

"We're right here!" Dev shouted, standing up, chin high, shoulders back.

Shro's jaw tightened, his stony eyes narrowed. "You have quite a knack for making dramatic exits and entrances."

"That's because we're performers," Maeve said, popping up at Dev's side, flanked by Tessa, Lewis, and Isaiah. "And this is our grand finale. Aten-hut!" she called.

Duna gave them a relieved look, smiling weakly. They had been searching for the cadets everywhere, to no avail.

"Guards! Seize them!" Shro barked, but Ignatia raised her hand, overriding his orders.

"No. I want to hear what they have to say for themselves." She studied the Earthlings, her horns shifting between colors. "You may approach the podium."

The five cadets marched, heads held high, sneakers and boots squelching with sea water, dripping down the illuminated aisle.

72

STATION LIMINUS

"WE'RE TELLING THE TRUTH," MAEVE SAID AFTER THEY HAD made their case.

"Lies! Ludicrous, outlandish lies!" Shro's voice was full of gravel and grit. "They insult us with their falsehoods and fabrications! Let us not be swayed by these delinquent Earthlings."

"We can prove it," Dev said intrepidly.

Duna cocked their head to the side. Ignatia leaned forward expectantly. "Can you really?"

"Show them," Maeve said to Tessa.

Tessa stepped forward. She pulled up her right sleeve, exposing her eChron watch. She tapped a button. An audio recording filled the air.

Shro's voice echoed throughout the chamber. His confession in Gate Hall, his devious plot, was laid bare for all to hear.

The other council members turned, eyeing him suspiciously, the air in the room shifting. His carmine face paled as he realized his plans were crumbling.

Ignatia closed her eyes and inhaled, processing the weight of the information. When she opened her eyes again, her violet irises were bright and determined.

"Guards!" she commanded. "Arrest General Shro. He is hereby stripped of all titles. He will remain in custody until a full trial can be arranged." She turned to address him directly. "You will be held accountable for your betrayal and manipulations. The Multiverse Allied Council will uncover the Empyrean One's identity and stop the malicious plans you set in motion before it is too late."

"Never!" Shro strained against the guards, kicking and thrashing. "This is not the end! This is only the beginning! The Empyrean One will not stand for this! Dimension8 will rise again! We will prevail. We will—" The guards zapped him with their stunclubs. Shro crumpled to the floor. They heaved him up, snapped electromagnetic shackles to his wrists and ankles, and hauled him out of the room.

"What about the vote?" Xol asked, addressing Secretary Leapkeene. "The fate of Earth must be decided."

The chamber doors flew open. A majestic woman entered, a crown of gilded narwhal tusks and limpets circled her head. A sweeping pearlescent carapace rose from her back, curving gracefully to frame her face and shoulders. She wore liquid turquoise silks that moved like ocean waves, with white frills cresting and curling at her ankles and wrists. A small child with wide, glacial blue eyes and a smaller carapace stood beside her.

"Virri!" Tessa cried out.

The child gave a shy wave and smiled.

The rest of the council immediately bowed graciously.

"Your Highness," Ignatia said with deep reverence. "We have been eagerly awaiting your return."

"As have I," replied Eryna, Queen of Klapproth.

"Your speech! It has been restored!" Ignatia held a hand to her throat. "We thought the silvox virus rendered you silent indefinitely. What a relief to hear your voice. It is needed now more than ever. Our alliance is in a state of great unrest."

"I am aware."

"You are? But how . . . ?"

"The plague that struck Klapproth was engineered by General Shro's biological warfare operative. Upon realizing that I had uncovered some of his more nefarious plans, he plunged my innocent planet into total silence and disabled all of our communication devices. Then he issued a multiverse-wide interdiction rife with inaccuracies and scare tactics, cutting us off from all our allies."

The Klapprothi queen gestured to the door. A teenage girl in a shabby maroon jumpsuit with a shock of white hair appeared. She bowed to the queen and council.

"Thanks to Kor, the resourceful Ebvarienne trader, I was able to circumvent the interdiction and transport my daughter, Virri, onto the Station clandestinely."

"That's a fancy way to say smuggled, right?" Lewis asked. Maeve nodded.

Eryna continued. "Working with Duna and the Earthlings, Virri was able to reactivate our dimension's triskaidecagon and transmit information back to me on Klapproth using the Earthlings' musical sound waves." She regarded the children with kind, serene eyes. "Once our communication channels were restored, Duna contacted their allies on Mertanya to bring me here today." She smiled gratefully at Duna, Kor, and the cadets. "If it weren't for them, I would not be here with you today."

"Is all of this true?" Ignatia asked in astonishment.

They nodded.

Eryna took her seat at the massive thirteen-sided onyx table. "I will gladly cast my vote in favor of assisting planet Earth of Dimension14. We must do whatever we can to halt Shro's latest pathogen before it infects us all."

"What about the others?" Dev asked. "Shro wasn't working alone. Dr. Scopes? The Empyrean One? They're still out there."

Ignatia's voice was firm. "We will identify each and every operative associated with this dark plan and deliver justice."

Quirg squirmed in his seat. Sweat dripped down his doughy face. "I confess!" he cried miserably, flopping onto the table with a damp squish. "Please! Forgive me! I was coerced, against my will and good judgment." He wailed. "Shro threatened to destroy my dimension if I disobeyed him. I have young Quomions at home. You know I would do anything to keep my thirty-nine children and fifteen wives happy and safe. I am sorry, so sorry!" He sobbed, racked with guilt and regret. "Punish me, but do not harm my families." He slid off his chair in a miserable heap.

"Quirg, get up," Ignatia commanded. "You will receive a fair trial for your misdeeds. But I appreciate your honesty. We will consider your case at a later date. Until then, you will be held on house arrest. Ira, please escort our disgraced delegate back to his home dimension and keep a close eye on him until further notice."

"Yes, Your Eminence." Ira nodded and led Quirg down the aisle, aided by a set of guards.

"And you, young Earthlings? Will you accept my apology for wrongly accusing you of heinous crimes and doubting your motives?" Ignatia asked. Her braids swirled in silvery eddies at her shoulders, her horns flushing pale pink.

"Of course," Maeve said. "We understand, and we want to help."

Ignatia's face brightened. "Very well. We have much work to do in the coming months. Together, I believe we can combine our skills and resources to advance the multiverse in wonderful, productive, and sustainable ways. But before we do so, I believe I must return something that belongs to you."

Seemingly out of thin air, she produced an oboe, a trumpet, a clarinet, a saxophone, and a set of drumsticks. "You may need these in days to come," she said. "And I am still awaiting a performance."

"We would love that," Maeve said, retrieving the instruments with her fellow cadets.

Tessa's wrist vibrated. She looked down at the messages streaming in.

> The Syntropitron gizmo worked!
> The quantum collider is fixed!
> Dr. Khatri says you need to get
> an exit point or gate thingamajig as
> soon as possible.
> Did you get that? ASAP!
> He's not sure how long the
> collider will be stable.
> It's sort of glitching out, but it's
> mostly good to go . . . we think.
> Anyway, HURRY!

Tessa bit her lip. "I think we're going to need a raincheck on the concert."

"Why is that?" Ignatia asked.

"We have to get home. Our families are worried and waiting." Tessa caught Duna's eye. She smiled. "We have to go," she repeated, "but we would love to come back. Soon. We promise."

Duna gave a quiet nod of agreement and understanding.

"Ah." Ignatia sucked in a breath. "About your return journey . . ." She looked at the cadets. "Unfortunately, there are no active portals that currently connect your home dimension to the Station. We can expedite the construction of a new Gate, but it will take some time. I'm afraid you're stuck with us here a bit longer."

"Actually, we may have found a solution," Dev said.

73

EARTH

"WHERE ARE THEY? WHY AREN'T THEY RESPONDING? DO YOU think something's wrong? Are they hurt? Are they sick?" Mayor Hawthorne paced back and forth across the lab.

"Mom! Enough. Please." Zoey gave her mother a reassuring hug. "I know you're worried, but there's nothing we can do right now except wait. I'm sure Tessa will send us a message as soon as she can."

Dr. Khatri tinkered with some buttons on the collider's control panel. Professor McGillum inspected the metal panels and rivets for the third time.

"Transfer: Initiated," a robotic AI voice said.

Dr. Khatri blinked. "We're ready to go whenever they are."

The collider hummed and vibrated; the crystal sphere overhead began to spin.

"Gate Materialization: Initiated," the robotic voice announced.

Dr. Khatri examined the console's curved screen. Coordinates appeared. He clapped his hands together. "Tell Tessa and the others to proceed to Gate FJC0629. According to this, a blue wooden door should appear within some sort of central transit node any minute now."

"Got it." Zoey quickly typed the message and hit send.

The ceiling-mounted crystal sphere spun faster. A web of light fell across the room.

"They need to hurry," Dr. Khatri said, becoming frazzled. "I can't seem to pause the countdown." He pressed a combination of buttons. Nothing worked. "If the kids miss this window, the collider may self-destruct again."

"Then what happens?"

"They'll be trapped outside our dimension for the foreseeable future," Dr. Khatri said, his hands beginning to tremble. "We don't have enough fuel to repower the Syntropitron a second time."

Mayor Hawthorne paced some more, nervously biting her manicured nails.

Zoey looked down at her watch, tapping its glassy surface impatiently. "Come on, sis. Come on, come on."

A second later, the watch buzzed.

74

STATION LIMINUS

"OUR RIDE BACK TO EARTH HAS ARRIVED. SWEET!" LEWIS SAID, skidding to a stop.

"Zoey was right!" Tessa ran through Gate Hall. She stopped beside Lewis at a blue wooden door. Above the transom, a code ticked across a narrow digital plaque.

"Gate FJC0629. This is it!" Dev cried, jumping up and down, high-fiving Lewis.

"Are you sure?" Maeve asked. "This door is red."

"Huh?" They blinked and the door morphed back to blue.

"What is going on?" Isaiah asked, his nose inches away from the color-shifting paint.

"The Gate may be unstable," Duna said, jogging to catch up with them. "This happens sometimes." They touched a finger to the blue door. It turned orange for a split second, then blue again.

"Okay, this is freaking me out," Lewis said. "Is this the right door or not?"

"You should wait and see if the atoms settle," Duna said. "There is a lot of entropic activity." The door shimmered.

Isaiah didn't mind waiting. He looked down the hall, hoping Ming would arrive, worrying about what had happened to him back on L'oress. Maeve followed his gaze.

"It's going to be okay," she told him, reading his face. "We'll find Ming. Ignatia and the council will help look for him and bring him home." Isaiah nodded, but he wasn't so sure.

Just then the door warped, its hinges sparking. Tessa jumped back, shaking her head. "We can't wait any longer." She glanced at her watch. "Zoey said the collider sequence has been initiated. They can't figure out how to stop it. Either we go now or miss our chance."

Dev turned to Duna. "Thanks for your help." The others nodded in agreement.

"Thank *you*," Duna replied graciously. "I know we will see each other again soon. Safe travels, Earthlings." Duna pulled the door open. "Go," they said. "Hurry."

In the blink of an eye, the door changed from blue to red, then back to blue again.

Dev nodded. "They're right. We have to go, before the Gate disappears completely."

"I agree," said Tessa.

Duna stepped aside and gave an encouraging wave.

"Okay, on your signal." Lewis smiled at Maeve. She reached out and held his hand.

"Aten-hut!" Maeve stepped closer to the Threshold, singing loudly, her voice rising above the fierce quantum wind and bursts of searing yellow lightning.

"We are Conroy Cadets, hear us roar. Look to the skies, watch us soar..."

EARTH, SORT OF...

"HOME, SWEET HOME!" LEWIS SAID, STRETCHING OUT HIS LONG limbs. His legs were tingling with pins and needles.

The whooshing, rumbling sensation stopped. The Transfer was complete.

"Isaiah, are you puking again?" Tessa asked.

"I can't help it if I suffer from extreme motion sickness," he said woozily.

"Let's get him some fresh air." Dev pushed against the walls of the shiny copper capsule they were encased within. It hissed and peeled open. Instead of floating in a foggy white oblivion, it sat in the center of a laboratory.

"We made it!" Dev shouted, looking around. "We're alive! I recognize that." He pointed to a bunch of cardboard boxes. "And that!" The NASA logo was painted on the wall. "Ha! Ha! We did it!" He gave his saxophone a happy honk.

"Hey, Dev?" Maeve said hesitantly as she helped Isaiah

to his feet and then picked up both of their instruments. "Where is your dad?"

"Wait." Tessa stopped in her tracks, almost dropping her sister's clarinet. "Where is Zoey? And my mom? I thought they'd be here, too."

"Maybe they're down the hall?" Lewis suggested, kneeling to grab his drumsticks. He was happy that both of them had made the journey this time. "Let's take a look."

The kids exited the room. The building was empty. It was decaying and poorly maintained. The windows were smashed, the paint chipped.

"Did we cause all this damage?" Lewis asked, wide-eyed. "We have a habit of doing that . . ."

"No." Maeve sucked in a breath, studying the cracked floor. Thick black root tendrils snaked between the tiles, cleaving them apart. "This is not the same NASA building we were in before, during the field trip."

They wandered down the abandoned corridor until they found an exit. They pushed the door open and coughed. Gray smog hung like a thick, noxious blanket across the skyline.

"Guys, I don't mean to get all gloomy and doomy again, but something is very wrong here," Isaiah said, peering out across the valley.

Smokestacks rose up where the Conroy city center should have been. The plazas, the parks, the commerce center were all razed, replaced by brutal concrete structures. Brush fires burned in the old soy and corn fields to the east, ash darkening the sky. Rusted cars with flattened tires were parked haphazardly along the road. Invasive vines ruptured the asphalt, strangling nearby trees.

"Where is the school? Where are our homes?" Tessa said, staring off into the distance. "Where are all the people?"

It was Earth, but not *their* Earth. It was like the apocalyptic visions and nightmares Isaiah sometimes had, come to life. Like a warning, a precursor to what their home would look like, if they didn't do something to stop the Empyrean One.

Dev's voice was weak and despondent. "I think we somehow crossed into a parallel dimension."

The roots at their feet twisted, sensing the presence of living creatures. A whispering sound, like a thousand small, quiet voices, drifted hungrily through the air.

"Are we the only ones here?" Lewis asked, listening.

"I don't know. It looks like someone, or something, is down there." Dev gestured to the puffing smokestacks and blinking yellow lights in the valley. "We should go and see if they can help us."

"Wait," Maeve threw her arm out in front of him. "Do you remember what Ira told us? If we cross paths with our doppelgängers in a parallel dimension, we could mess up the space-time continuum."

The whispering voices grew louder. Motes of dust and ash floated in the air. As his nausea faded, Isaiah felt a thrumming within his chest, like a premonition. Or maybe it was a call to action?

A gust of wind swept dry leaves into the sky. A scrap of paper fluttered to the ground and landed at their feet. Dev picked it up.

If you think you can stop me so easily,
you are gravely mistaken.
The Empyrean One

Lewis guffawed. "That's the cheesiest prank I have ever seen. Isaiah, your uncle is hysterical!" He slapped his knee and doubled over laughing.

"I know Uncle Ming sent me some cryptic notes in the past, but I don't think he left that one for us," Isaiah said, feeling a pang of sadness. "I wish he were here, but I think he's still stuck on L'oress. He never arrived on the Station, remember?"

The cadets were silent, all of them thinking of Ming and their own families, who seemed farther away than ever.

Isaiah removed the cipher Ming had given him. He ran his finger over the symbols, sighed, then returned it to his pocket. Before the field trip, Benni the bus driver had wished Isaiah a bold journey, one that might lead him to the answers he was seeking. And he *had* found answers, about the multiverse and more. He'd reunited with his beloved uncle and discovered an untapped power inside himself. He knew he should be grateful, but somehow all those answers only led to more questions.

Lewis's smile drooped. "So, let me get this straight:

We're trapped in a parallel world? Pursued by a mysterious enemy? All by ourselves?" He blinked. "Honestly?"

"Tessa, does your eChron still work?" Dev asked.

She looked down. The face was shattered. "No," she said. "I think it's broken. For good this time." Tears pricked her eyes. She wished she could hop in a time machine and reverse everything that had happened. But then she realized that changing the past wouldn't make anything better. She had to set her sights on the future. She had found her voice and now she needed to use it, even if it meant getting out of her comfort zone. Way out.

"Well, Captain," Lewis said, turning to Maeve. "What exactly do we do now?"

"That," she said, "is an excellent question." She took a deep breath, gathering her thoughts, formulating a plan. "We find another portal. We get home. We fight this thing with everything we've got. We save the world."

"Right, that sounds easy enough," Lewis said. He was surprised by the feeling in his chest. A competitive drive, a fierce desire to win. He thought about his family, the silly motto they always repeated: *Wynners never lose.* But it didn't seem quite so silly anymore. It felt important.

Only two days earlier, Dev's mother had told him that if he wanted to be a knight, he would need dragons to defeat. Well, the Empyrean One wasn't exactly a dragon (not that he knew of, at least), but Dev understood that whatever came next would be the biggest challenge he had ever faced. He was grateful to have his friends by his side.

Maeve put on her best game face. She was a performer. A survivor. A leader. She straightened her shoulders and looked her friends in the eyes. "All I know is that the show must go on. Aten-hut!"

ACKNOWLEDGMENTS

Some books take years to write, simmering slowly, emerging line by line. This was not one of those books. This story rocketed onto the page at warp speed, propelled by the guidance of my fearless editor, Anne Heltzel, and the fantastic team at Abrams. Thanks to Amy Vreeland, Jessica Gotz, Margo Winton Parodi, Laura Bernier, and everyone else who worked hard behind the scenes to bring this book to life. I'm grateful to Christa Heschke and Daniele Hunter of McIntosh & Otis for championing my work and opening up portals to new creative opportunities. Thanks to Chris Skinner for creating such dynamic and beautiful cover art, and Marcie Lawrence for excellent design work.

I'm thankful for the insight and friendship of my trusted critique partners, especially Erin Cashman, Diana Renn, and Sandra Waugh, who read each draft with the keenest eyes and fullest hearts. Shout-outs to my wonderful community of creative friends and collaborators, including the Lucky13s, the Electric Eighteens, the Concord and Littleton kidlit writing groups, NESCBWI, The Room to Write, and The Writers' Loft. Utmost appreciation to the librarians, teachers, and booksellers who help put books in the hands of young readers. High fives to all the independent bookstores, especially the Silver Unicorn Bookstore in Acton, Massachusetts, and the magnificent middle grade book clubbers.

There are numerous theories about the multiverse, each more mind-boggling than the next. When I began writing this book, I immersed myself in the research and writing of Carl Sagan, Brian Greene, Stephon Alexander, Barry Parker, Bernard Carr, Tom Siegfried, and many other brilliant thinkers. Edward Elgar's *Enigma Variations* provided the perfect musical backdrop while drafting this story.

Most importantly, I offer a galaxy of love to my family, especially my wonderful parents. Thank you for your encouragement, unwavering support, and patience. Writing and revising a book is an exhilarating but difficult process, and there were many times when I felt as though I had stumbled into a black hole. Thank you, Stefano, for pulling me back to Earth, calming my nerves, and feeding me lots of snacks. I couldn't ask for a better partner in love and life. Lastly, to my bold, brave, musical daughters: My love for you is infinite. If anyone can save the world, it will be kids like you.